J . S . HARMAN

DARK
TIDES

BOOK TWO OF THE DARKWORLDS SAGA

Also by the Author:

DARK SANDS

Contents

A Note From The Author   IX

PRELUDE   1

PROLOGUE   12

PART ONE: UNKNOWN   19

1. WHAT STRANGE PROVIDENCE   21

2. A FIRST BREATH   29

3. QUESTIONS   39

4. MALEFICUS   53

5. A BANQUET OF PASTE AND BROTH   69

6. A NEW PURPOSE   77

7. DIVE   85

8. WARNINGS   93

9. A FRIGHTFUL WONDER   104

PART TWO: UNSAFE   113

10. THE DEPTHS   115

11. THE GRAVE PILLARS   125

12.	SHIFTING SANDS	135
13.	FAKE CAPTAINS AND REAL SALAD	144
14.	OMNIA MORSAE	152
15.	PHANTOM COMFORTS	167
16.	VIGIL	173
PART THREE: UNRAVEL		187
17.	THE SWARM	189
18.	WHISKY AND DESPAIR	200
19.	TRUST	204
20.	A LIGHT IN THE SKY	208
21.	A DEPARTURE	218
22.	COLOSSAL	226
23.	THE LAST, SLOW SWIM	234
24.	THEY ARE INFINITE	244
25.	AS IT ALWAYS WAS	253
26.	ASCENSION	264
27.	FALLEN	269
PART FOUR: UNDONE		275
28.	THE RISING DARK	277
29.	TENDRILS	282
30.	THE LAST MESSAGE	291
31.	SANCTUARIAL LIMBO	298

32. DEVASTATION — 305

Acknowledgements — 314

How To Support The Author — 316

About The Author — 318

A Note From The Author

Dear Reader,

Thank you so much for being here. Of all the millions of things you could be doing right now, you've chosen this, and that will never not be awesome. Thank you to everybody who took the time to read *DARK SANDS*, and review and recommend it to others – the response this release received was, simply put, staggering. And guess what, we've made it to the sequel! As you know, most of those involved (the characters, at least) *didn't* make it this far. I have a few notes before going into the novel proper.

Firstly, this is Australian English. I'm an Australian author, and until I have a publisher who wants to pay for multiple edits in multiple languages, *The Darkworlds Saga* will remain in Australian English. Thank you for your understanding.

Secondly, on trigger warnings. I want to acknowledge that retraumatisation can occur at any time, and warnings don't always do that justice – what's often equally important is the way this kind of content is handled by the creator. As far as conventional trigger warnings go, be prepared for scenes involving death, grief, and trauma for our characters. Also, very high heights and deep, dark oceans. This is a thriller/horror novel, and brutal things will happen. Take your time, and know that I have approached everything as mindfully and sensitively as I can.

Thirdly, in lieu of a synopsis, I made the creative choice to write a Prelude before my Prologue. This Prelude is plot-essential and designed to re-immerse you in the dangerous worlds of my series without the flow-halting labour of chewing through a synopsis – but it does mean we have a strangely structured introduction wherein my book includes a Prelude, and a more-standard Prologue after it.

Oh, and one last thing: the *DARK TIDES* Prologue directly follows on from the Prologue in book one. I hope it works for you!

Thank you so much for reading, and I hope you have a great time with the novel.

With love, JSH.
January, 2026.

PRELUDE

"SHE'S GETTING WORSE," Mon said, grim shadows playing across his face.

"Pointless an observation, in't it?" Han snapped. "She's been getting worse since she first got hurt."

"This is different. Not just fevers. It's like, her leg. It's all... puss-ey."

Han ran a coarse palm through his thinning hair. "Sol help us, Mon, do you think we're going to have to... go through with it?"

They'd had this discussion before. Mon shook his head, furrowing his bushy eyebrows. A pained moan drifted between them from the other side of the door.

"I told you, we'd be just as likely to kill her with our clumsy hands."

"I don't think a saint would sit and watch her go slowly." Mon huffed and entered the room. Han knew what he was trying to say. *Inaction begets complicity.*

Through all the crises they'd faced since coming to Cahros, this was the first that had come between them. Han had always been a firm believer of doing what he knew and only that; it had kept him out of trouble so far. But with it being just over fifty hours since Jame and Mai had led the rest of the colonists into the storm, he was starting to think that he and Mon were *it*.

Maybe Mon was right, and it would be best to at least try something. They'd worked miracles so far, in restoring half of the power grid after the sandstorm, who was to say they couldn't work another? A human body couldn't be that different from a solar panel... right?

Han shook his head, and crept into the dorm where Mury lay in fever. It all started when she'd snapped her ankle during the chaos of the Sunfall. One of the doctors had tried to reset her ankle, but they'd done a poor job of it, and infection began to take hold as the long Cahros night wore on.

Mon was at her side, staring sullenly down at their companion. Han ran his hands over Mon's left shoulder and drew him in a little closer.

"You're right, Mon. We can't just watch her fade away. But I'm not going to do the cutting," he said gently, his voice barely a whisper by the end.

Mon turned to him and smiled. "Knew you'd see the light. Thanks, Han." He skipped out of the room, probably to go rummage through the medpacks in the vehicle bay. Han wondered how long it would be before the thrill of being right faded, and the pressure of the upcoming task set in.

He waited expectantly for Mon to slink back in, or perhaps call out, but neither transpired.

"Mon?" Elhanto called.

Nothing.

"Okay... Hang in there, Mury." Han glanced down at her one last time before leaving the room. Her skin was blotchy and sweaty, and facial twitches suggested the pain had infested her dreams.

The corridors of Catal were almost pitch-black to conserve their limited power, and eery. Since the Sunfall, Han always felt disturbed whenever he walked through them now. *Too many ghosts.* The faint smell of burning ozone persisted – residue from the damage – bringing with it the lingering fear of a final, deadly breach.

Han ignored the echoes of screams and hustled down to the V-Bay, from which a crack of light shone. Just as he reached the button, a firm hand clasped his right arm.

"What game is this?" Han exclaimed, but Mon hushed him.

"Someone is here. Come." He led Han back the way they came and through to the command centre.

"I've got it up on the main screen," Mon said, but Han had already seen it. A large, dark-grey carrier charged towards Catal, dispersing waves of orange mist in its wake.

"A D6? Could it be…?" Han asked, and Mon nodded. Still, their growing hope was cut with tension. It had been over two days, and nobody had survived out there for longer than ten minutes since—

A hash of static burst from the comms station in the corner of the room.

"I can see you chews have been busy," a familiar voice growled. "How about you get busier and let an old man in?"

Relief flooded across them both as Elhanto ran to the station. "Jame! Ohhh, your voice is a sound for sore ears! Are you with everyone?"

There was a short delay before Jame spoke again, his words sobering, "No. Just me."

Mon looked ready to ask something, but Han touched his arm. "Not now," he mouthed.

"I'm suited up," Jame said, "so I'll park the D6 then move into the Decon-room, if you can open it all up for me."

"Absolutely. We'll see you soon."

They followed his instructions, and a few minutes later, met him in the darkened hallway.

"You boys have done well. Better than well. And lucky for me too, I was down to fumes in there." Jame seemed in reasonable spirits, and while his grin was infectious, Han held back.

"Turned out things weren't as bad as we thought," Han said. "And since the storm, the things have stayed away. So far."

"I can see that. Well done, really... But I guess you're wondering where the others are?" Jame said, his smile fading. They nodded.

"I wish I could tell you. Did all I could to call them an evac, but Binson said... Argh, Sol to it. Here's what happened. Some of the others died before they even got to the van, but the rest, all those brains, they thought they'd try their luck in the caves while I tried to radio in evac. Surprise, surprise, that request was denied by the brave man upstairs. I went back to the caves... but all I found was a pile of bones. Weird bones, too. But no suits. Bizarre."

By the end of the monologue, Jame had started to sound like he was talking to himself, and Han wondered how long it had been since he last slept. Jame must have noticed their bemused looks, but he didn't seem to mind.

"Figured this was as good a place for me as any. And given you're all still alive... that means the bugs haven't gotten in?" Jame pushed past them, suggesting the question was rhetorical.

"And how is dear Mury? Doc said that she set her leg properly, but I had my doubts." He strode down the dark corridor, still rambling to himself. It had only been a few days, but he seemed... different. Jame had always been focused, canny, and calm, but right now, he seemed borderline eccentric. Mon noticed too, and they traded a nervous glance before following Jame down the hall.

Han caught him just outside the dorm-room where Mury lay and pulled him aside, speaking quietly.

"She's worse, chew. Her leg looks all infected. We were just talking, we think we're going to have to... *swish*... you know what I mean." He made a cutting gesture with his hand.

Jame's eyes narrowed, and his bubbly demeanour fell away.

"So you two have taken all the fun jobs but left the best ones for me. Well, if you want something done right." Jame stalked into the dorm and surveyed Mury, who tossed and turned on stained sheets. Mon came in behind them with the medical equipment.

"Sol, you couldn't change her bed?" He looked back accusingly, and Han wilted under his glare.

"We didn't want to disturb... she seemed so pained and all," he replied meekly.

"How do you even know it's infected? Fever could be caused by anything. Sol knows she had to sit awake in pain for hours."

"Her skin. On her leg..." Han stammered, but Jame understood what he was trying to say. He ripped the sheets from Mury. She was only wearing underclothes, and Han and Mon instinctively looked away, but they couldn't escape the smell.

"Fuck. That's infected all right. Looks like it's only the foot and ankle, but fuck me if there is anything we can do to salvage it. Well then, we'll have to get this over with quick, and hope there's nothing internal. Got a T-4? She's allergic to seds."

Mon paled and backed out of the room, returning shortly after with a handheld tranquiliser.

"Jame... Ever done anything like this before?" Mon said.

Jame turned back to him, then looked over at Han.

"No. Hand me the sharpest thing in there."

Mon rustled around through the bag, and Han wandered over to look over his shoulder.

"There, that one," he said.

"Thanks," Mon retorted sarcastically, lifting a small case labelled OSTEO.

He gingerly passed it over to Jame, who cracked it open and fingered the gleaming silver handheld tool. After a moment, Jame laughed with disdain and shook his head.

"The blind leading the fucking blind. Even if I get her leg off, there's no way in Sol we're sealing the wound properly, or treating it. If the shock doesn't do for her, she'd bleed through the tourniquets in a day." He tossed the tools down and went back to Mury's side.

She stirred at his approach, and the two shared a few words Han couldn't make out.

"Come on then," Jame said, leading Han and Mon from the room. "I'll change her sheets and clothes in a moment and try to get some nutrients into her. In the meantime, do we have comms?"

"Yeah, we got the dishes back up, but they're uncalibrated, storm really wiped everything out."

"Well, it really is your lucky day. It so happens I learned a thing or two about calibration since we last met."

Jame disappeared for ten minutes or so while he tended to Mury, and then spent another hour or so cursing and panting at the comms terminal. Han and Mon didn't say anything, but they were beginning to doubt Jame had learned as much as he claimed when he finally exclaimed in triumph.

"Can you really do it all?" Mon said gleefully.

"All except what matters." Jame shook his head, a dark look spreading across his face. "Poor Mury."

A series of clicks rang through the command centre before anyone could speak again.

"Catal? Binson here. We weren't expecting to hear from you."

"Good to see you too," Jame growled. The slightly manic mood he'd been in on his return was already a fast-fading memory.

"Talwyn...?" The tinny voice sounded incredulous.

"Yep. Back from the grave." Jame smiled, clearly enjoying the surprise of the fleet officer on the other end of the line.

"But... how? Never mind. Last we knew, Catal was dysfunctional and abandoned. And you were..."

"A ghost in the making. But alas, here we all are. Situation is secure and the storms have abated. Word is..." He glanced at Han and Mon, standing idly before him. "The bugs have had their fill, we're back online, and more than happy to sit on our hands until the mothership gets back. Can I get a status on that?"

"Same as it's always been. Three standard weeks from landing. So, eight days to go."

"Shit. I don't know if Mury is going to last that long."

"Who? You've got wounded in there with you? Need I ask if they are compromised?"

Jame's eyes narrowed, but he checked himself. "Not compromised, not exposed at all. Just broke her ankle during the chaos, and it hasn't set right. Looks infected."

"Where?"

"Like I said, ankle."

"Sol-damnit, then it's easy! Tourniquet the limb and feed her some antibiotics, even if there's a wound, it's unlikely to kill her in a week."

"Thanks," Jame's voice oozed with sarcasm, "I've done that. But what about sepsis?"

"I don't suppose one of the, how many of you are there, happens to be your onsite medical professional?"

"Four, counting Mury, and no."

"Well, I don't know what to tell you. *Nitimini* will return in eight standard, and they'll be able fix her up. Keep her clean, comfortable, and alive until then. Start a prayer circle if you need. Anything else?"

"Yes." Jame hesitated.

"Spit it out, Talwyn."

"The group at the formation... what happened to them?" Jame twitched, and the suggestion of a tear pooled under his right eye.

"Nothing. No sign of them, dead or alive. And yes, we flew out to them, but no, we didn't land. But... they'd set up a short-range transmitter, we got to see everything that went down. Looks like one of them went insubordinate, and the rest chased him down the caves. Nothing after that."

Jame cursed under his breath and blinked several times, regaining a semblance of composure. Curiosity burned Han's mind – there was so much he had missed – but now wasn't the time.

"Binson. With everything that's happened here... what are we going to tell everyone back home?" Jame continued.

"Leave that to the spin doctors on the *Nitimini,* and Earthside. As far as home is concerned, we have successfully erected and maintained our first extraterrestrial settlement."

"And the losses?"

This time it was Binson's turn to pause.

"Nobody was expecting we wouldn't have losses."

Jame shook his head, aghast. "The entire population down here is dead, missing, unaccounted for! This isn't *losses,* it's a fucking catastrophe! What about the other base, gone too, right? They going to throw that one out there? What about the second colonisation fleet? Surely they can't be still sending—"

"Enough. I fail to see your point. Your findings have been essential, and the next wave will have plenty of time to implement them. Your... our expedition can only be described as a success." His coldly delivered words raked through Han like poisoned scythes; such a trivialisation of all who had lost their lives.

"So that's it then? Business as usual?" Jame spat.

"In a term, yes. Keep the place together, and the *Mini* might even be able to drop a few extra bodies down for you to help maintain the place, and get Mury back on her feet."

"Maintain the place? As if anybody would want to come down *here*...What about our evac?"

Binson simply laughed. "You really think the UCI is going to just walk out on all this? Have you forgotten about the many interests these expeditions represent? Forget it, CO, orders are orders, and besides, I don't see what you can do about it."

This time, Jame had nothing to say, and it seemed the news about his friends at the formation was starting to take a toll. He stared straight ahead, seeing and saying nothing. Uncomfortable, Han stepped up to the comms console, gently shouldering past the older man.

"We read you. Reinforcements in a few weeks. Then we proceed as usual. How long until the second fleet's meant to arrive?"

If Binson noticed the change in speakers, he didn't care. "The *Nitimini* will return to Earth, with news, in a little under three months subjective. Six months for them to develop whatever response is needed to properly contain the threats of Cahros, then another six to get back to you. Do the math. Now, is that everything?"

Han tried not to envy the cold, unempathetic officer in the sky. How was it that a man like Binson got to go home after all this, when dozens upon dozens of worthy people had fallen to an agonising demise?

"No. End comms," Han murmured, feeling heavy.

"They never cared if we lived or died down here," he whispered.

"Yep. Just a bunch of guinea pigs," Jame said, still staring straight ahead.

Han remained at the console for a time, until he felt a warm hand creep into his, restoring a little bit of hope.

"Come now, eighteen months isn't so long. Just a'cos they don't think we'll make it, don't mean they're right. And the company could be worse." Mon's tanned face was creased in a smile, and crow's feet stretched from the corner of his eyes.

Jame looked over them, and Han braced for a reprimand, but his face softened.

"You boys are lucky, you know. Just four people left on the planet. What are the odds your bed-friend is one of them?"

Han felt another flash of encouragement. He'd worked with Jame a long time, and the man was as capable as any. And Mon... was the gentlest soul he'd ever known.

He allowed himself a little smile. "Good enough for me."

PROLOGUE

New London, Earth   CD: 20-06-2220

Crisis Correspondent

"A COMPLETE, UTTER, unmitigated disaster!" The wailings of the beady-eyed man echoed through the conference room, causing the row of dull-suited executives to shift uncomfortably. As if to emphasise his despair, he dropped his tablet to the conference table with a melodramatic swish.

Outside, a light rain fell, leaving dirty brown streaks on the old, ill-maintained windows, and a light in the corner flickered as the room held its breath. Eventually, all eyes drifted towards the crisis correspondent. She grimaced, suppressing the flurry of emotional punches in her stomach. Her job was about to be difficult enough without all this scrutiny.

"So... just to confirm..." she began carefully. "Ninety-six out of one hundred colonists were lost? All dead?"

The beady-eyed man shook his head, skin flaps around his neck quivering. "Unaccounted for. The first colony had forty-one confirmed deceased. Five missing. The second... no survivors, no reports, all *presumed* dead. But none confirmed."

"Right." She weighed up her response, knowing the words would feel like razors as they departed her throat. "So, if you want the spin, the best thing to do is be sparing with information. Oversharing just opens you up to targeting. Ergo, we don't report on presumptions. Nor do we openly specify exactly how many were missing in action – ambiguity breeds doubt. What is the status of the facilities?"

"Both intact. One abandoned, but can be salvaged."

"Good," Lenza, the CEO, interjected, rolling her eyes. "So they got *something* done at least."

The correspondent fought the impulse to retort. Did Lenza really believe this disaster was the fault of anyone but the UCI?

"It seems simple enough to me," the correspondent continued, hating every word she breathed. "We advertise the success of the facilities, the discovery of new life, and praise the sacrifices of those lost. Run tributes, specials, interviews, all the like. Send out the farewell vids they all recorded. Build some memorials, have the families lay the wreaths."

"But we tell them nothing," Lenza said pointedly.

"They are going to need an explanation, even if it is not the tardigrades. A freak construction accident. Someone falling asleep at the wheel, activating the airlock, decompressing the base. Something like that, I'll work out the kinks."

"We're going to need a scapegoat. Or two. Maybe three," Lenza said.

The correspondent looked down at the table, her breath catching. None of this was fair. It was bad enough they'd sent these people to their deaths, now they were blaming them?

"I needn't remind you the importance this does not get out. We have several colonist ships we still need to fill, and public relations are precarious at best already." Lenza's tone sounded somewhere between stern and annoyed.

"Fine," the correspondent said through gritted teeth. "I'll pick the ones with no family, no connections, nobody to remember them... or stick up for them."

"Good. We will... need to include a sizable military force this time around. Market to everyone, but ensure we screen for those in the service."

"Forgive me, ma'am," the beady-eyed man said. "But about squashing the message. Won't the prospective reinforcements find out anyway? Once they get there? Not to mention the R&D teams, if we're going to go military..."

"I don't care. Tell them we need more soldiers to protect our interests. Once they're in the air, we put together a little presentation. Tell them how important they are and why they couldn't know everything until that moment. Then equip them with all they need to fight these... tardigrates."

The correspondent surveyed the room. Not a word of resistance came from those present. She wondered what strange, hellish world she'd stepped into. That she was now a part of. Another wave of nausea kicked at her stomach.

"What about everyone else? Don't you think the world deserves to know about what we found?" a clean-shaven, short-haired man asked.

Lenza turned to him and smiled. "Of course. Once the ships have launched, we break the news worldwide."

She rose from her seat and spread her arms in a magnanimous gesture. "Life, in outer space! Ancient Tardigrames, frozen in the sands. Predatory, but easily contained. They're the size of a fleck of dust, after all!"

The correspondent couldn't control herself this time. "Tardigrades."

"What?" Lenza said sharply.

"Tardigrades, not tardigrates." The glare Lenza shot her could have drawn blood.

"That's what I said. Tardigrades. You've got a lot of work to do, yes?" The unceremonious dismissal may have been embarrassing, if she wasn't so relieved to get out of there. While waiting for the lift, she listened to them waffle from the other side of the room.

"Now, who was the one who discovered them?"

"Credit attributed to one of the scis," the beady-eyed man said, casually. "Tarlo, looks like his name was." The correspondent's breath caught in her chest. She'd long given up hope of ever hearing—

"Not sure if he was one of the deads. Probably was though, considering..."

"Shame," Lenza said, equally emotionless. "But let's say they did, unfortunately, pass, their sacrifice does have some poetic sway! Have the species named after them, or something. Tarlo-grates, it's almost perfect already!" A smattering of sycophantic chuckles spread through the room.

The lift finally arrived, and the doors opened with a shudder. The correspondent leaned back against the brown walls, ignoring the grime, and emitted a shuddering sigh. The lift came to a halt with an uncertain, off-pitch ping. She drew in a deep breath and mapped out her route. Coffee machine, cubicle, shutters, safety.

Two dozen anxious eyes followed her as she wove through the room, but she kept her gaze to the floor and mouth glued shut.

There was more to her frustration and anxiety than just some moral objection. Sure, what the UCI were doing was disrespectful – at best – but that wasn't news to her.

She took the coffee, bitter and burned as always, but still comforting in its predictability. Reaching the safety of her cubicle, she activated the privacy shutters, and in the darkness, logged into her terminal. She'd have access to all the dossiers now, as well as all the information about what had really happened. But first, there was one person whose fate she *had* to know.

Ignoring the growing curiosity in the room, she opened the report labelled COLONISTS and began scrolling through. Each file contained information about the history, profession, and now, the fate of everyone who had been on the expedition.

Why was this taking so long? Assailed by her worst fears, she kept losing focus and must have scrolled up and down the list three times already. *Where is he?*

There.

TARLO.

A surge of anticipatory nausea pummelled her, and she took another deep breath. For all her words upstairs about "ambiguity", the law of averages suggested his demise was nigh-certain, and she knew that on a remote, non-terraformed planet, "missing" might as well have been "dead".

But still, she had to know.

With a shaking hand, she clicked.

27. MALE. BIOLOGIST. NEW LONDON. MISS-
ING AS OF 05-04-2220. FATE UNKNOWN. PRE-
SUMED DECEASED.

Despite the coverings, everyone on her floor heard her single, involuntary shriek of despair.

PART ONE
UNKNOWN

1

WHAT STRANGE PROVIDENCE

A GREAT WEIGHT pressed down upon Tarlo as he staggered through the dark, but a sense of growing wonder propelled him forwards. Warning lights blared in his visor, signifying his suit's power levels were critical, and his head ached like never before, but all of that faded into the background – he needed to find the source of those waves.

Tarlo stumbled through the cave's exit, and his boots immediately sank into wet sand. *Sand!* Alarm coursed through him, and he jumped back to the sharp rocky ground at the edge of the cave to catch his bearings. Though it was night, an array of stars provided ample light to the vista ahead, and in the far west – according to his vis-compass – bright glows suggested the imminent rising of at least one celestial body.

Tarlo turned his attention to his immediate surroundings. Less than twenty metres from where he perched, the edges of a great tide foamed a muddy sandbar. Mesmerised, he watched the waves loom high, casting shadows taller than he was. They hung in the air for a few, long seconds before thundering into the shoreline, darkening the sands with their moisture.

He realised then that their small islet of sand was a brown oasis in the midst of being swallowed by a sea of navy blue. Despite its size, it seemed to function almost as a microcontinent, drawing the waves upon it from all sides like inverted ripples. Beyond the shoreline, there were no landmarks. Just an endless sea of indigo.

"Tarlo, wait up!" A voice echoed in his headset – the vocal register had been damaged, so he had no idea which of his companions it belonged to. Turning, he saw that all three of them had caught up, but his attention was quickly drawn to the sight behind them. Through a large, previously unnoticed gap in the cavern's ceiling, two great towers rose: parallel bars of obsidian that stretched far into the sky, darker than the darkest night, and blocking the shine of the stars behind them.

Disorientation struck. These monoliths directly resembled the ones he'd seen before entering the cave, but now, the sands of Cahros had been replaced by these endless oceans. His mind scrambled as he remembered the visions, the feeling of being shocked by a thousand bolts of lighting, then falling through the dark.

Tarlo raised his hand, index finger outstretched. They all turned, following his gesture.

"It's a Blackrock formation. Just like... the other one," someone said.

"The other one? Are these not the same rocks?" another voice shrilled.

"Where in Sol... are we?" A third voice, still garbled, but deeper. Tarlo attributed it to Terrus, who lagged at the rear of the group, clutching his left arm. Tarlo winced, recalling the scuffle with Yerald that caused it, and hoped the wound had not been reopened by their mysterious transit.

"Cahros. Where else could we be?" Matter of fact, minimal words used – Ashelyn.

"No. No. No! There is not a drop of water on Cahros, now or for decades before! This... we are somewhere else now." Judging by their hurried words and agitation, it must have been Mai.

"What? You make no sense," Ashelyn said. Detecting her frustration, Tarlo felt a wave of sympathy – she had never coped well with the abstract.

Despite the reality-defying nature of their experience and growing distress around him, Tarlo felt a flush of relief. Somehow, after everything, they were still alive. "It must be some trick of the rocks. Some vision, like those before," Mai said. "I'm... Sol, my head hurts."

Their voices faded into the background as Tarlo knelt to the ground. He trailed a gloved hand through the sand, feeling a mix of wonder and awe. "No. This is real. I don't know how, but it's real," he said, staring at the clumpy, brown grains as they tumbled from his grip.

"My suit is low. Really low," Mai said, the panic in her voice being translated into a high pitch that might have been comical at any other moment.

"Mine too."

"And mine. Sol, what do we do? Should we go back?" Terrus said.

"We were nearly fully charged before we came here. There's no way our suits survive another trip," Ashelyn said.

Tarlo ran his hands through the sand again. It was markedly different to the dusty, lightweight grains of Cahros. With a start, he realised the cause of the heavy lumpiness. *The sand was wet.* He flicked his eyes back to the ocean with a growing sense of urgency. The metronomic thundering continued, and the shoreline had crept a couple of metres closer already.

"The tide! It's coming in!" he shouted, stumbling back towards the others. Mai was gripping Ashelyn tightly, and behind them, Terrus had gone quiet and was teetering a little to the left.

"Coming from where? And where are we going?" he said woozily. The impact of his wound seemed to be worsening.

"It's moving slowly, but it's coming in. This whole area is going to end up under water!" Tarlo said. Concern spread through the others. Their suits would be able to keep them warm and afloat, but only as long as they remained charged.

Then Tarlo saw it. A red light, flashing by the entrance to the cave. *A distress beacon.* There was no time to speak or debate, he darted towards it and slammed his glove on the obvious red button.

"Come back this way. It's drier. I think." Terrus made it to him first, collapsing on Tarlo. At this range, Tarlo could see the details of his face behind his visor. Terrus's features were as proud as ever, but his eyes were rolled and forehead soaking wet. With an effort, Tarlo shifted the dead weight, propping Terrus as gently as possible against the beacon.

The others joined them. Ashelyn firmly instructed Mai to sit beside Terrus before she crouched in front of him.

"He's unconscious. Probably a good thing for now, will use less resources. And Mai, listen to me. The quieter you are, the slower you breathe, the less oxygen you use. What's your favourite song?"

"Anaesthesia, by Purple Works."

"Does it have lyrics?"

"Yes, a lot—"

"Sing them in your head. If that fails, count in sevens back from three thousand."

"Okay."

"Stay with Terrus. We're going to scout around for a moment."

Ashelyn turned to Tarlo and gestured back towards the tides. The entire islet was only a few hundred metres squared, and shrinking fast, but he suspected she wanted to get away from their companions for a moment.

"Wait!" Tarlo said. "Sand... water... we can't know it's safe. There could be—"

"We've only got a few minutes of juice anyway. If they're here, they're here. I want to look around." Ashelyn strode forward. Against his better judgement, Tarlo found himself caught in her slipstream, and followed her towards the water's edge, exiting local comms range.

"I'm so tired," Ashelyn murmured, staring out into the waves. "And so lost. I thought I had made sense of everything. The spirits of those... creatures, their messages. But now we're somehow stepping into solid rock and being spat out in a totally different place? Help me, Tarlo."

Tarlo stepped beside her, and laid a hand on her arm, just above the elbow. She jerked a little, reflexively, but leaned in towards him. He felt a small thrill.

"It doesn't make any sense. It can't make sense. But wherever we are now... people have been here. The beacon... It's UCI," he said.

Ashelyn raised her arms in an exaggerated shrug. "That's no more insane than anything else that's happened here. Logically, I'd suggest the chances of rescue before our resources run out are impossible, but I just don't know anymore." She started pacing and wringing her hands, as if trying to stimulate an answer. "If the beacon actually works, maybe people are around here somewhere. Somehow. We need to get the others back safely, especially Terrus. Back? Somewhere? Safe? Sol, I'm so tired."

They trudged back towards Mai and Terrus and watched as the tides closed in on all sides. They could have fled back through the cave, but it was all downhill, and the water was sure to follow them. They could have scaled the rocky walls to put a few metres between them and the encroaching tide, but not while bearing Terrus's deadweight. Instead, they hoisted him up onto the highest piece of ground they could manage. Mai clambered up beside him, but there wasn't room for all of them, so Tarlo and Ashelyn chose to stand grimly at the cave's entrance like sombre, stone guardians. Despite the panic such a situation should have caused, a distracted numbness descended upon the group. There was nothing else they could do, and they had been running for so long.

The encroaching waves consumed the remains of the sandbar. Water slid against their ankles, and the sand sucked at the soles of their boots hungrily. In the distance, a bright white light pierced the skies as a small, white-grey moon crested the horizon.

"That settles it," Ashelyn breathed. "This definitely isn't Cahros. But how…"

"I don't know." Tarlo's reply hung in the air, and they shared a moment of stillness. He remembered the first time they had spoken properly, all those days ago. On that occasion, they'd been gazing out at an orange sea instead of a navy one, and his greatest anxieties were only what she thought of him. Back before the Sunfall. Before the deaths.

"It sure is pretty," Ashelyn said.

It was, but still, the only thing Tarlo wanted to look at in that moment was *her*.

"A nice enough place to watch the world end," he said.

"Maybe just ours." The waves crashed against their knees with a force that activated their stabilisers. Absently, Tarlo thought about the excess power this would use.

"I can't believe we're alive at all. For now, anyway," he said, marvelling at the strange moonrise.

"Nor I. Whatever made us so special?" Ashelyn sighed. "I can't stop wondering if this has all been one big experiment."

"If it is, maybe you think it's time they pulled us out?" Tarlo laughed weakly.

His breathing slowed as he imagined the four of them from a bird's eye: a little copse of broken bodies clustered together on a world unknown, soon to be consumed by the blue nothing. For all they'd been through, all they'd survived…was this how it was meant to end?

An uncharacteristically hearty laugh from Ashelyn brought him back to the ground. "Guess the experiment isn't over yet." She pointed towards the moon, and for a moment, Tarlo thought she'd lost her wits, but then he saw it, too.

First, it was the smallest of shadows, a silhouette against the rising moon. As it grew larger, Tarlo made out the artificial white of headlights, and then the shape of a small, shuttle-like vehicle, hovering just a few metres above the ocean's surface.

"What strange providence," Ashelyn said dryly, but Tarlo's mind was occupied only by thought of rescue and safety. His energy returned in a flash, and he joined her in waving his arms vociferously, screaming for the shuttle to come their way.

2

A FIRST BREATH

THE VEHICLE DREW nearer. Small and sleek, it was something between a boat and an aerial shuttle, with a flat, rectangular body and triangular cockpit. The passenger compartment was small, with a shallow roof that would make it impossible to stand fully upright while inside, though the cab stretched back with deceptive length. Beneath the shuttle, dual rows of splashes flurried across the surface of the water. The exterior of the shuttle was a uniform light-grey, with a single, aqua stripe around the hull that dappled in the moonlight.

It reached them in short time, drawing to a graceful halt a small distance away. Tarlo noticed a series of digits – X098 – painted in black beneath the stripe. The cockpit popped open in a fashion that reminded Tarlo of the BBF buggies they'd used back on Cahros, and two women rose to their feet. While they wore suits similar to Tarlo's E12, amazingly, neither of them had helmets on.

Ashelyn saw this at the same time, and gasped. "Sol! Are we back... on Earth?"

Their rescuers must have had earpieces in, for they heard her words and shook their heads. One beamed with laughter, while the other appraised them sternly.

"No, we're not on Earth, but there is a Bermuda back there too! Though we'd loooove to know where on *Alantia* you've popped up from?" the laughing one said, her voice ringing out clearly thanks to some kind of microphone device.

The two women leapt from the shuttle, landing in the thigh-deep water with a synchronised splash. Now the place was submerged, the ferocity of the waves had notably lessened. Tarlo noticed his E12 stabilisers power down as he and Ashelyn walked towards their visitors.

"I'm Mauve," the jovial one said. A wave of red hair framed even redder cheeks, and a pleasant smile occupied her face. Now they were closer, Tarlo could see a small, clear device attached to each of their cheeks, connecting an ear and mouthpiece. Their noses were free though, suggesting they really were breathing in the air of this place.

"I'm the personnel liaison here. Colonial HR, if you will," Mauve continued. Where she was short, heavyset, and welcoming, the lady beside her was tall, thin, and taciturn, and did not offer a name or greeting.

Tarlo looked over at Ashelyn for guidance, and she nodded. There was no benefit in surreptitiousness; they were at the mercy of these people.

"I'm Ashelyn, lead Neurosurgeon of Catal, Cahros. This is Sci Tarlo. We have two companions with us, another sci and a squaddie, who is wounded. I'm sure you are aware the tide is coming in – we also have seriously low charges on our suits. There is much we can share, but first, we request your help."

Mauve laughed again. "Why, so formal! But just to confirm, did you say Cahros?"

"I did."

Mauve's eyes widened, and she exchanged a quick glance with the stern one, who took their turn to step forward.

"I am Elís, the lead sergeant of Tuwia, the local skybase. We will be able to aid you, so long as you agree to follow strict quarantine, and adhere to my authority."

Tarlo noted how she said *my* authority, and not that of the settlement or a governing body. Then there was also one of the words she used... *skybase*... he remembered talking to someone about such a thing a lifetime ago but couldn't remember who.

"We will adhere," Ashelyn said simply. Elís nodded to Mauve, and they jumped back in the vehicle, piloting it past the two colonists and over towards the rock formation. Tarlo and Ashelyn jogged to keep up, and their suits were sodden by the time they reached the pair, who were surveying Mai and Terrus.

Ashelyn's grounding exercises appeared to have worked well for Mai, who was on her feet, babbling excitedly with Mauve.

"Go on, take your helmets off!" Mauve said. "The air here has been safe for human consumption for months!"

Mai complied, and her haggard face split with joy as she sucked in a great breath.

"It tastes... sweet. And hot. Tarlo, Ash, did you hear? This is Alantia, the *water planet*. Tarlo, you should know, we used to speak of this place!"

Tarlo's memory flashed with an image of a shuttle, buckled up, Mai beside him, discussing the planets chosen by the Martellus Index for colonisation.

Elís climbed up the outcrop where Terrus rested and perched beside him. "How long has he been this way?"

Ashelyn cautiously popped off her helm and took a deep breath. "Not long. A few minutes. However long since we hit the beacon." She spoke calmly, but Tarlo detected a slight edge in her voice.

"Minutes? We got your signal two hours ago," Elís said. "But never mind. We know all about the tricks these rocks can play. As far as he's concerned, it *has* only been a few minutes. What is wrong with him?"

"He was wounded. By... someone. They cut him with a shard of the Blackrock."

"Blackrock? Do you mean—"

"That." Ashelyn pointed at the black towers.

"Huronium? Given it was named for someone on Cahros, I'd assume you are familiar with the name." Elís gave them a suspicious look, which morphed to one of concern upon seeing Terrus's physical state. "We've never seen anyone cut by it... though we know it can be deadly in other ways. He will need to be cared for quickly... and uniquely."

Tarlo felt a wave of concern for his friend, followed by guilt as he remembered how Terrus had been wounded in coming to his aid.

"I won't touch him. You will have to get him onto the shuttle. Get your friend to help you," Elís ordered, before nimbly turning and leaping back into the cockpit.

Ashelyn called out to Mai, who jumped back into the water, still babbling excitedly.

"The skybases, they really got them to work! I don't know how, but those rocks took us to another planet. And not just any, to the second planet on the Martellus Index, one of the ones targeted by the other expeditions! By Sol, we have so much to talk about!"

"Yeah, well, we have some lifting to do first," Ashelyn grunted in reply. With great effort, the three of them bore Terrus to the rear of the shuttle, fighting against light swells that compounded their intense fatigue. They nearly dropped him at the craft's edge as Tarlo tripped in a footmark, but Ashelyn somehow jabbed an arm out to steady him just in time. Once they got the top half of Terrus into the shuttle, the rest was a simple, if clumsy process of shoving with all their might.

"Tarlo. Won't you take off your helm?" Mai prompted. Beside her, Ashelyn nodded, but still he hesitated. It had been so long since he breathed clear, fresh air from anywhere, he almost didn't trust it anymore. Beyond that, his mind was still whirling. Elís had said it was hours ago when they heard the distress call, and what Mauve had said... months of clean air? Had they not only travelled in place, but time too?

"Come on," Mauve called. "We'd best be leaving. If we're not back in eight hours objective, they'll think we're in trouble. And according to our gravitationally adjusted mental watches, we're sitting on about six now. You'll get all the fresh air you want back at base!"

Mai shrugged and crawled into the passenger space of the vehicle, where four seats were suspended against the side panels, between which lay Terrus. Ashelyn did the same, as did Tarlo, bumping his knee and clanging his helm multiple times as he tried to slalom through. The vehicle whirred smoothly to life, and they skimmed the waves in the direction of the first-risen moon, whose bright light reflected across the endless seas in shimmering ripples.

"Once we're out of interference range we'll run your IDs. But if I'm correct, you four are among the last unaccounted colonists from the first wave over in Cahros," Mauve said. "They've been looking for you for a good while. Well, actually, they gave up a long time ago, but more on that in a minute. So, tell us, what was it? I see you're mostly scientists; did you throw together some kind of bastardised spaceship, skip your way out? Sol knows I would have, with what you all went through back there. Better to take my chances against the cosmos than a megacolony of *Maleficus*. And there was enough tech missing from the sites that you could have scrounged something up. Then what? Run out of fuel, crash-land here? Or maybe your expertise only extended to building the ship, not charting it, and you hurtled off in whatever direction you were facing? No, too much of a coincidence you'd find the one planet you might get help. My oh my, you've all some explaining to do! The UCI have declared you dead, martyrs in fact. If you were to show back up here though... deserters, I should think. That won't look too good for you. You know, they tried to desert the fourth planet, the jungle one, on account of the spider-lizards, but they—" Mauve was cut off by a sharp gesture from Elís, who turned from her position piloting the shuttle.

"Never mind her. You, at the front. Tarlo? Tell us how you got here."

Tarlo's head was still spinning from all the information Mauve had just unwittingly shared, and he fumbled at his helm, still hesitant to remove it. Elís must have noticed the heaviness of his face and droopiness of his eyes, for she redirected the question to Ashelyn.

"There were no ships," Ashelyn replied. "And we did not wilfully desert Cahros, although we were awaiting evacuation. I doubt you'll believe the rest of our story, though it might be best if we shared in a... more comfortable space. We are tired and have been through... a lot."

Elís looked them over, narrow-eyed. After a moment, she nodded once and turned around.

"So be it. Your disorientation is clearly not being simulated. Once we arrive back at base, we will quarantine all of you, but shall send some specialists in to aid your friend how we can. Then, the rest of you will be medically examined. Staff will be under firm instruction not to engage with you, due to the questionability of your sudden appearance, and we expect you will conduct yourselves with discretion. Am I understood?"

"Yes. Thank you," Ashelyn replied simply. Elís made it clear the conversation was over through a series of commands barked into her mouthpiece.

A final warning flashed on Tarlo's visor.

ENERGY DEPLETED. REMOVE HELM TO AVOID CARBON DIOXIDE INHALATION.

The choice was out of his hands now. Tarlo raised his aching arms and fingered the release button on the back of his neck. He leaned forward, the helmet clanged into his hands, and he took his first breath of fresh air in months. He coughed reflexively, but it was clean and warm, surging through his greedy lungs with a wheeze.

Mauve turned to them again, her cheeks rosy and merry, despite the tenseness of the previous conversation. Tarlo noticed a faint scent wafting from her red hair. *Was that... floral?*

"How did you know to look for us out there? As in, to leave a beacon so conveniently placed? And what did you call it, Bermuda? What does that mean?" Ashelyn asked.

"It's funny you ask. We've been running deep-sea expeditions here for months, and some of these missions, well, as *you* would know, can go awry. People get lost, navs fall away, all that kind of thing. For some reason, they kept resurfacing right where you good people popped out. There was an old folktale on Earth that it reminded us of – the Bermuda triangle. A dead zone in the ocean where early ships, even planes, often disappeared, never to be seen again! So we figured, let's set up a little doorbell for them, so that we might, you know, have a hope of getting to them in time."

Her words tailed off, and Tarlo wondered what growing pains they'd faced here, and how they compared with the disasters that had taken place back on Cahros. The expedition to settle this planet, Alantia, had departed Earth at the same time as their own. For Alantia to have a leadership structure, a human resources liaison who had access to such a luxury as *perfume*, not to mention conducting months of exploration and terraformation, and somehow having news of what had happened to Cahros...

"Mauve? What date is it?" he blurted, and she gave him a confused look.

"What date do you think it is, chew?"

"I... I can't remember," he said, suddenly embarrassed.

"Last we knew, it was oh five oh four," Ashelyn said, sparing his blushes.

"Sure. That was only a few days ago."

"Wait! Oh five oh four, twenty-two twenty," Tarlo interjected, the date finally returning to him.

Mauve laughed, thinking he was jesting, then frowned a little. "My friends... Your confused act is mighty compelling, but you don't need to lie to us! It's twenty-two twenty-two! A once in a millennium year!"

The blood drained from Tarlo's face, and beside him, Ashelyn looked similarly stunned. If Mauve noticed this, she remained unperturbed.

"We know that these rocks slow one's perception of time in quite a way. Are you sure you were only waiting for us a few minutes?" she posed.

"Yes. We... we fell. Through a similar place like this... Bermuda. Just on Cahros. It was similar... but different. Two black rocks just like..." Tarlo's words slurred as his exhaustion mounted, and it wasn't until he fell into Ashelyn that he realised he was losing consciousness. She caught him firmly, and once she propped him back up, he could have sworn her hands lingered on his shoulders for an extra second.

"There will be time to fill us in on your grand misadventures soon. We're almost there!" Mauve said cheerily, though her eyes were a little more wary.

"I'd suggest you all look ahead through the cockpit. You only get to behold Tuwia for the first time once!"

With her words, the ship lurched upwards. Tarlo squinted through the glassy cockpit, weariness tugging at the tips of his eyelids. A dense, grey fog swallowed the shuttle, and he fell into its colourless embrace.

Just a little further... Just a little...

Sleep took hold of him right as they peaked beyond the clouds, denying Tarlo the first sight of his new home.

3
QUESTIONS

Tuwia, Alantia   CD: 08/04/2222

Tarlo

THE JOLT OF the shuttle docking with Tuwia was enough to startle Tarlo back to consciousness. For a moment, he was disoriented, wondering what had become of the dark sands of Cahros, but lucidity quickly returned when Elís popped the cockpit. A stern breeze accosted them – the first burst of natural air Tarlo had felt in months. It was brisk and cool, sharpening his fuzzy senses, and his exposed skin tingled all over. Just as quickly as the gust began, it ended, and Mauve gestured for them to crawl from the cargo-space.

The sky around was all grey, but the fog had cleared somewhat, allowing Tarlo a view of his immediate surroundings. Their docking area was small – it seemed they'd taken the facility's only shuttle – although two other strange, spherical vehicles were suspended in place nearby. On opposite sides of the docking area, two gunmetal staircases stretched upwards, leading to alternate sides of the facility.

"Pretty cool set-up, hey?" Tarlo didn't know what Mauve was referring to until she gestured back towards the shuttle. Rather than clamps or straps holding it in place, it seemed to have melded directly into the base. "All magnets. Don't need power, don't need heavy machinery – the only thing that could compromise them would be the sun falling on top of us. Meaning, heat. Which at this altitude is never a worry, except for lightning – but that only comes from above, and we have plenty of protection against it. Expect things to stay a chilly five or ten degrees Celsius outdoors."

Mauve led them to the foot of the staircase on the left side and continued her lecture, "Gusts here get pretty fierce, can knock a woman right overboard! That said, they are somewhat sporadic and we can usually see them coming. Keep your ears out for a single klaxon – if you hear it, you'd best grab a handrail." As Mauve bellowed, she procured several harnesses, which she tossed to them, gesturing they attach them to their waists. As Tarlo clicked the harness to his hip, his vision flickered, and for a second, he saw golden bonds leading into the deepest dark...

"Can't be too careful. Policy is to always be hooked up when you're outside," Mauve was saying. "Now, follow me. We'll get you quarantined, treated, and inoculated. Air is breathable and safe, sure, but too much of it and your E12 waste tanks start feeling real small, real quick!"

Tarlo's stomach flipped, and he reduced the depth of his breaths. He knew he should have kept his helmet on! He'd eaten so little in the past twenty-four hours; he dreaded to think what kind of impact this seemingly "fresh" air might have on his immune and digestive systems.

"All hooked up? Follow me then. Don't worry about your friend, we'll have him brought in once staff are suitably... protected."

"I'll see you in decontamination," Elís said to Mauve. She shot them all one last glare before striding up the alternate staircase, all rigid posture and square shoulders. Mauve beckoned to Tarlo and the others to follow her. She took the stairs confidently, not even trailing a hand on the rails that lined the area. Ashelyn was first to follow, though Mai lagged behind, choosing instead to peer over the fence.

"Tarlo, look!" Warily, he tiptoed beside her, fastening his gloved hands so tightly to the railing they might have fused there.

"See, the clouds are about to clear!" He fought the rising vertigo and peeped over the edge, at first seeing only a floor of wispy white clouds.

"Prepare for incoming gust," a metallic voice rang out, followed by a piercing horn. Tarlo held his breath and braced. This gust was significantly stronger than the first, and nearly brought them to their knees, shaking the entire facility. Mai paled and dry heaved. Tarlo fought hard against the urge to do the same, but when he saw what was below, he lost all control.

His first viewing of the parting of the clouds might have made for a beautiful moment, were it not once again ruined by his discomfort. A small portion of brown bile spilled from his mouth, and he watched it bashfully as it trailed slowly through the sky towards the ocean below. He lost sight of it after a few metres, and tried to push it from his mind, but the new vision of the cobalt-blue waves rising and falling was in equal parts mesmeric and nauseating. He had spent so long fearing the sandy grounds of Cahros, but to now be somewhere where the ground simply *didn't exist...*

"Manage not to keel off?" Mauve's chipper voice echoed from above. "Come now, there will be time to sightsee later. The sooner you start quarantining, the sooner you stop!"

Tarlo and Mai crept up the staircase, and he felt very aware of the growing pain in his throat and stomach. He felt a peculiar sense of relief when they were shown into a drab room, also in that dull-metal colour.

"You lucky ones will get the penthouse suite," Mauve said. "While Elís and will I have the *ignominy* of decontaminating in the old broom closet. Not exactly UCI HQ, but it will be your home for the next few hours. Three, to be precise. There is an enclosed bathroom on the far side, you'll be pleased to note, though you'll have to take turns with it. Once this is all done, we'll have worked out a plan for what we're going to do with you all. Elís might want to radio you in, let the UCI decide what to do with you, but that will take days to get anywhere. Besides, I've got a better idea. But worry not! The docs will bring in a few energy bars and the like, but nothing too exciting given what your digestive systems will be going through. Hydro caps too, of course. Anyhow, I've got schemes to make, I'll see you all in a few hours!"

With that, she left the three of them alone. Apart from the occasional roaring gusts of wind – accompanied by the same, prerecorded warning announcement, the area was silent.

"How high up do you think we are?" Tarlo asked, refusing to approach, or even look at, the windows peppered around the room.

Mai was far less concerned and had already made her way over to one. "I don't think we're too high, though it's hard to tell by eye. Going by the fact there are clouds beneath us, I'd guess around two to four kilometres... but the conditions here might make for a lower cloud ceiling."

"It feels wrong… not having a ground below us. Like we might plummet at any moment."

Mai laughed, though there was a strain in her voice. "Tarlo, you've spent months of your life in a spaceship, and potentially just had the first human experience of teleportation, and you're worried about that? You heard them, they've been up here for years."

"I'm still trying to process Cahros. Sol, I'm still trying to process the Sunfall! Things are moving so fast, I don't even know how to… what…" His words failed him, and he rested his head in his hands for a moment. He felt like he just needed some space, some time, maybe a warm drink, to slow down and make sense of everything he had been through.

"Every time I start thinking about what's happened, I feel the urge to throw myself out into these winds. But the brain has a funny way of shutting itself down when it needs to. Maybe you should let yours?" Mai said.

Tarlo looked over at her, musing over the many mood swings, exclamations, and general unpredictability that had overcome her since they reconvened in the D6, before travelling to the Cahros formation. It didn't seem she was shutting anything down, but he guessed this was her best attempt at being helpful.

"What do we think about our rescuers?" Mai continued, evidently looking for something to focus her mind on.

"Or our captors," Ashelyn grumbled. "I don't trust them. That Elís… she's by the book. And the book says to throw us overboard, be it into the ocean, or on a ship and into what they call a *professional debrief*. If it was military, they'd call it a court marshal."

"Mauve seemed to have a different idea."

"Yes… she is a little harder to read. I wonder what purpose she thinks we could serve? Hopefully not as the subjects of research." Ashelyn's words hung in the chill air for a moment, heavy and ominous, as another gust of wind howled against the facility.

"Could be they want to put us to work," Mai said.

"Could be. I just hope they update us on what the hell we've missed."

"Back on Cahros, do you think anyone else…" Mai trailed off, the suggestion clear.

"I don't know. I doubt it. It's probably just us now."

Tarlo understood her doubt. What was the point of hoping?

"What do we do?" Tarlo asked, hugging his legs to his chest. "About the tardigrades? The formation? The… ghosts? What do we say?"

"The smart thing to do would be ask what they know and share nothing that might cause them to mistrust us, or doubt our mental soundness. As before, Tarlo, I think we should keep what we found in the caves to ourselves for now," Ashelyn replied. She looked tired, and her vivid jade eyes lacked their usual lustre.

"But, I can't help but think they were trying to tell us something back there."

"I agree," Mai said, looking similarly concerned. "You all had those visions, yes? Of green trees, forests… I think I saw the history of Cahros, before those *things* came."

"I had a vision too, although not of trees. I saw planets, five of them. One was Cahros, one was Earth, though the others... I don't know," Tarlo shook his head as bright, piercing lights bounced around inside his skull.

"Interesting. Ashelyn, what of you? When you touched the rocks, what did they show you?"

"Much, though it was different again to what you both mentioned. I don't want to talk about it here. They will have us under surveillance. But... it felt like a warning of some kind."

"If it's a warning, should we not share it with everyone we can?" Tarlo protested, frustrated at the doctor's seeming insistence on solving everything on her own.

"I will share it when I know what it is that I'm sharing," Ashelyn snapped. "Spouting gibberish will not help us, nor the credibility of our message."

"Has it really been two years since... we were at Cahros? If so, a lot may have changed. Ashelyn is right, we should find out as much as we can before making fools of ourselves," Mai said, just as three new colonists joined them in the room, bearing the limp form of Terrus on an orange stretcher. Contrary to the enviro-suits Mauve and Elís had worn, they were clad in full white hazmats.

They laid Terrus down and began silently prepping him, removing his suit with a precise roughness – they were in a hurry. One of them came over to Tarlo, Ashelyn, and Mai and addressed them with a pleasantly deep, masculine voice.

"We're not supposed to talk to you, but I always like to know what I'm getting injected with, and by whom. I'm Alesio, the lead clinician on base. Single immunisation is all you need here. It's based on Ciprofloxacin, a fluoro-quinolone antibiotic. Good for bacterial stuff, particularly

E. coli infection. Can't tell you why, but breathing in the air here sets off an internal chemical reaction that the human gut just does not like. Anyway, the Cipro. Rather than this being a pure antibiotic, it's been synthesised into a genuine inoculation. Be warned, the first six hours or so can be rather unpleasant, but afterwards, you'll thank us. We'll be taking some bloods too, to ensure you're not carrying anything we need to be worried about."

Most of what he said flew over Tarlo's tired head, but the idea of six hours of suffering did not appeal to him at all. Alesio came to Tarlo first, briskly assisted him with removing the top half of his E12, and jabbed him with a small needle.

"Second is for bloods," Alesio said, anticipating his next question. Tarlo had never loved injections, so was relieved that they were relatively painless. The 'sucking' feeling that came with the second needle sure wasn't pleasant, though.

"This is the easy part," Alesio grinned, visible through the clear panel at the front of their headpiece. A hearty brown beard framed a rugged, handsome face, with messy dark hair and straight, white teeth.

He pulled out four fresh needles for the others, before circling back towards Terrus, who was now fully de-suited. Ashelyn followed him closely, with Tarlo and Mai trailing behind a little more hesitantly. Peeking over two sets of shoulders, Mai gasped and recoiled. Words of concern babbled from the suited workers, who continued to act as though Ashelyn, Tarlo, and Mai were not there at all.

"Sol save me, I've never..."

"Should we still? Should we call in...?"

"Forget inoculations," Alesio said, his voice suddenly a lot more authoritative. "We can't operate or expose him either. He's going straight into cryocoma. Viola, get the anaesthetic kit and two other scis to come help."

"What's going on?" Mai cried, as Tarlo tried to bounce onto his tiptoes to get a look at all the fuss. The doctors continued to ignore them, but curiosity drove him around the pack to get a clearer view of Terrus's arm. He only managed to look at it for a second before he was forced back by a mix of repulsion and guilt. The wound was no longer red at all, but a lurid purple that spread several inches down Terrus's left arm, like an otherworldly infection.

The doctor's aide – Viola – returned with the kit as instructed and babbled that the others were still a few minutes away.

"It seems to be spreading, can we afford to wait?" the other assistant asked nervously.

"Forget them. Let me assist," Ashelyn barked, imposing herself on the group. Alesio appraised her sceptically, though Tarlo detected a hint of admiration in his eyes.

"Do you know what you're doing?"

"What *you'll* be doing, rather, and I know enough. All you need from me is a leg held down. Tarlo can assist too."

Alesio considered her for a second before nodding. "Fine. Three jabs, neck, shoulder and hip. We'll get a mix of reflexive and hypnogogic jerks, each more intense than the last, but keep your grips firm. Pulse will slow and he'll run cold, by then the others will be here. At which point we get him out of here and hooked into life support immediately. We'll have two minutes. Ready?"

They nodded, and Tarlo took his place beside Ashelyn at Terrus's feet and made his best imitation of her restraining grip.

"Shot one," Alesio said calmly, and the spasm was largely absorbed by the two aides holding Terrus's arms. Tarlo tried not to wonder if Terrus could feel any of what was happening. He knew little about this "cryo-coma", having only heard sparse mentions of it as a speculative, experimental treatment back before leaving Earth.

"Shot two." This time, Terrus jerked his left leg, though Ashelyn barely moved. Alesio shuffled his way down towards them, crouching beside Tarlo for the final shot.

"And three. Hold tight." Alesio's warning was well founded, and if weren't for his steadying hand, Tarlo likely would have been kicked clean free, such was the force of the muscly quadriceps as it lurched upward.

"Keep your hands on him for a little longer," Alesio said, returning to his kitbag. Tarlo watched in morbid curiosity as Terrus's skin became pale, then blue. The strained furrow in his brow relaxed, and his skin became smooth all over. His legs were unnaturally cold, and cooling by the second, and Tarlo withdrew his hands as his own skin began to prickle uncomfortably.

"What are you going to do with him?" Ashelyn asked through gritted teeth.

Alesio glanced over at her again. "We haven't seen anything like this before. Quarantine and contain. Some might suggest amputation. I'd rather observe, learn what we can."

"You should amputate. What if the infection spreads? Nobody's life is worth—" Ashelyn protested, but Alesio waved her silent.

"Actually, you're wrong. Learning about the threat these rocks carry to others is highly important. How do you think we came up with the inoculations?" He gave her a hard look, his eyes challenging, and she conceded.

Just then, the other aides made it into the room, similarly clad and bearing a wheeled stretcher.

"Medbay two. Section it off. Nobody goes in without my clearance," Alesio instructed, and the four aides scrambled to action his words, leaving him with the three of them in a sudden quiet.

"I know he was... is your friend, but I won't apologise. I have the safety of everybody in this facility to worry about. My people."

"Your people. What does that make us?" Ashelyn scowled.

"That remains to be seen. You, you speak with a certain air... what is your name, your profession?"

"Ashelyn. I'm a neuropsych."

Alesio appraised her, and his gaze, unprotested by Ashelyn, awakened something in Tarlo. Was it... jealousy?

"Well, Doctor, what do you know about cryocoma?"

Ashelyn paused, as if hesitant to spill information that might give their story away. "I know it's new. Was new. And unless legislation has changed, is illegal on any planet or facility where a functional hospital exists."

"That's right. Only in the lawless frontier of these colonies can we engage such risky endeavours. Your friend may never wake. Do you not see the advantage in learning what we can?"

Tears welled in the corners of Tarlo's eyes. While he had always liked Terrus, he hadn't spent much time in his company – but that hadn't stopped the trooper from throwing himself to Tarlo's aid without thought or question. And for what, to be unceremoniously jabbed and prodded by people from another planet, who may as well be aliens themselves?

"If that is what is going to happen. Allow me onto your team. As discussed, I have the qualifications."

Alesio smiled approvingly. "We'll have to see what the bosses say, but we've recently had some vacancies across our science teams. You two, what do you do?"

Tarlo paid little heed to the question and felt himself drawn to the window. A grey mist had gathered around the facility, obscuring the seas once more. Distracted by throes of guilt, he barely heard Mai respond.

"We're biologists, I'm Mai, and he's Tarlo."

Alesio made a *tsk*ing sound. "Interesting indeed. Now, that's more than enough from me. As I said, we're not supposed to talk to you. Oh, and have these." He tossed a transparent bag towards them and left the room.

Ashelyn joined Tarlo by the window. "You should try to eat. It will help your body handle the inoculation."

The bag Alesio had left contained a selection of pastes, in three colour varieties – a dull pink, a dull brown, and a dull beige. Tarlo wrinkled his nose and shook his head, while Ashelyn and Mai both chose beige.

"So, looks like you made a good impression," Mai said to Ashelyn.

"I thought, if one of us was on the team looking out for Terrus... I might be able to keep him from the worst of it. Make sure they actually treat him."

Tarlo breathed a heavy sigh. "He is only hurt because of me! Because I couldn't even fend for myself. Just like Jame. Just like Jontie. Just like Vel. Just like everyone else... I watched them all... and did *fucking nothing*." In that moment, he longed to scream, or to cry, but the fatigue, dehydration, and hollowness of everything hit all at once, causing his despair to manifest only in a few pathetic, choking sobs. A moment later, he felt suddenly crowded. He opened his eyes and saw that both Ashelyn and Mai had both come a little closer.

"There was nothing any of us could do. For any of them," Ashelyn said, though her voice shook. Tarlo knew that, as a physician and a person, she bore the weight of each death even heavier than he.

"You, we... did everything we could, with what we had," Mai said shakily. "We have to believe that. But after all the madness, I can't help but wonder if there's a reason we made it through. Terrus too. The things we saw... I think there's a reason for all of it. Though I don't have a clue what that might be."

Tarlo shook his head. "I feel the opposite, like my being here is only a waste. Like it should have been my arm that caught Yerald's rock, or feet in the sands, or anything else that happened."

"Survival is not something to apologise for. You know this, Tarlo, you've studied it for years," Mai said. Her words helped a little, painfully logical as they were, but he still felt hollow.

"Things won't ever be the same again," Ashelyn said, leaning into him a little. "And there's no point pretending we will be, either. But I think Mai is right. Whatever we stumbled upon in the caves... it's big. Maybe really big. But for now, just take it one moment at a time. And we need to stick together."

Tarlo turned and looked at them both – two people who, for most of the time he'd known them had been intimidating strangers, yet were now the only familiar faces this side of the galaxy. There had never been any attraction between he and Mai, and her mannerisms and tangents sometimes still moved too fast for him to keep pace, but he felt they now shared a sense of familiarity, friendship. After all, she was the one who had been there when he first discovered the tardigrades. And Ashelyn... *Ashelyn.* He felt lots of things about Ashelyn.

He sniffed, and his stomach rumbled, eliciting an embarrassed laugh. "Thank you both. And you're right, Ashelyn, one thing at a time. I guess the next great challenge is surviving the next few hours with our dignity intact?"

The two women looked at him stoically, neither of them seemed to be in much discomfort yet. "You go first, Tarlo. We'll pretend we're none the wiser." Mai laughed.

As Tarlo shimmied to the bathroom on the far side of the room, he couldn't help but wonder how the colonists here managed their waste containers.

He decided he'd rather not know.

4
MALEFICUS

Tuwia, Alantia   CD: 08/04/2222
Tarlo

THEY WERE MADE to wait a little longer than the three hours promised, passing the time with anxious conversation and occasional bashful trips to the lavatory at the far end of the room. After all they'd been through, Tarlo did not appreciate the uncertainty that came with waiting, but he lacked the energy to protest.

When a sharp rapping finally clanged against the metal door, the relief was short-lived. Elís strode into the room, garbed in grey fatigues and tense suspicion, portrayed by perpetually scanning eyes and hands that never drifted far from her holster. The fatigues were interesting – on Cahros, colonists either wore casuals, underclothes, or their enviro-suits. Maybe this *was* Elís's version of casual. Either way, the lack of hazmats was a good sign.

Ashelyn, Mai, and Tarlo rose to their feet in acknowledgement, but did not approach their new guest.

"It's time to go," Elís said. Her unwavering stony expression could have been chiselled in concrete.

"Go where?" Ashelyn replied. Tarlo and Mai had agreed to let her do the talking.

"What difference does it make to you?"

"Little, to be fair. But, consider our situation, in a new planet, surrounded by strangers whose intentions are equally unclear. We'd like to know, are we your guests, or captives?"

Elís's eyes narrowed before she shrugged her square shoulders. "It's not been fully decided yet, but the best answer? Neither."

"Please elaborate." Tarlo wished Ashelyn wouldn't be so curt.

"If you follow me, you'll find out. We're going to be moving you to slightly warmer quarters, where we will be interviewing you. Following this, there may be opportunity for you all to make yourselves useful. Now come." Ashelyn hesitated for a moment, and Tarlo stepped forward.

"Warmer sounds great." He forced a smile. "We understand your caution and appreciate your welcome. Let's go."

Ashelyn bristled at him, but he gave his best attempt at a reassuring smile as he passed her.

"Play nice," Mai added quietly. "We can negotiate later."

Elís did not speak again as she led them from the room. It was cold outside with the wind whipping at their faces, and they harnessed themselves to the handrails of another silver staircase. At its summit, they were greeted by a platform supporting a much larger grey building than the one they'd just left. At each corner, tall watchtowers rose into the mist, and on the roof sat an array of perhaps two dozen small windmills, their propellers spinning furiously in all directions. A general static of machine noise rumbled through the air, getting louder as they ascended. Tarlo wondered how much the whole facility must have weighed, and how the engineers at the UCI had pulled off such an ambitious concept. *The same way they pulled off post-light travel, I suppose. Teamwork, and lots and lots of money.*

"This is the main hub," Elís said. "Level three. Inside, we have everything you'd be accustomed to, including habs, biolab, and command centre. Since we've expanded, there's a small mess and a medbay too – that's where we'll be briefing you. There are obviously going to be other colonists here, but they know not to engage, so don't be surprised if they don't give you the warmest welcome. Follow me."

They unharnessed and stepped inside, and Tarlo was immediately struck by how *familiar* much of it felt. This was half a galaxy away from Cahros, miraculously suspended in the sky, but it seemed UCI interior decoration was all cut from the same cloth. The walls were white, possessing that rough quality of Moonsalt, and there was even that similar, slightly stale smell of recycled air. Not all things were the same, though. A few steps in from the entrance, the lifeless walls were decked with thin, wide enviro-screens, identical to the ones he'd had on his little room back on the *Nitimini*. Currently, they were synchronised to display a lush jungle clearing where several small campfires glowed. A light crackling wafted from small speakers at the base of each screen, putting Tarlo at immediate ease.

"The crew tend to go for dry, warm patches of ground," Elís said, perhaps noticing his relaxing shoulders. "Sometimes even deserts. Not too many beaches or oceans, though."

The place was warmer than he ever remembered Catal being, too. After shivering in the quarantine room and being buffeted by the winds outside, it felt positively *luxurious* in here.

They arrived at the medbay, where Mauve enthusiastically waved them in. The room was brightly lit, but most of the light was absorbed by a series of dark green curtains that obscured the back and sides of the room. Tarlo was trying to work out which one Terrus might be laying behind when Mauve called for their attention.

"Hello chews, lovely to see you again! Firstly, I am happy to confirm your bloods have come back clean – I knew you weren't smuggling in any superviruses!" Her insistent positivity helped set him at ease.

"We have a few questions... if we may?" Ashelyn took lead again.

"Why of course," Mauve beamed at her. "Though I am *dying* of curiosity myself. What is it you'd like to know?"

"This colony... Tuwia... it's so advanced. You said it has only been two years, that means there could only have been one real resupply since you set up here?"

"Great question, and an easy answer. As far as we were told, the UCI were so impressed at our first reports, they doubled their investment in the return expedition."

"Wait!" Mai interjected, sounding alarmed. "I played a major role in planning during the early months of the Project. There was to be no playing favourites between the four planets that were to be settled – there wasn't enough funding even if they did want to. Resource allocation was determined for at least a decade!"

Mauve's smile wavered, and Elís, who'd drifted into the background, came forward.

"You were part of the ECP?"

"Yes. I was one of the coordinators on the Martellus Index. Got access to a *lot* of higher-level data." The admission surprised Tarlo – he hadn't expected Mai to share this information so soon. As Mai's expression rapidly switched from confused to concerned, Tarlo realised she hadn't either.

"Unless..." Mai stammered. "What do you all know about Cahros? About the other planets?"

It was Mauve and Elís's turn to share a look.

"Actually... rather little, apart from what Mauve shared when we picked you up," Elís answered. "Same with the other planets that they sent the expeditions to. That's a large part of what we want to ask you about."

"One thing we do know," Mauve said. "Is that that one of you is a *major* celebrity back on Earth." She turned to Tarlo, and he blushed.

"Does the name *Tarlosius Maleficus* ring a bell?"

Tarlo's heart quickened. *Did she say Tarlosius?*

"That sounds taxonomical," Mai breathed. "But no, it does not."

"Indeed it is – taxonomical, I mean. It happens to be the name given to the UCI's greatest success story: the first non-Earthan lifeform officially discovered. Which remains credited to you."

Tarlo's head began to spin.

"Sol... So you know about the tardigrades? And... someone named them after Tarlo?" Mai said excitedly. "That means our messages were heard! Jame must have gotten through to someone!"

A confused frown teased Mauve's brow. "Your messages? And who? I thought by the name... Did you not name those creatures?"

Tarlo's skin felt hot.

"We didn't get the chance – given you know about these things, I'd presume you understand the challenges we were up against," Mai continued. "But one of our friends reported their existence and their discoverer. Someone must have pored through the data and come up with the name as a kind of... tribute."

Tarlo's stomach dropped. His whole life, he'd dreamed of making such a momentous discovery, and to one day be immortalised in the name of a new species.

But not for *this* species.

"These things killed everyone... and they named them after me?" The words escaped his closed throat so quietly he didn't know if anybody even heard them. Whatever strength he had left fled his body, and he sank to his knees on the cold, white floor. Shudders travelled up and down his spine as the corners of his vision went dark.

Tarlo surrendered to the panic.

He forgot his company, and choked sobs ripped from his throat. The floor pulsated beneath his frail, red hands, and he imagined a vicious mouth surging towards them, wrapping torn lips around bloody fingers, and longed that it would consume the rest of him, too.

He didn't know how long he was incapacitated so, but when he came back to, the only thing he noticed was Ashelyn. She had crouched beside him and laid a cool hand against his brow. Her eyes oriented him, and she spoke in a soothing voice.

"It's okay. It's okay." Shakily, he leaned against her side. Her embrace was firm but brief as she rubbed his shoulders and helped him back to his feet.

Mauve gave him a sympathetic look, and he was startled to realise everybody else was still in the room... and the same places. Had he only been out for a few seconds?

"It seems you've been through more than we know. But as we said, we need your collaboration before we can confirm our next move," Elís said.

"How do we know we can trust you?" Mai replied.

"You don't," Elís said. "But I believe you have already reached the sound conclusion that you have little choice. My belief in your integrity is the only thing between a safe job for you all, and..." She made a pointed gesture of sliding her fingers across a holster at her hip.

"What do you need to know?" Ashelyn replied, still standing close to Tarlo.

"As we said before, information from or about the other colonies has been hard to come by. We have feared, as Mai said, that perhaps our extra resources were a reallocation due to some kind of mishap elsewhere." Mauve looked ready to say more, but Elís intervened.

"What can you tell us about Cahros?"

The trio shared uncertain glances.

"Where to begin?" Ashelyn said. "Firstly, if it really has been two years since we were there last, then any information we do share will be seriously outdated."

"We know," Elís said simply.

"As I said, what information we have been provided, has been very... watered down," Mauve added. "We know that your expedition was the first of any of us to encounter life, and said life was very dangerous, but little beyond that. I'm sure you can imagine our surprise at the four of you arriving here, of all places. I am still waiting to learn where you hid your ship."

"Whatever disorientation you feel, I assure you, we can empathise," Ashelyn said, almost smiling. "But, so you know, it doesn't bring us much joy to relive events that, as far as we are concerned, happened only yesterday."

Mauve gave them another sympathetic look, though her eyes were tinged with another emotion. Confusion? Annoyance? Impatience? "Everything you say mixes me up a little more than the last... but please, share what you can."

Ashelyn took a deep breath. "We arrived at Cahros on schedule, although the place seemed very different to what we'd been promised."

"Now, that we *can* understand," Elís said.

"Alantia was hypothesised to be a humid world of temporal seas, comparable to a pre-continental Earth," Mai chimed in. "Apart from maybe few degrees of temperature, I am unsure what differences you could be referring to?"

"For one thing, carbon sampling from the area around the inlet where we picked you up revealed that Alantia is in fact much older than Earth. We have also identified evidence that it may once have been home to entire continents – but more on this later. What happened after you landed on Cahros?"

"Well, we established our settlements, followed protocol and then, roughly a week later, these *Maleficus* things showed up and took the lives of almost everyone in the colony. They were awakened from anhydrobiosis, and attacked us en masse, as if they were coordinated by some hive mind. They—"

"You misunderstand, Doctor. The *Maleficus,* and their capabilities are the one thing we do know about, including... what they did to your friends. What we want to know more about is what *you* found there, how it brought you here, and the state of things you left behind," Elís said.

Even through his daze, pieces started to come together in Tarlo's mind. These two clearly knew something about the strange rocks that had served as some kind of conduit between worlds and had brought suspicions into this meeting that were far bigger than just he and his companions. An image flashed into his mind of two planets side by side. The first, a brown-orange marble, was Cahros, and the second, once shrouded in shadow, cleared into a shifting blue-grey mass before his mind's eye. *Alantia.*

"It was a formation, just like the one where you found us," he blurted. "Except we were in the middle of a sea of sand, not water. Entering it, we fell through a cave, which contained… phenomena… that defied belief. And we found a message."

A look of alarm shot across Mai's face, and she pulled them aside and whispered, "Hush! Shouldn't we…?"

"Yes. I know what we discussed… but whatever we have stumbled on… we can't deal with alone." Tarlo said. "I think we can trust them. I think we need to," Ashelyn nodded.

"We have cam coverage in here, you know," Elís said lazily. "And have the ability to play back anything that we can't hear in the moment."

Ashelyn straightened herself up. "Back on Cahros, in the formation, we found a communication of sorts, that looked like it had been left behind by a sentient race of some kind."

"What kind of message?"

"A warning. But we don't really know what for, though the tardigrades were clearly part of it. We need to convene, debrief, put together our learnings. There is some link between this planet and Cahros, and maybe others, too, though we are yet to understand what it is."

While Ashelyn spoke, a pensive look came across Elís's already stern face, and Mauve began to fidget.

"What about things on Cahros? You said many lives were lost, were there any survivors you left behind? What about the facilities?"

"The facilities seemed largely intact, though this will have changed fast once we evacuated. We left... three people behind."

"Only three?"

Mai winced at this. "One was hurt, and the others... didn't want to leave. But as far as we're aware, the facilities are salvageable, and our frigate was a couple of weeks from returning. Whether or not they gave up on the planet... I really don't know."

Suddenly, Elís relaxed. "I sense you are being honest. You have nothing to fear from us," she said. "Nor the UCI. They have no real jurisdiction here anyway – apart from that which we provide them. In all honesty, our... concerns... are not directed at the four of you."

At last, the tension in the room began to dissipate. "Despite being told we did such a great job here, we have heard very little in the way of directive or encouragement from those in charge back home. We have come to think of ourselves as our own nation-state, in a way. Or planet-state, perhaps," Elís said.

"How many times have you connected with the UCI since your frigate left?" Mai asked.

"That's just it. Once the ship we arrived on left the system, bearing all of our good news, the only contact we received was when the next one arrived here. We have sent dozens of messages using our solar arrays, but not once have we gotten a reply. We didn't even know the second expedition was coming until four weeks before they showed up, with all the extra luxuries and tech we could ask for. Although there was one important resource they supplied none of."

"Colonists," Mauve said, and Tarlo finally began to make sense of their intentions. The interviews, the suspicion... had it all just been a glorified job interview? *Maybe they need us as much as we need them?*

Elís paced about as she continued speaking. "They did leave us with one other piece of information, that we were not initially forthcoming with you about. Within the caves here on Alantia, there are these rocks... They contain an element named Huronium, which we know was first identified by one of your compatriots on Cahros. This Huronium appears to have two states of activation, black and blue, though we've only ever seen it black here. We can't confidently speak on its true properties yet, but have observed numerous anomalies that, while they don't explain your sudden appearance, render it on the edge of believability. I would have you stay and continue to aid our research on these formations, as well as our ongoing priorities to terraform and explore this planet."

The room fell silent. After a few seconds, Elís gave Mauve a terse nod and strode from the room. Mauve's face split into another great smile. "Well done! It takes a lot to change that one's mind, I can't believe you did it so fast!"

"You mean... That's all? We're in?" Ashelyn asked.

"Yes! To be honest, I was expecting she'd have you in here for hours! Can't run a place like this without some healthy suspicions, I guess. Anyway, we have discussed what to do in the event you gave a good impression. I'm happy to offer the three of you places with our research teams, although don't be fooled, there is a lot more 'doing' going on at the moment than there is 'thinking'!"

"What do you mean by that?"

"That's a discussion for after you've taken rest." Ashelyn moved to interject, but Mauve forged on. "Ashelyn, you'll be in the medical team, answering to Alesio, which I'm sure is welcome news given your concerns for your friend, Terrus was it?"

Ashelyn swallowed hard but nodded in acceptance. "How is he?"

"He's right here, in fact." Mauve pointed to the curtain to their right. "Stable and sleeping. Well, cold and comatose, but that still counts, right? Our primary hope is that the cryo halts the spread of his infection, but we're proceeding with caution. We have no reason to believe that he is contagious, but for now, it's just Alesio who will be tending to him – he's the one you need to convince if you'd like a closer look. Now, Tarlo and Mai, you'll be working with me in Bio."

"Bio? I thought you said you were a personnel liaison?" Mai said.

Mauve laughed. "I am a lady of many hats! For now, I'll show you all to your quarters, where we have laid out some supplies and sustenance for you. And before you ask, we do grow fresh food here, but thanks to your inoculations, it'll be protein paste for the first twenty-four hours. Right, any questions?"

In his right mind, Tarlo might have had a thousand questions, but all he could think of in that moment was finding some place quiet to rest. That, and how much he hated protein paste.

"Yes, one, for now. What are we telling people? About our... getting here?" Ashelyn said.

"Elís will be dealing with this already. Official word is that you escaped by ship and crash-landed here, and I'm thinking we might throw in that you found the place due to Mai's know-how from her time on the Martellus project. Pretty sound, right? You'll have it easy the next day or so, while you're officially 'recovering', though I suggest the three of you meet and bring your thoughts together on exactly what it is you went through. When we're ready, I'll call you all in for another briefing, and after that, you're on the job! Now, are you ready to go?" They nodded, and Mauve led them back out into the facility.

They followed her past the mess area – from which a brief splash of noise and light echoed – and down a dark corridor. There were no enviro-screens here, and in their place, dozens of small doors lined the hallway, each no more than two metres apart. Tension crept between Tarlo's shoulders... when had he started fearing the dark?

"No shared dorms here?" Mai asked.

"Dorms?" Mauve snorted. "We haven't had dorms since training back on Earth." Maybe this place wasn't as similar to Catal as Tarlo had initially thought.

"Unfortunately, you'll be a bit all over the place. Mai, this first one is yours. Tarlo and Ashelyn, your quarters will be across from each other a little further down." Mauve procured three tags and passed them out.

"See the doors with orange lights above them? Just rub your fobs against the handle and you'll sync them to your room. I'll let you all be now. Let's see... it's 1440 now... Usually we muster at 0800, but consider yourselves on leave until this time tomorrow! I'll meet with you all at 1500 to discuss what's next. Oh, and we run on Common Time here – the days are actually about twenty-nine hours long, but it was too much hassle to have two versions of time. The light up here is a pretty constant grey or black anyway." With that, she shot them one last smile, turned with a flourish, and left them alone.

"To part after everything feels... strange," Mai half-raised her arms awkwardly, as if to initiate an embrace, before quickly changing her mind. "But this is the safest I've felt in... too long. Do you think we should meet later? Or in the morning?"

"Perhaps in the morning, I think. Though I'm not sure I'll get much sleep," Ashelyn said.

"Yeah, me neither. But maybe some time alone, in the quiet, will help," Mai said. Tarlo tensed at the very thought. "Okay," she said, "how about 0800? Or so." Ashelyn and Tarlo nodded.

"Okay," Mai said again. "I will see you both then?" She fiddled with the door for a moment before shuffling into the room. Tarlo caught a brief glimpse of the quiet tears on her face as her door slid closed.

He was very conscious of the distance between him and Ashelyn as they walked towards their rooms – too close to be natural, but still further away than he might have liked.

A faceless anxiety began to rise inside of him as they neared their point of parting.

"Mai was right. It will be strange, being apart after everything we've been through," Ashelyn said, putting words to his fears. He realised there hadn't been more than a few metres between them at any point since everything went to hell back on Cahros. Subjectively, that was only a couple of days ago, but it already felt like a lifetime.

"We lost everyone..." Tarlo stuttered. There was something about the orange light above Ashelyn's head that disturbed him, initiating a strange instinct that screamed at him to *step back.*

"Even the planet beneath our feet. But not each other." Ashelyn reached out and took his hand gently. Despite the comfort of her gesture, his sense of alarm deepened.

Ashelyn released his hand, looking hurt. "Tarlo, what's wrong? Did I...?"

The light faded from her eyes and her expression twisted into a contorted rigor mortis grin. Tarlo stumbled backwards, slamming against the door to his room. He fell to the ground with a thud, curling his arms around his knees. Ashelyn spoke again, but all he heard was the sickening *splat* of faces slamming into Moonsalt floors, accompanied by shrieks of despair. He smelled blood, and salt, and fear, and the world around him fell through a black tunnel. It was only when Ashelyn synced her bracelets to her door that the light flashed green and his vision of his surroundings returned.

Gently, she guided him into the little room and sat beside him on the bed. She didn't touch him, nor did she speak, instead sitting calmly nearby while the tremors raked his body. As time passed, their severity lessened, and he became aware of her breathing. Its slow, deep, reliable rhythm grounded him, and after a few more minutes, his breaths began to match hers.

"It was the helms, wasn't it?" she said quietly, after a time. Still not ready to speak, he nodded.

"Would you like to stay with me in here?"

Tarlo felt as though he were watching them both from the corner of the room, a pathetic little man beside a patient, ever-capable woman. He scrunched his face up and buried it in his arms, head spinning.

"You don't have to... It's okay." *Enough, Tarlo.* He reached out his left hand until he found hers and squeezed with the last of his energy. He barely noticed as she stood, and gently shifted his body so that he was lying down. By the time she'd taken a watchful position seated on the ground, Tarlo had fallen into a restless sleep.

5

A BANQUET OF PASTE AND BROTH

Tuwia, Alantia   CD: 09/04/2222
Tarlo

TARLO WOKE AT noon, covered in sweat and still in Ashelyn's bed, feeling like he was nursing a full-body hangover. He lay disoriented, nauseous, and miserable, immobilised by half-formed thoughts that went nowhere. Whenever he opened his eyes, the world felt too bright and loud, but whenever he closed them, he felt tendrils weaving at the corners of his mind, as if searching for something...

Finally, a knock at the door brought about some relief. "Tarlo, it's Mai. I know you're probably not going to want to hear this, but I think it's time you got up."

Tarlo groaned, which Mai took as encouragement, and he heard the door slide open, admitting a waft of cool air into the room.

He rolled to face her. Mai stood at the door with her hands on hips, looking down on him like he was a hapless teen.

"Come on, you'll feel better with some food and fluid. Ashelyn's already eaten, I think, but Alesio said the food should be good for a while."

"Alright, *Mother*," Tarlo groaned.

Mai laughed and helped him to his feet. "I was going to say you could do with a shower too, but that might be laying it on a bit too thick. I'll show you where they are after we eat."

Tarlo nodded, and they trudged back up the darkened corridor towards the light and noise of the mess hall.

"And the last of the crash crew have arrived!" Alesio declared with a grin. "Pretty simple, the stuff you're looking for is over there, by the wall. It's self-serve, as always. I'd keep it light if I were you, stick to pastes and liquids. Now, I'd love to introduce you to everyone, but I need to go check on Terrus. Please, make yourselves comfortable." He gestured to one of the tables, where a handful of colonists sat. Tarlo vaguely recognised one of them from the quarantine room, but the rest of the faces were all new.

"Thank you, Doctor."

Tarlo and Mai headed for the food station. A lovely array of vegetables was arranged, buffet style, in four silver trays, beside a deeper bowl containing an ambiguous brown, vaguely meaty broth. Beside the soup, two white, cubic machines loomed, casting dour shadows over the collection of lovely, delicious-looking food. Tarlo's mouth dried at the sight of the protein dispensers, but the tribulations of the day before encouraged him to opt for the beige edition, along with a small cup of the warm broth.

The militaristic monicker of "mess hall" was something of a misnomer – this was the liveliest room they'd been in. Easily the largest singular room of the facility, the hall was split into dining and recreational areas. The former contained the food station and two long tables, while the latter held several exercise machines and VR consoles. Bright, wall-spanning windows welcomed lots of natural light, and a playlist of lyric-free synth-pop contributed to a pleasant, almost mundane atmosphere.

The tables were flanked by two long benches that required an awkward straddling motion to mount. Tarlo was grateful to be at the back of the line, as most of the other colonist's attention was on Mai when he spilled broth on his left thigh.

A diminutive, dark-skinned woman on their side of the table wrinkled her nose as they sat down. "Ah, got you on the protein paste still, have they?"

"Doctor's orders," Mai said solemnly, while Tarlo tried to decide what to consume first.

"He's a good one, I'd take his advice." the woman said. "I'm Mawie. This lovely one is Viola." She pointed to the woman sitting across from them, who smiled shyly. Tarlo knew he'd recognised her cocoa skin and skittish eyes, and the name confirmed her as one of the aides from quarantine.

"And here we have Zhang and Johann," Mawie gestured to the other two colonists. Zhang gave them an awkward smile, but Johann barely mustered a grunt.

"And I assume you've met Elís." Tarlo hadn't noticed the sergeant, who sat on her own a little way from the crowd, her fatigues almost blending her in with the grey flooring. She worked through her meal with the efficiency and precision of a combat operator and was already standing to leave by the time Tarlo had choked down half of his paste. It tasted dry and wet at the same time, with a sweet, almost milky aftertaste that left him clicking his tongue in disgust.

"Good stuff, isn't it?" Mawie gave him a look of mild amusement.

Elís stopped by the table on her way through. "It is good to see you all now up and about. Briefing at sixteen hundred." Without waiting for a response, she continued her march from the room.

"Another good one," Mawie said. "Don't mind her attitude. She's *always* looked after us." Viola and Zhang nodded.

Tarlo moved on to the broth, which wasn't as good as it looked, but at least helped banish the paste from his tongue.

"So, they told you much about the place yet? Alantia, I mean?" Mawie asked. Whether by arrangement or otherwise, it seemed she was going to do most of the talking.

"I think they're saving it for the briefing," Mai said between slurps. "Anything you think they'd want us to know?"

"Mauve said she's happy for us to give you a bit of general background. You two are the biologists, aren't you?" Tarlo and Mai nodded. "Well, long story short, everything changed here when we discovered the DSL."

Johann got up suddenly, despite still having half a plate of carrots and kale. Tarlo could've sworn the man treated him to a particularly venomous look before he shouldered past and headed over to the exercise machines. Bashfully, Zhang picked up his plate and made for the cleaning stations over beside the food.

The others didn't seem to notice. "As in Deep Scattering Layer?" Mai was saying. "Like on Earth?"

"Yes. Funny history with it, the old navies used to think it was the sea floor on SONAR, until it moved... and they learned it entirely comprised marine organisms."

"Yes, we all know the story. Humans are idiots."

Mawie gave them a little smile, and in a gesture that appeared to be unconscious, yet practiced, took Viola's hand. "Well, turns out they have one here. And when we finally figured that out... we found life. And lots of it."

Tarlo and Mai gasped in synchrony.

"How long were you here for when—"

Mawie ran her free hand across her shaven scalp. "Longer than some of us care to admit. Long enough that we missed out on the claim to being the first to find life..." Her awkward pause caused Tarlo to wonder if word had spread about his episode in the medbay the day before. "Anyway, we've found some amazing things down there. Even started to map out entire food webs."

Food webs? For a moment, Tarlo forgot his worries, enchanted by the idea of a new ecosystem. "What kind of things? Creatures? Like, what are the best ones?"

Mawie laughed. "Yeah, it's pretty awesome, once you get over the constant fear of being crushed. We've had car-sized molluscs, and *lots* of bioluminescence, but—" Her smile faded. "It's not all sunshine down there. Well, it's not ever, but you know what I mean. I should probably let Mauve and Elís handle the rest."

The conversation wound down, and Tarlo couldn't help but wonder why nobody had brought up the strangeness of his group's sudden appearance. Had Elís been that convincing, or were the colonists under strict orders? He knew there was more to what Mawie had hinted at about the oceans, too, but his sense of wonder overshadowed his worst fears. They were floating above a world of strange, new creatures, just waiting to be discovered, categorised, *understood*. Was he going to get the chance to go down there?

After an hour of gradual hydration and acquainting himself with the resident "steam and clean" hygiene station, Tarlo was feeling a lot better. He met Mai again, and they made their way to the command centre. The hallways today showed a series of gentle green hills.

Mauve and Elís were the only two in the room when they arrived. Noticing them, Mauve waved them in, while Elís sealed the door behind them.

"Thank you for coming in. There's something we wanted to talk to you about... before the others got here," Mauve said, uncharacteristically austere. She sat on the edge of the conference table and kneaded her temples.

"Elís, if you don't mind?"

Tarlo stood a little straighter. He was starting to notice a trend where Mauve tended to handle the safer topics, leaving the harder-hitting conversations to Elís.

Elís stepped forward. "Mai and Tarlo. On Cahros, you had a cousin-colony, did you not?"

"Yes. Unfortunately, it fared even worse than Catal," Mai replied.

"Catal?"

"That's what we called home. Our cousin had a name too, although I can't recall."

"Casarabe," Tarlo said. "And from what we know, they were... wiped out. All of them."

Elís's eyebrows creased in what could only be sympathy – the sudden expression of emotion surprised Tarlo.

"Why is that… Wait, there should be another skybase here on Alantia, right?" Mai asked, voice tinged with excitement.

"There…was. Until three weeks ago."

Tarlo's stomach churned so fiercely he could taste the dreaded paste again.

Elís took a deep breath. "We had a system. Scheduled comms-contact at the start of day shift, every day. At first, when they didn't answer, we thought it was just interference – it had happened before, and it was a windy morning here. Our distress beacons aren't impacted by the storms though, or electromag, as you found out at the formation. We figured if they were really in trouble, we'd know about it."

"But we heard nothing," Mauve added, her voice low.

"That's right. When the skies cleared the following day and we still hadn't heard, we sent a team over."

"And we found… nothing," Mauve almost whispered.

"As things stand, we are yet to find a trace of our friends in Alvolito."

Tarlo felt cold. For a brief second, he'd allowed himself to believe that things would be different here. That Alantia might be the planet Cahros had been promised to be, and, after all his suffering, things might finally be about to change.

"I know you'll have a lot of questions, but believe us, so do we. You now know everything we do," Elís said.

"I ask that you keep this information in mind as we proceed with this briefing," Mauve said. "And any mixed emotions you see among the team here. These dives... We aren't just looking for new life. We're trying to find out what happened to our friends."

"Well, at least that explains the... mixed reaction we received at lunch," Mai said.

"Oh?"

"Yeah. Mawie was the only one who was able to string a sentence together."

Mauve smiled. "Some people don't like to dwell in silence during times like this. I'm glad to hear you've spent some time with the others already. Look, I know this might feel sudden, but we need to get our next search underway. Elís, should we get this thing going?"

Elís nodded. "I'll get the others. You won't need me back, will you?"

Mauve shook her head. "Thanks again."

Once Elís had gone, Mauve turned towards Mai and Tarlo, a small smile had returned.

"So... I don't suppose either of you would be up for a dive?"

6

A NEW PURPOSE

Tuwia, Alantia   CD: 09/04/2222

Tarlo

"BRIEFING COMMENCING. CD oh nine oh four, time, 1600. Attendance reading in no particular order, Elís, Mauve, Johann, Zhang, Viola, Mawie, and our two new team members, Mai and Tarlo." Mauve's pleasant introductions belied a strange mood in the room, where none of the colonists seemed enthused to be there, and most eyes were trained on the floor. Only Johann's eyes roved, but that was just to subject Tarlo to another unsavoury glance.

Mauve pressed on, seemingly oblivious to the atmosphere. "The purpose of our work today is as usual. We'll be setting down ten kilometres east, and dropping past the Deep Scattering Layer, which, as we know, begins at half a kilometre down. We're expecting standard DSL rising time of approximately 2200. You'll be moving against the traffic, going down while the wildlife travels up. High chance of some sightings."

Tarlo tried to pay attention, but his thoughts kept drifting to the fate of the other colony. Disappeared, without a trace, falling to the seas below... What could have caused such a thing? These people on Tuwia had seemed welcoming enough, for the most part, and he knew how lucky he was they decided to take him in... but what circumstances had they taken him into?

"Now, we've already mapped this region extensively, and have a true sea floor depth of around three kilometres. We're expecting a range of phytoplankton, and various representatives of the local food web."

Despite the horrors that made a home in his idle thoughts, Tarlo still felt the occasional thrill of excitement. To explore these oceans, to see creatures of unprecedented form and purpose. And maybe a chance to find something, some clue of what had happened to Alvolito...

"For the dive conditions, winds are expected to decrease steadily throughout the evening, with an optimal dive time set for 2100, right after sunset. Thanks in part to our two new team members, we should easily manage a full, three-person team tonight. Now, who wants to go down?"

"I do!" someone declared. Five full seconds passed before Tarlo realised that it was his own voice that echoed through the room. *What am I doing?*

Mauve flashed him an appreciative smile. "That sounds wonderful. Now listen, everyone, I know that these two are new, but they have much to offer – they've been through a lot, too, and are uniquely positioned to understand the feeling of... loss we are enduring." From across the room, Mawie gave Tarlo a little smile of encouragement, but nobody else reacted.

"If it's all the same, I'd prefer to remain here," Mai said. "I'm much more useful when I have the bird's eye."

A thick, guttural voice piped up from the other side of the room. "I will go," Johann snarled. "I am not scared."

Tarlo felt a flash of anxiety – Johann seemed scarier than anything he might find in the ocean.

The room stayed quiet for a time. Finally, Mawie spoke up, her voice wobbling. "I... I guess it's my turn. I haven't done a dive for a little while." She ran a hand over her scalp, uncertainty written over her face.

"Thank you, Johann and Mawie! There we have it, our crew is decided!" Mauve said with forced brightness. "Now, you three can spend the next few hours as you see fit, but Tarlo and Mai, I ask that you remain here for further briefing. For the rest of the dive team, I'll see you at 1950."

Once the others had left, Mauve leaned over the oaken table wearily. "I'm glad one of you signed up."

"What was with that?" Mai said, gesturing vaguely at the now-vacated space where the others had been standing during briefing.

"It's complicated... What happened at Alvolito is affecting everybody differently. We ran the story, but these people are smart. I imagine they've figured there's more to how you got here... and during times like this, uncertainty breeds distrust. That's why I'm *so* happy you volunteered, Tarlo, I think this will really help get you off on the right foot."

"I noticed your people weren't exactly leaping to volunteer," Mai replied. "What exactly are you throwing Tarlo into?"

"After what you've been through, this should be a walk... or a swim through the park," Mauve said, not looking directly at either of them.

"I've already signed up," Tarlo said. "There's no need to gloss over anything. If you mean to send me into more danger, you should at least let me know."

Mauve sighed. "Technically, we're always in danger. Frontier life, and all that. But yes, you deserve to know a little more about the place. As far as conditions go, the wind is important, as it can affect the currents, waves, and the accuracy of first drop and eventual surfacing. The layer you'll be entering though, the upper pelagic, is rather calm. Water temperature is a balmy thirty-one Celsius, though it drops as you get lower, hitting five degrees around a klick below the DSL."

"This is all useful, but hardly explains the lack of enthusiasm of your team," Mai interjected. "You've had a skybase disappear out of thin air, I'm sure you have theories on *why*." Tarlo was beginning to notice a tension between Mai and Mauve. *We've only just been accepted here, please play nice.*

"I'm getting there, chew," Mauve nearly snapped. "Look, one of our recent expeditions... there were some issues. Nobody died, just... some strange behaviours from those who went down there. It led to a rapid resurfacing, which had some, well, complications. They're all in the recovery ward at the moment, hence the spaces in the lab for the two of you."

"And by your eagerness to get us in the team... I'm guessing they won't be out soon?" Mai said.

"You are shrewd. It will be... good to work alongside you, Mai. But yes, they will be incapacitated for some time." Her smile wavered.

"What exactly happened down there? What do you mean by strange behaviours?" Tarlo asked.

"Well, therein lies another purpose for your mission tonight. They found something, and it panicked them pretty good. We're hoping that you can work out what that was – minus the pandemonium, and if it might somehow contain a clue to what happened at Alvolito." Mauve flicked a red lock behind her ears. "I really do believe that, after what you've been through, this should be easy."

Tarlo wasn't so sure. After all he'd been through, would that not make him the *last* person capable of dealing with any kind of danger? But there she was, tantalising him with the prospect of more discovery...

"Do you have anything else for us?"

Mauve wandered over to the main console and input a few commands. The large screen suspended over the table shuddered to life, displaying what appeared to be a static-rimmed cam-feed.

"Passing twenty-five hundred metres, all systems steady," a smooth voice intoned. "Recording an update per standard reporting measures, a hello for every two hundred. Scanners state we are approximately six hundred metres from the sea floor. Visibility is nil, water temperature stable at seven degrees. Pressure at seven twenty bar."

"Eight degrees and seven twenty? That's significantly warmer and heavier than what we'd have on Earth. And colder than I thought it would be here," Mai remarked.

"Ahh, but you aren't on Earth, are you? And like we said, Alantia wasn't all that we thought it would be." Mauve said. The transmission continued.

"There is some disagreement between the crew regarding our next move. Arkans thinks we can go deeper, but Bjora disagrees. Oxygen looks good for at least another hour before surfacing. Wait... is that—" The transmission cut off with no further warning or context.

The room fell quiet, and Tarlo felt another strange cocktail of emotions. Stomach-sinking dread lined with enthusiastic hope. A desire to survive, clashing with a need to learn more. Was his blind decision to volunteer for the expedition really made from desire to help? Or just some self-destructive urge to try to take control back, to plunge headlong into the gnashing teeth of—

"That's all?" Mai said, brow furrowed.

"Now you know what we know. They surfaced half an hour after this message, and all three of them were in near-critical conditions. We stabilised them quickly, but in the three days since, they're yet to stir."

"So, let me get this straight? You've just had three people inexplicably incapacitated, and your first decision is to send more back down there?"

"There's more to it. The ship, the cams, they were only cut off thanks to *internal* tampering. We've scanned the vehicles up and down, back to front, and there is no sign of damage, fault, or external attack."

"So what, you think it was one of the crew?"

"We know for a fact it was one of the crew. Bjora, whose name you heard, suffered some kind of mental... lapse, commandeered the vessel and brought it to the surface." Mauve gave them a determined look. "We have no safety concerns for anyone returning to the area."

Tarlo *wanted* to trust Mauve, the promise of exploring the deep seas here was so compelling, but Mai still didn't seem convinced.

"So let me just get this one more time. You lost an entire colony, nearly lost a deep-sea dive, and you'd like us to go back down there again?"

Mauve's veneer fell away completely, and this time, the smiles did not return.

"That is exactly right. And before you say another word, I ask you to consider that if there *was* some kind of threat in the skies or seas that led to us losing our friends, or some way we could learn what happened to them – would that not be *extremely* worthwhile for us to learn what that is, to ensure our own safety ongoing? This has gone well beyond sentimentality, chew. This is about survival."

Mai was stunned silent. She lowered her eyes and murmured something akin to an apology.

"So just to confirm, you still want us to keep a lookout for new life, too?" Tarlo said, aware of the uncertainty in his voice.

"Absolutely. It will provide a nice focus for you. Keep your mind and eyes busy."

Sol knew he needed something like that.

"And you trust me?"

Mauve gave him a long look. "I do. Your enthusiasm, your credentials... I get it, you've barely been here twenty-four hours, perhaps it is irresponsible. The truth is, we don't have the luxury of vetting you for months. Something washed the four of you up here, and after everything we've lost, I'm not going to turn down having more hands on deck."

Tarlo nodded.

"Any other questions? I *promise* you, whatever life you find down there, you'll be amazed. Each dive unearths an average of seven new species! You'll find the seas of Alantia to be quite the melting pot of wonderful and peculiar lifeforms."

These people were going through something similar to what he had been through... and maybe there was a way

he could help, and in the process, right his own wrongs –
by discovering new life, something other than the dreaded
Maleficus. Or maybe, he could just take refuge from the
horrific memories that had pursued him all the way from
Cahros. Doing *anything* felt better than sitting and waiting
for them to overwhelm him.

"Tarlo, I don't like this," Mai said. Mauve pursed her lips
at this but elected not to interject. "We can find another
way, you don't need to—"

"No. I want to do this." Tarlo felt a familiar sensation, a
compulsion, just like the one he'd felt while surging through
the sands of Cahros, drawing him towards that fated rock
formation.

"I need to do this. Just tell me what I need to know."

7
DIVE

Tuwia, Alantia   CD: 09/04/2222
Tarlo

THE SETTING SUN cast a white-orange glow over the western side of Tuwia, its fading rays doing little to penetrate the growing chill. Mauve shared that Alantia maintained an ovular orbit of its resident star, Exon, and at this time of year, when its distance was greatest, daylight only lasted ten hours. This wasn't a huge issue, as the light of the moons bathed the facility in a similar bright, grey hue for most of the night. The season came with a change in conditions, wherein global humidity was at its lowest, particularly during the night, while the altitudinous winds were at their fiercest.

Tarlo relished the feeling of the cold air against his skin – for a long time, this was something he thought he'd never experience again. He paused during his descent between the two silver staircases to appraise the distant skies. Exon was not as dominant as Exsar had been from the surface of Cahros, or Sol from Earth, so the sunset was understated – the heavens were a simple, dull grey reflected in the gunmetal seas. As predicted, the clouds beneath the facility had cleared with the coming of the winds, so he now had a clear view of the eternally swelling waves far below. In this mellow calm, the skybase didn't feel quite as perilous as it had before.

Mauve appeared beside him. "As we discussed, let Mawie and Johann do all the piloting. You're there as primary observer, so keep your tablet handy at all times." It was a nifty little device: a thin, translucent rectangle capable of taking high resolution photos even in near darkness, while enabling freeform observations to be recorded through text or speech.

They finished their descent towards the deployment bay and Tarlo spotted two shadows inside one of the spherical vehicles.

"Formal designation for these things is R16, but we tend to refer to them as 'Rocks'. They may look like balls of glass, but they are much sturdier than they seem. Not even glass at all, in fact, but an ionised, glazed variant of Moonsalt. Crazy, I know, and expensive like you wouldn't believe. Just one of these things cost about the same as Tuwia itself – so look after it."

Mauve pulled him up just before the vehicle. "Now, look, Johann can be a bit... well, I think you might have seen already. But don't worry, just don't get in his way or try to piss him off and you'll be fine. Any final questions?"

Standing in the dark deployment bay with hundreds of metres of air, and thousands of metres of ocean beneath him, Tarlo's expeditious spirit lessened just a little. He thought for a moment of Ashelyn, and their quiet night together. He hadn't seen her since, as she'd been deployed to the medbay with Terrus, so there'd been no chance to check in with her about what had happened. He felt like a part of him had spilled, messily, and there'd been no chance to tidy it back up.

"And one more thing." Mauve's words brought him back to the present. "Thank you. We appreciate you being so ready to help out, after everything you've been through. There's no better way to earn respect than to get involved. Now go get them!"

Tarlo forced a smile and tiptoed over to the R16. Inside were three seats, two beside each other at the front, and one at the rear. Johann sat at the far side, right hand resting on a steering lever while the left flurried over a series of buttons on a console. Mawie sat quietly beside him.

Johann shot him a derisive look as he entered, and neither of the Tuwian colonists spoke.

"Should we... is there anything I need to put on, or ready?" Tarlo stammered as he climbed into his seat. There wasn't much room either side of it, thanks to it being flanked by two internal jet thrusters.

Johann choked out a laugh. "Bah. If anything punctures the hull, you're good as dead no matter what." He jammed a button, and the exit door slid shut. The bottom of the R16 was as transparent as the rest of it, and Tarlo's head started spinning as he looked down on the waves tussling below. It was one thing to stand on the sturdy platforms, gripping the handrails for safety, but in here, the glazed Moonsalt was so clear he could have been floating.

"It's always a fright sitting up here," Mawie offered him a hint of a reassuring smile. "Look forward, or above, until we're down there. It helps." Tarlo took her advice.

"Alright team, you are green for departure," Mauve's voice rang through the R16 speaker. Even though they were still in base, it sounded tinny and compressed. "We'll have comms all the way until you breach the DSL, after which things tend to get patchy – just make sure you record updates every couple hundred metres. Area is clear and forecasts are pristine. We'll check in again once you're at the dive zone. Ad Aeterno." Tarlo noted how Mauve's delivery of the UCI slogan – while still entirely devoid of gusto – lacked the irony that had been typical of the Cahran expedition. Even in the brief interactions he'd seen between Tuwian colonists, things here didn't seem as playful as they were on Cahros during those early days. But he had to remember, this *wasn't* the early days. The Tuwians had been here for years and had just endured a frightening tragedy.

"Confirmed," Johann said, and with a slight, groaning buzz, the magnetic clamps holding the vehicle in place were released.

Tarlo braced himself for a sudden plummet, but Johann timed the thruster initiation to perfection. He guided them from the bowels of the facility with impressive fluidness, but Tarlo still felt his breath catch as they soared free.

The setting sun gave him a welcome point of orientation. He remembered a similar moment, plunging from the shuttle in the first descent to the surface of Cahros. There, he'd been distracted by a warm, hopeful sunrise as he soared above a sea of orange. Here, it was a cold, nervous sunset shining over a world of grey and blue. Despite it all, hope still burned within him.

"Hover altitude reached," Johann grunted, stabilising their vehicle a few feet above the waves. They were so close Tarlo could have touched them, had there not been several inches of impenetrable material between them.

Barely a word was spoken during the first leg of the journey. Johann focused only on his steering, while Mawie busied herself with various checklist tasks, and acted as the primary communicator with Mauve back on Tuwia. Tarlo tried to stay present, fiddling with his tab while observing the gentle ebb and flow of the waves around them. They went on forever, it seemed, just like those sands of Cahros, and their vastness communicated a similar uncaring majesty.

"Alright. This is the spot," Johann said eventually, pulling the vehicle to a sudden halt. The sun had begun to drift beneath the horizon, its departure darkening the surface of the seas. A thrill of excitement and fear swept through Tarlo's chest, and he could have sworn he saw shadows dancing beneath the indigo sheen.

"Good work, team," Mauve's ever-cheery voice flicked through the vehicle, accompanied by an eerie burst of static. "So, planned dive time is four hours, one for ascent and descent, two for general shenanigans. You are clear to proceed."

"Just another day at the office," Mawie muttered, as if coaxing herself.

"And down we go, back to vertical drive," Johann said, flicking the steering switch.

As they submerged, Tarlo instinctively braced for the cold, wet feeling of water on his skin, but of course, it never came. The tides rose around their sphere, swallowing them quickly, and it was only a few seconds before they were in complete darkness.

Inside the vehicle, Johann seemed unperturbed, but Mawie breathed deeply, clutching at her armrest.

"Is everything okay?" Tarlo asked.

"Yeah," she said, almost gasping. "Just, that moment when it goes dark, always hits me." She took another breath and regained some composure. "I do this every time. We'll be okay." Again, it sounded more like she was trying to convince herself. She adjusted the internal lights in the R16, setting them to a comforting yellow glow.

"Okay. I'm just... Mauve told me about what happened last time. With the rapid surfacing. I'm down here now, so there's nowhere for me to run. Do you know anything else about what happened?" Tarlo gave a little laugh, trying to soften the situation, but his discomfort continued to rise, not least helped by sitting in the darkness with two near strangers.

"Mauve has a way of putting things, that's fer sure," Johann said. "Look, these dives aren't easy. It's dark, it's scary, sometimes the local wildlife can jump out at you, and everyone is scared of the bogeyman. Bjora was always skittish, and that was that. I trust *you* aren't made of the same weak stuff, *hero* that you are." The way he said it, the word "hero" was an insult.

Once, Tarlo might have taken these words meekly and apologetically, but a newfound indignancy burned in him. "We do not know each other, but you've quite the way of speaking to me, Johann. What is it you think you know about me?"

"I know enough," Johann said, scoffing.

"So this area is usually very quiet," Mawie jumped in. "It's exceedingly rare to find anything in the upper pelagic. We originally believed these oceans were completely empty, and the DSL zone was the sea floor. It was only thanks to Johann that we discovered that wasn't the case."

"*Very quiet*, she says," Johann huffed. "We spent three months running around in circles up here, and didn't make a single discovery."

"But beneath this Deep Scattering Layer... well, you'll see," Mawie concluded. None of this helped explain what Johann's problem was, but Tarlo decided to watch his words. Johann seemed wired tightly enough that too much prodding, and *he* would be the one to snap and send them surging to the surface.

"What is this DSL made up of? I know it's biomass related, but what actually *is* it?" Tarlo asked.

"Well, its equivalent on Earth is much more exciting – most of that layer comprises deep-living fish and wildlife. Real animals. Here, it's a little different – and almost solely consists of an incredibly dense population of phytoplankton and prokaryotes. But still, life. Just as we'd always hoped. Sitting right beneath us all that time."

"And this layer... does it shift, same as Earth? Is that why we set forth at night?"

"In a way. Though where on Earth it's the predators that surge towards the surface, here, it's the prey. And they aren't coming up to feed. They're fleeing."

"Fleeing?"

Mawie smiled, warming for the first time during the trip. "As I said, you'll see."

Another question had been bothering Tarlo. "With the others... why did surfacing impact them so? I mean, if these things are so indestructible—"

"We don't know," Johann said. "Didn't Mauve tell you that?"

"What do you mean, you don't know? Was it the bends?"

"No, Rocks are pressurised. No sign of physical trauma, either. Best we can tell, they just... shut down."

Tarlo shivered.

"We have you coming up on the DSL." Mauve had keyed in again from Tuwia, and her forced cheer was starting to grate. "Which means radio darkness for the next two point five hours or so. Stay safe, and keep recording. Any final updates?" Tarlo felt cold as he thought of their contact with the surface severing.

Outside, everything was the same level of dark and quiet, while inside, he couldn't even see the navs consoles spread in front of Johann and Mawie. He imagined this was how it would feel to be an asteroid, lost in space.

"Negative, liaison. Proceeding," Johann said.

Mawie turned to face Tarlo, her enthusiasm continuing to grow. "Get ready, sci, things are about to look real different, real fast!"

Tarlo braced for an imaginary impact as they plunged through the layer of microscopic animals, wincing as he thought of the thousands that were being torched by their thrusters. A thought wormed away at the back of his mind, of the little creatures rallying against this threat, uniting together and fighting – biting – back, chewing through the hull, his clothes, his skin... Ludicrous. Except... it had happened before.

Then they were through, and a whole new world opened up before him.

8
WARNINGS

Tuwia, Alantia   CD: 09/04/2222
Mai

THE BIOLAB IN Tuwia was similar to the one where Mai had spent most of her time back on Cahros. Large oaken desk in the centre, and dozens of purpose-built monitors around the edges of the room – but, to her dismay, no glass ceiling to provide a glimpse of the heavens. *I guess they didn't have any Elhantos here.* Mai had been pleasantly surprised when he came to her with the idea to customise Catal in such a way, having always assumed him to be a bit of a grunt. She wondered what had happened to him, Mondes, and Mury after the she had fled Catal with the others. How long had they lasted, alone and surrounded by the vicious sands?

Mauve's demeanour had changed after the dive commenced, and she now stood rather sullenly at the comms terminal, speaking only when checking in with the expedition. Viola flitted in and out of the room, attending to various small errands, but otherwise, the facility was quiet. The lack of action led Mai to the realisation that, in an entire day, she had only seen seven colonists throughout the facility, not counting the three who were incapacitated in the medbay.

Many questions burned in her mind, and she recalled one that Mauve had cut off, somewhat patronisingly, when she tried to broach the subject earlier.

"All our metrics about Alantia pointed to it being similar to a pre-continental Earth, complete with hot weather and boiling seas," Mai began. "The air temperature here is significantly cooler than I would have thought."

"I would have thought you and your friends on the Martellus project would be used to being wrong by now," Mauve snapped, refusing to look at her.

Mai's jaw locked in frustration, but she maintained her composure. "I'll have you know that I only signed up on these expeditions to get *out* of that team, having pointed out numerous flaws in the metrics used. And before you say anything, you don't need to impress upon *me* the consequences of those errors."

Mauve paused in her preparations, weighing up a response. "Well... maybe in this case your friends weren't correct *enough*. What was it, a thirty-four point six chance of a life-match?"

"Thirty-six point four six."

"Yeah, well, it should have been much higher. The planet is covered in *water*, the cornerstone of all carbon life, for Sol's sake."

Mai was hit by a realisation. "It was when I mentioned I was ECP, wasn't it?"

"What?"

"Your attitude... it changed. Look, I am sorry for how things have played out. I'm sorry you lost people. Everyone at the UCI... they were irresponsible."

"*They*? Not *we*?"

"Do you see any of them out here, risking their lives to test their theories?"

Mauve grimaced. "I get it. You're stuck out here just like the rest of us. But Sol help me, I lost a lot of friends, and it really, really hurts. It's easy to blame the UCI for all this. So to have a company person, even a former company person, land in our laps?"

Mai digested this information. Having spent her life battling bureaucracy, she understood Mauve's disapproval of the Martellus project. But Mai had suffered too, and the liaison's words came across as slightly sanctimonious. Who *hadn't* been misled by the UCI?

"That wasn't what you said in front of the others. What was all that about having much to offer?"

"I'm upset with you, but that doesn't mean I want to sabotage you," Mauve huffed. "The people here trust me, and it is imperative those on the dive trust Tarlo, too."

Mai swallowed and took a breath. "That was... professional of you. Thank you."

Mauve finally softened. "Just... give me some time, okay? And keep the questions to business. I'll get there."

Mai nodded. Business suited her just fine – even if that was what had got them bickering in the first place.

"So, about the oceans... what can you tell me?"

"Well, you... they, were correct about the seas. The surface level is *hot*, as far as oceanic waters go. But the Deep Scattering Layer – comprising your prokaryotes, among other things, seems to work as an insulator of sorts. Once you get below it, there is quite a variance in underwater climates. As for the weather – our terraformation has had some say in that. Getting the nitro-ox balance right in the atmosphere resulted in a lot of extra cloud formation, and as a result, winds and rain. You're floating above a very different Alantia to the one we first landed on, two years ago."

They spoke on this for a while, and the mood between them calmed, but Mai's thoughts kept returning to the case of how small the staffing at the facility seemed to be. Eventually, her concern and curiosity won out.

"There was something else I wanted to ask."

Mauve sighed. "Go on then."

"I haven't seen many other colonists since we got here. Have you lost... I mean, how many people are here now?" Mauve shifted awkwardly, avoiding eye contact.

"We're a frontier colony, you know what it's like."

Mai knew now wasn't the time for this, but a mixture of anxiety and compulsion drove her to keep pressing. "What do you mean?"

"We have had some accidents, over the years. And some... who've left. But please, this was not what I meant when I said to keep it business. With the others in the field, I can't really think about this right now."

"I'm sorry, it is bad timing. It's just, we've had so little time to adjust, I'm all over the place," Mai said. "I think what I am trying to ask is, do you think they're in danger down there?"

"Look, most of our losses occurred in the early days. Construction accidents, ignorance of what we were up against. Then again when we started risking direct exposure to the air – hence the inoculations. Last time out was the first time a dive really went wrong, apart from the occasions people have gotten lost and wound up in Bermuda." Mauve turned to her and gave her a weary but patient smile. "Now, I know you mentioned you are most comfortable in the overseer position, and have experience doing so, but now they are underway... there is precious little to do here."

"Understood. Apologies, for my forwardness, I'm still trying to get my head around... everything, really. Comms me in if there's anything I can do."

Mauve nodded. "Not a worry. See you soon."

Mai departed the room and followed the signage to the medical area, intent on finding the only person she knew to be more sceptical than she was. Again, she noted the quietness and lack of activity throughout the place.

An eruption of raised voices echoing from the medbay suggested that her confrontation with Mauve had been positively diplomatic.

"You HAVE to amputate! You have no idea what he's been through, you can't just freeze him like this and hope for the best. These stones work in strange ways, and look, you can see that the cryo hasn't stopped the spread!"

Mai had only seen Ashelyn so animated once before, when she'd learned of her role in awakening the tardigrade threat back on Catal. Mai preferred her this way – as when the doctor was quiet and distant, she was much harder to read.

"We shouldn't tamper with the patient," a deeper voice replied. "We don't know what's safe."

Mai paused outside the room, unsure what to do.

"If it was airborne, we'd all be impacted by now, certainly those of us who came with him," Ashelyn said.

"I need to do what's best for my people," the man replied. It sounded like the doctor who'd inoculated them... Alesio?

"I'm not sure you heard the news, but we are your people now, too! We are UCI colonists, Sol-damn it, just like you. Do you think we chose to have all our friends killed, and be thrown halfway across the galaxy? This man is only hurt in the first place because he was trying to protect us."

"We don't know the risks."

Mai couldn't resist any longer. She strode into the room, adopting a confident posture that did not reflect how she felt at all. Bright white light bathed the grey walls and silver shelves, and a drawn curtain on the right-hand side of the entrance revealed Terrus. Alesio and Ashelyn, both wearing hazmats, stood beside his bed, casting large shadows against his limp frame.

"Doctor, Alesio..." she said, hesitating for a moment. *Do I have any idea what I'm talking about?* "For all we know, the risks will only increase as the infection spreads." *Yes, that sounded good. Keep going.* "Where are your ethics?"

Wait, what are their ethics?

"The scientific potential of knowledge gained is always superseded by the preservation of life, unless that knowledge is essential to preserve the lives of others," Ashelyn recited with a small smile.

Alesio's eyes flickered between them, and Mai was surprised to see his face lined with worry, rather than indignance.

"It's... been a long time since somebody mentioned the code of ethics out here. But that's exactly my fear... what if we do need to monitor this, to correctly ascertain the risk to others?"

Ashelyn shook her head. "Eliminate the risk. Then there are no risks to others. Monitoring him only increases the danger."

Alesio stared down at Terrus, hands clasped behind his back. Suddenly, he shook his head and turned to face them both. "What in Sol was I thinking? Of course, you're right."

Mai and Ashelyn both heaved relieved sighs.

"I can assist you," Ashelyn said, moving swiftly to prepare an operating station. It was only now that Mai noticed the three beds in the corner of the medbay, each bearing a sleeping colonist.

"Should we be worried about waking them?" Mai asked, but Alesio shook his head.

"Any sign of life from them would be a good thing at this point. They've all been cold since they resurfaced. Also, you aren't sterile. You can observe, but I ask you come no closer and do not touch the equipment or the patient."

"We will keep him in the cryocoma while we operate, yes? Should slow any blood flow and give us ample time to clean up," Ashelyn said. Mai knew she was well out of her depth – a feeling she did *not* take kindly to – but here with Ashelyn and the Alesio seemed a better option than antagonising Mauve in the command centre.

"Yes, you're right," Alesio said. "They really make them with thick hides on Cahros. My thanks to you both for holding me to account."

"We were there for barely a week, I'm not sure that's long enough to develop a culture," Ashelyn deflected.

"Sometimes these things happen without our consciousness of the fact. But truly, only a week? That's a long time to be cramped up on that getaway ship." He eyed them at the last statement. Mai wondered how many other colonists found this story suspicious.

"It was," Ashelyn replied.

"Alright, alright. Bigger things to focus on now, I get it. Now, Doctor, you speak like you know your way around an osteo, but I would be remiss if I didn't ask, have you ever completed a surgery like this before?"

Ashelyn blushed. "Actually, no. My field is Neuropsych, so it's generally basic first aid only, and I can't say I'm wonderful at that, either. Though, you pick up a few things. I set a compound fracture not too long ago..."

Alesio laughed. "Then forgive me, but I might ask that you play the role of second hand here."

Ashelyn made a show of rolling her eyes, but a small look of relief washed over her when he turned away for more supplies. "Okay. But do NOT call me nurse."

"I wouldn't dream of it. Mai, what about you, do you need to be...?"

"I'm free for the best part of an hour, I'd be happy to... observe? Don't worry, I've seen this kind of thing before." That was mostly true. She watched a lot of med-flix.

"I don't doubt that." His gaze lingered on her. "You know the code better than I'd expect in the average biologist."

Mai smirked. *And you have no idea I was bluffing.*

"And you take feedback better than the average doctor," she said, instead.

A smile spread across his dark features as he rustled up an array of sanitary equipment.

"I've spent a long time sitting on my hands out here. Maybe I just want an excuse to do something."

Mai smiled. Alesio came across as genuinely caring. Perhaps it was the gentleness with which he marked out the operating lines on Terrus's upper arm, or the respectful way he'd addressed his assistants back in the quarantine lab, but he seemed cut from a different, altogether warmer cloth than most of the colonists she'd met on *either* world.

The procedure was completed with surprising swiftness – and cleanliness, thanks to the effects of the cryocoma slowing all blood flow – and it wasn't until it was over that Mai started to think about what it would mean to Terrus. Brash, confident, heroic Terrus had been whole when he fell into this feverish sleep. Since then, he'd been infected, partially frozen, amputated on, and soon, unfrozen. Plus, he'd be coming out of all that missing an entire limb. For someone who had been an ultra-fit, survivalist type, the mental consequences of this revelation could be scarring. And all that was the best case, if the infection was actually contained to his now removed arm.

"How long before we can wake him up?" Mai asked, concerned.

"Hard to say, depends on his individual resilience, but I'll bring him out of cryocoma as soon as possible. After that, ideally, we monitor him for another week, and ensure that no further spreading occurs. Given the... infection... was unimpeded by the coma, we can assume that if it does not spread further in the next eight hours, it has been contained," Alesio said, fishing about in the corner of the room. He made an "ahhh" sound, and procured a bright yellow, radioactive-waste bag.

"What are you going to do with... his arm?" Mai said, feeling just a little queasy. She hadn't looked at it much, but what she'd seen had been a rather ghastly purple-black, almost like a deep bruise, with tendrils that stretched from his wrist to about an inch below his shoulder.

"This needs to be locked down, and all the operating tools and equipment too. Even the bed will be disposed of. Though I'd love to still observe the arm..." Alesio said, and Ashelyn and Mai shared a wince.

"Are we really in a place that can be done safely?" Ashelyn asked. Another strange expression came across Alesio's face, somewhere between troubled and contemplative, but a noise in the corner of the room – something between a groan and a shout – startled them.

"Bjora!" Alesio exclaimed.

Ashelyn and Alesio rushed to her bedside, but Mai kept her distance. It seemed Bjora was shouting words, though they were barely legible.

"Jörmungandr! Hafgufa! Jörmungandr!"

A shiver of dread crept up Mai's spine. "What is she saying?"

"She is Danish, perhaps something in her tongue?" Alesio said, grabbing Bjora's shoulders as she continued to thrash. Her eyes were wide and bloodshot, her skin pale as death.

"Alesio, her vitals!" Ashelyn exclaimed, gesturing at the wildly fluctuating electrocardiogram. Mai was no medical professional, but from what she could see, Bjora's heart rate was surging and plummeting almost *simultaneously*.

"Hold her. Sedating," Alesio said, fingering a needle.

Then Bjora broke from her rambling and used a new word, one whose meaning long transcended the native tongue that had birthed it.

"KRAKEN."

9

A FRIGHTFUL WONDER

STREAMS OF NEON red pierced the blackness, flurrying around the R16 like elegant, twirling ribbons. At least six feet long, they chased one another through the waters in a sleek, unknowable dance. Occasional white pulses travelled the length of their long bodies, and they twitched and changed directions spasmodically. They were hunting.

"*Aquavermis Nodae,*" Mawie said. "Social and bold, as far as the locals go. Usually the first to greet us."

Tarlo watched in awe as the *Nodae* danced about, trying to get a count. At least a dozen wove through the currents around them, lighting up the realms beyond the headlights of the R16.

"Ahh, and here comes *Cyanea Multiforma.*" Beneath their feet, a colony of bright blue triangular domed creatures floated gently towards them.

"Closest thing on Earth would be a jellyfish, though with some key differences. We've observed *Multiforma* to be at least somewhat aware of its surroundings. Look."

Sure enough, as the ship drew nearer to their ranks, the colony delicately parted. Tarlo pressed his face against the transparent glass, marvelling at stubby tentacles and transparent stomachs containing dark, mulchy masses.

"So, we've got two and a half kilometres of this?" Tarlo said, wide-eyed.

"Yes. Well, in the time allotted, we can cover perhaps half of that, if we're doing it right," Johann said.

"We're meant to be mapping, yes? If so, should there be… probes of some kind?" Tarlo asked.

"Obviously. But no." Johann laughed mirthlessly.

"We tried using probes, but they always disappeared once they hit the sea floor," Mawie said. "Either the pressure was too much for them, or some so-far undiscovered species took a liking to them. Well… that is new. Look!" Mawie pointed to the right side of the R16, where a dark mass floated by. "That looks almost like… vegetation?"

Johann pivoted the vehicle, shining its headlights onto the mass. It was a dull, dark green, and roughly the same size as their submersible, with small dark strands protruding all around it. They trailed out in different directions, heedless of the currents, and whenever one of the *Cyanea Multiforma* or *Aquavermis Nodae* came close, retracted.

"Are you getting this?" Johann said, and Tarlo remembered his tab, drawing it up to his eyeline. The photos it captured were amazingly clear.

"Hit the microphone button and have it transcribe for us," Mawie said, and she began to describe the oddity.

"Unconfirmed if this is vegetational or animalia. Observable behaviour in alignment with terrestrial predatory vegetation, or oceanic coral – possessing awareness of surroundings and reactivity to same. Run a quick match-test, see if anything like this has been observed before. Once you submit the recordings and photos, the option appears automatically."

Tarlo complied, and the system advised of no matches.

"Well, there you go. Discovery one for the expedition. We'll worry about names later."

Mawie didn't sound particularly enthusiastic, but then again, they'd made dozens of discoveries already. Tarlo thought back to how monumental – and surprising – his finding of the tardigrades on Cahros had been. Here, it was just another name for the list.

Not for him, though. He'd just made his second discovery, and it couldn't be further away from the first. Calm, vegetational, floating through the seas in a blissful—

Suddenly, a series of silver beams shot through the dark green mass. At first, they looked like bolts of pure light, slicing through their prey with merciless pace. Chunks of green sprayed out into the water. The dendrites on each piece waved about furiously but were powerless to do anything in the face of the onslaught. Each time the masses were torn through, Tarlo felt a spark of pain through his chest. They were so helpless...

The bright lights continued their attack, impossible to accurately discern until one of the entities halted right in front of the vehicle. It possessed the appearance of a fish, with a rigid-rectangular body, replete with several rows of small fins and what looked like a bio-electric current coursing from nose to tail. It turned on its side, revealing a wide, lidless eye. It bore into the shuttle, flickering between the three of them almost as if in... recognition.

"Ugly fucker," Johann said, but Tarlo was transfixed. A little chunk of green hung from the creature's mouth, and it continued to eye them warily, little silver charges rippling up and down its slender frame.

"*Eleccillia Carnipiscis*. Not actually a fish, but as close as you'll find here on Alantia," Mawie narrated, as Johann resumed piloting the R16.

Noticing their movement, the creature baulked, jerking up two previously hidden cheek fins. They flared like a lion's mane, and a vivid red glow emanated from within, similar to the colour of the eel-like creatures above them. The *Carnipiscis* held its threatening pose for a moment, but seeing the R16 was "retreating", retracted its fins and returned to the feeding frenzy. By the time they sank beyond the killing field, Tarlo's first discovery on Alantia was no more.

The seas around them calmed and the initial flurry of life subsided. The perpetual blackness became familiar, but the sense of insignificance never lessened, nor did the feeling that something was out there in the gloom, just beyond view, watching them all the way.

The coldness crept upon Tarlo with the oppressive dark, and his hands grew numb and heavy. He rubbed his shoulders and checked the time on Johann's console, careful not to nudge him by accident. Had it really been over an hour since their dive began?

"Fifteen hundred metres. Starting to feel pretty deep now, hey?" Mawie said, and, noticing his shiver, "Most of the power in here is dedicated to life support and pressurisation, they figured we could suit up if we were in environments that were too hot or cold."

"Is it usually this quiet? Mauve said there's often... I think six or seven discoveries on a dive like this?"

"There was, at first. As usual, Mauve exaggerates. Still... it has been a little more sparse than usual," Mawie replied.

Her eyes never calmed, rapidly scanning the area around them while Johann continued his rigid-shouldered steering. Tarlo gazed out at the depths below, struck by their eternal stillness. They could have been drifting through the depths of space or the bowels of a planet; it all would have looked the same.

Then he noticed it. A serene blue, directly beneath them, stretching as far as his squinting eyes could see.

"What's that below us?" He exclaimed.

"I don't know! But I... I like it," Mawie said, sounding dazed.

"That *is* different." Johann agreed, slowing their descent.

The layer of blue rose towards them, and Tarlo made out that it was actually several round shapes, delicately floating towards them like azure lily pads. More than just a curious sight, they seemed to elicit a feeling, an *energy*, bringing with it a sense of calmness and safety, like an oasis in the night.

Tarlo fumbled for his tablet, heavy hands warming as euphoria began to pulse through him.

"Do you feel that, too?" Mawie called in a high-pitched voice. Johann laughed, and for a moment, Tarlo basked in the emotional embrace.

"These creatures... must be emitting some kind..." Johann brought the vehicle to a halt and stood, laying a hand on the against the inner shell of the R16.

The giant blue petal-like creatures were all around them now. Mawie was next to stand, pressing her cheek against the ionised Moonsalt and closing her eyes. Tarlo felt a similar compulsion to give himself to these beings, but his cold feet were his undoing, and he tripped over his chair while trying to stand up. The clank of his head against Johann's ankle broke the spell just in time to see an opening growing in the nearest of the entities.

"What in Sol…" The opening widened from its centre point, getting larger and larger until…

It was big enough to swallow them whole.

"Johann! We need to move!" Tarlo shouted, but it was no use. Both his companions had fixed their bodies against either side of the vehicle.

It seemed that whatever power the creature used to influence them had been halted when it switched to *digestive mode*, and Tarlo's clarity of mind remained long enough for him to lunge over the chair and yank one of the steering levers downwards. Thankfully, the controls weren't as complicated as Johann's hyperfocused attitude made them look. The vehicle lurched, scorching the nearby creature enough for it to retract. The other beings scattered, confused – as if such a response was totally unpredicted. As quickly and serenely as they appeared, they faded back into the ocean, their only residue a strange tickling in the back of the mind.

Johann and Mawie slowly returned to their senses.

"Sol praise you, Tarlo, what just happened?" Mawie asked, while Johann rubbed his head, grouchy and embarrassed.

"I take it we haven't run into those… things before?" Tarlo said. A dull ache was growing on his right temple.

"No. Fucking hell, was that thing about to *eat* us?" Johann said, sitting down in a huff.

"Maybe. Or try to, at least. I'm not sure any creature would be able to digest Moonsalt," Mawie remarked.

"You might be right. Not even the tardigrades we found back on Catal were able to chew through it," Tarlo said. Even here, even now, it felt *wrong* to actually talk about what had happened back there.

"Right. So, any ideas on what the hell just happened?" Johann said.

Tarlo took a moment to gather his thoughts, and a murky theory began to crystallise in his mind. "Best I can tell, it was a pheromonal attack. There's precedence for this, in animals and plants, like *Nepenthes*," he checked his tablet to ensure it was recording. "I'm not sure how it got to us through the Moonsalt with pheromones alone, but it was clearly incredibly powerful, enough to trigger some kind of excessive oxytocin rush, resulting in a trance-state, and paralysis. This attack must have been a finite blast, as once I snapped free, I was able to think more clearly while it focused on preparing to digest. This must be some kind of slow, delicate ambush predator."

"Beware the blue," Mawie said. "Sol, I think I'm quite ready to leave now. I wonder if what just happened to us... something like that happened to Bjora and the others. Sol, maybe she *saved* them by—"

"The speculation is pointless," Johann said. "But I agree, we should leave. These expeditions have been a fucking accident waiting to happen, regardless of what they think we could learn about Alvolito. We should prepare to ascend, as long as it's not straight back through that pack of blue bastards."

Despite their predatory intention, Tarlo disagreed with the labels Johann so readily assigned these strange new creatures. This was their realm that they had blindly entered, so confident in their machines and their tech.

Not for the first time, he wondered if the same rule applied to the Cahran tardigrades.

Did we really invade their realm?

No, that was different. We meant them no harm.

Tarlosius Maleficus... your legacy.

At least half of their name was appropriate: those creatures had been *evil*.

"We'll travel horizontally for a half hour, then commence our ascent. Should be easy enough, with the sea floor a constant navigational..." Johann cursed.

Mawie leaned over him and emitted a panicked gasp.

"What is it?" Tarlo asked, though he decided not to wait. He clambered as close to Johann as he dared and peered at the navs console. It was difficult to make sense of the various numbers and archaic looking SONAR, but finally he found the readout for the depth to the sea floor.

"Another one point five kilometres, right? What's the issue?"

Johann said nothing, and Mawie dropped to the floor, as though she was searching the abyss below.

"Wrong. That is the distance to the Deep Scattering Layer above us. *This* is the distance to the sea floor," Johann said, raising a shaky finger to another number. The only difference was this number was shrinking rapidly. Time slowed as Tarlo stared at the screen, watching it count down in chunks. *Two hundred metres.*

One seventy-five.

One thirty-five.

One ten.

Ninety-five.

"So that means..."

"What we thought was the floor... is coming towards us. We need to get out of here. Now."

PART TWO
UNSAFE

10
THE DEPTHS

Uncharted Seas, Alantia   CD: 09/04/2222
Tarlo

SILENCE. COLDNESS. DARKNESS. The ocean pressed down on them like an omnipresent, ravenous deity, squeezing the air from their lungs and smothering their thoughts in a dense fugue.

None of them moved. If, as they feared, some kind of seismic creature approached, they had no chance of outpacing or outfoxing it. Their only hope was that it would not find them. Tarlo snuck a quick breath. The air in the R16 tasted of stale oxygen and fearful sweat.

The counter indicating the supposed distance of the sea floor continued its inexorable creep towards zero. *Forty metres. Thirty-two metres. Twenty-four metres.*

Sixteen...

Eight...

The screens fizzled and cracked as a series of gibberish numbers burst across the interface. Then, all electronics in the vehicle short circuited and the world went so dark that Tarlo couldn't even see his own hands.

He held his breath.

Quiet.

Still.

Hoping that whatever was out there would pass them by, and the lights would turn back on.

Instead, an ear-shattering *boom* echoed from somewhere beneath them, setting his nervous system alight.

There's something down there...

Then came the impact.

The cabin rocked fiercely, sending one of his companions flying across the pod. They slammed into the wall behind Tarlo with a sickening *crack*. The other was also flung from their seat, clubbing him in the temple with a stray elbow. Strangely, Tarlo was unaffected by the gravitational changes, as a familiar, firm force held him in place. While the world shook viciously, something dragged him to his feet and drew him to the front of the R16. He pressed his eyes against the glassy surface, oblivious to the plights of those behind him.

Then he saw it. Deep within the pitch-black abyss, a flickering, fluorescent grey outline. Tarlo peered through the spectral presence, seeing a great maw, easily the size of a starship, spasming and contorting. Two four-fingered hands protruded from within, tearing at the shattered lips.

He had seen this before. Deep in the caves of Cahros, a similar cosmic battle had raged, and it had nigh consumed him before it was abated only by the arrival of a blissful, kaleidoscopic show of lights.

Only this time, there was no lightbringer to save him.

Cold thrills of terror sparked across Tarlo's skin, and he stood immobilised by this force that was so much greater than he. The warring entities continued, their conflict sending tremors through the waters, their density so great that they generated a gravity of their own. Their perilously small vehicle – once a great symbol of human innovation – was drawn towards the writhing mass, and Tarlo could do nothing but watch in horror as they came to within a few feet.

From this range, the shapes of the entities were lost, and a new vista emerged. In the centre of the mouth, a mass of tendrils squirmed, each glittering with an otherworldly glow. Gazing into the depths of madness, Tarlo realised these tendrils were attached both to the fingers and the mouth and twitched away at them like a Lovecraftian puppeteer.

You are one and the same.

Their R16 drew closer still, so close that even a nudge would send them tumbling into the maw to merge with this paradoxical creature forever. Tarlo sensed its tension, its confusion, its *hatred*, and a terrible fear flooded through him. What he'd seen in the caves... had it been an apparition, a reflection of this great monstrosity? Or had it been... a warning?

Whatever it all meant, it was far too late to do anything about it now. As always, he'd blindly rushed to his doom, headfirst and ignorant. The R16 shuddered as a final wave propelled them towards the chasmic creature – and Tarlo braced for the final, eternal fall...

But it never came. Just as they were about to merge with the fiendish entity, the oceans came alight, and a blinding beam of power rent through the being, illuminating the black seas like a galactic storm.

For a moment, Tarlo could not tell if he was deep underwater or deep in the heavens, before another thunderous *boom* sent the R16 surging through the seas, away from the entity. He was fortunate to land on Mawie's empty chair, which cushioned what could have been a bone-shattering impact, and he clung on with all his might.

Tarlo came back to his senses a few moments later, as the lights in the R16 reactivated. The waters around them were dark as ever, but they no longer seemed so heavy or so cold. He stumbled to the rear of the vehicle, amazed to see Johann looking relatively healthy – he'd been inadvertently braced between the back wall and Tarlo's seat, sparing him the worst of the impact. He groaned but didn't open his eyes.

Then Tarlo saw what remained of Mawie.

The multiple impacts had thrown her into the rear of the sub, where she lay in a crumpled heap. The first thing Tarlo registered was her left eye, still wide open, but her nose and the entire right side of her face had been crushed. Blood and refuse pooled around her face and terribly bent neck. The turgid scent of bodily fluid reached him, and fiery bile burned at his throat. With heavy limbs and sluggish thoughts, he turned back to a stirring Johann and clumsily helped him back to the front of the shuttle. Seeing Mawie, Johann let out a vicious curse, before shoving Tarlo down into her seat.

"Figure this out later. Got to go," he slurred, his voice barely audible over Tarlo's pulsing heart.

Somehow, Tarlo had managed keep his wits so far... but the thought of spending even a minute down here with a broken corpse just a metre behind him was too much.

"Don't," Johann grunted, hearing Tarlo's ragged breathing. "Not the time."

Johann's curt words were a tonic to the panic, a cold plank of clarity amidst turbulent seas. Tarlo suppressed the urge to vomit and regathered control of his breathing while Johann moved the vehicle into ascent. Another heavy feeling collapsed upon him, and he grabbed at Johann's arm.

"G'off me," Johann said, but the distraction was enough to slow them just in time to see what loomed above. Another bolt of pure energy flashed through the seas, illuminating something truly colossal.

The mass filled the oceans, a semi-translucent, grey-black mass spreading in all directions as far as they could see. Several appendages dangled beneath it, each easily the size of the hand-mouth entity, and they flapped through the seas in the most gradual fashion, slowed by their own bulk. Tarlo and Johann watched in terrified awe as the nearest limb completed its swing, and a few moments later, their sub was hit by another massive underwater impact.

They hurtled back down to the depths.

When their momentum slowed, any relief at being out of range of that *thing* was tempered by the knowledge that it still loomed above them. *And Sol help me, maybe below us too...*

Their seats had protected them from the worst of the whiplash, but Tarlo still felt as though he'd been tossed through a tumble dryer, and the rapid changes in pressure caused sharp pains to bubble behind his ears.

"We can't go back up." He gasped, and Johann swore again.

"Fuck else can we go?"

"We're not going to be able to get through them. We'll have to go around."

Johann smacked his armrest. "Don't know about you, but I'm not spending a second longer down here, with *her* like this."

"I don't feel any better about it. But whatever those things are, we can't just swim through them."

Johann said nothing, but the veins on his forehead looked as if they were about to burst.

"Just my fucking luck, stuck down here with a body, and *you*."

Another wave of uncharacteristic frustration pierced Tarlo's panicked mind. "You know, you actually are lucky to be down here with me. Otherwise, you could be here with two corpses, or with someone equally clueless to what we might be up against."

"Oh, and how could you know anything about what we're up against?"

"You don't know about what I've survived. What I saw, back on Cahros."

Johann laughed contemptuously. "And you don't know what *we've* survived here. You think you're the only one who's seen a bit of action?"

Johann's admission chilled him – had these people been through even more than what Mauve let on?

"Well, if you have survived half as much as I have," Tarlo snapped, determined to hold his ground, "Then you know we need to stay calm."

Johann glared at him but grunted in acknowledgement.

"How deep are we?" Tarlo asked.

"Says we're only five hundred metres deep. Those things... they're huge, if our scanners are bouncing off them and thinking it's the surface."

"Makes sense, considering we thought they were the sea floor when they were beneath us. Speaking of, how far down is the sea floor now?"

"Shit. Readings say two point five klicks."

"Sol..."

"Yeah. We were about 1500 metres when we were hit, give or take. Now we're at least 500 lower, meaning the *true* sea floor actually could be as low as five klicks. What now, professional survivor?" Johann said.

"We've just got to go around them. How long can these Rocks function for?"

"Oh, easily twenty-four hours. Just run the expeditions so short because it's so common to get lost."

"You mean... this has happened before?"

"Fuck, no, you think we'd come back down here if we knew *they* were here? No, just, the disruption thing, half our expeditions end up on the same sandbar you were picked up from."

Tarlo remembered Mauve saying something similar while ferrying them back from the formation. "Did you ever work out why expeditions washed up there?"

"Not really. It wasn't the current, though. Nothing magnetic either, though it seems to function the same way – almost like it pulls people there."

"So... we need to get lost again."

"What?"

"Nothing. Just... if we can't trust navs or line of sight, we should probably hope we wind up there again."

"Chew, we're going to be lucky if we make it anywhere again."

Tarlo didn't appreciate the negativity, but he controlled himself. "We should move. It doesn't matter where. Keep an eye on the ceiling and floor, see if those numbers change."

"Fantastic idea," Johann murmured, but he complied. It was only when Tarlo saw his dilated pupils and shaking lips that he realised how frightened Johann really was. *Doesn't excuse him for being an arse.*

Johann urged their sub through the darkness. They decided it best to keep the interior and headlights off, lest they attract any further attention, relying on the depth indicators to navigate forward.

Tarlo wasn't sure what was scarier – the infinite darkness above them, home to gigantic, deadly creatures, or the unknowable depths below, whose contents he daren't fathom. Again, he cursed the transparent design of the R16. Total visibility of the world around them felt like the last thing he needed right now.

After a time, a large group of small, silver-blue creatures found their ship, frittering about them like little sparks in the night. At this point, Tarlo and Johann realised that even the lights of their internal consoles may as well have been giant beacons down here, not to mention the heat from the sub's exhausts, and flicked the primary headlights back on.

As before, the lights did little to pierce the gloom, but Tarlo became fixated on a peculiar phenomenon. While the seas around them looked black, it would be more accurate to describe them as having an *absence* of colour – almost like a sad, empty grey. This was contrasted by these small little lifeforms, whose skin seemed to be a *true* black, which was at once both deeper and darker than the seas around, contrasted by the silvery bioluminescence in their skeletal system. Tarlo wondered whether black should be considered a colour in its own right, or only as the absence thereof like everybody always said. But if black wasn't a colour, then that meant these creatures should, in their silky denseness, be assigned some *new* hue. And they definitely weren't grey... which meant black was in fact *something*, but now he forgot what that thing was...

Anything to avoid thinking about the still-bleeding body behind him.

Eventually, the little creatures scattered, and for a while, they were even half-heartedly chased by a blind, wormlike creature that gave up after a few licks of their hull. Tarlo did his best to document them all on his bent-up tablet, where he also opened up a dossier for the massive deities that sent them to these depths.

But he never really stopped thinking about Mawie.

There was a haunting, cold feeling to this place, that couldn't be dispelled by even the brightest of creatures. It was as though whoever had painted the canvas of this world had simply forgotten to fill this part in, and their negligence had invited unspeakable, strange things.

Among them were the wisps.

Tarlo nearly jumped from his skin the first time he saw one, and Johann let out an uncomfortable, involuntary noise. It floated through the dark seas, oblivious to whatever currents abounded; multi-formed and light-grey, headless and with a single, gaping hole for a mouth. Despite its lack of features, it seemed to look directly at Tarlo, outstretching an impish, finlike hand.

Then it screamed.

Tarlo heard nothing at first, just noticed the hole in the centre of the thing's head expand, but after a few seconds, he became aware of a soft, whining noise, the kind that burrowed into his ears and rooted in either side of his brain, before steadily growing in volume and intensity.

The mouth widened further, and the noise ascended to a shrieking moan. Tarlo tried to cover his ears, but it was no use, the sorrowful lament only grew in fervour, reaching a point he thought his ears would bleed and his head would implode—

Only for the creature to shatter into a thousand ghostly pieces.

The oppressive silence descended upon them once more.

11

THE GRAVE PILLARS

EVERYTHING FELT COLD. Tarlo's head still rung from the piercing scream of the deep-sea wisp, and he was troubled by the nature of its demise. What was the purpose of that thing?

The seas were quiet but for the whirring of the R16's engines. Johann was a picture of terse silence: brow furrowed, jaw clenched, and hands firmly on the steering levers. Occasionally, strong currents brushed against the vehicle, ricocheting reminders that they were never truly alone down here.

Tarlo still couldn't look back at Mawie. When she had woken up that morning, had she known her life would come to a brutal end thousands of metres away from the light? She'd been kind, in her awkward way, and done everything she could to help him settle into his first day here. And now...

Now she was gone. And another truth had been revealed.

Not even falling to a new world had allowed Tarlo to escape the grasping hand of death.

An eventual grunt from Johann distracted him from his moroseness.

"What is it?"

"Looks like we're getting closer to the sea floor."

Tarlo fought back against a momentary alarm. "Like, it's coming to us? Again?"

"Negative. This is gradual, like the sloping of the land. We're headed for shallower waters."

Relief.

"What about above us?"

"We're having moments where the numbers jump, then settle back down again. For now, it seems those things have risen as far as they're prepared to go. As for the fluctuations, I'm guessing that we're getting occasional glimpses of the true surface when they move their limbs... we're not through the other side yet, though. By Sol, I just hope we don't see another one of those screaming little fuckers."

It was the first Johann had mentioned them, and it was comforting to hear. Thus far, his demeanour had contributed to the lonely, harsh atmosphere of this place.

"Agreed." Tarlo said.

"What was its problem, killing itself like that?"

"I can only guess. Kind of resembles an escape strategy, scream to scare away predators. Maybe the explosion was an illusion of some kind. Or maybe it's just haunted down here."

Johann laughed, and the room felt a little warmer.

"Did you notice the legs?"

Tarlo had not, but Johann wasn't waiting on a reply. "You're a biologist, of course you did. What I'd like to know, is why the fuck any creature on this planet would have legs?"

Tarlo rubbed his temples, unsure what to say.

"Reminded me of a siren. Or souls of the lost. Mythological shit. Just doesn't really make sense."

"Let me know if you see anything that *does* make sense." Tarlo groaned.

Johann turned his head, treating Tarlo to a strange look. "You wanna know why you pissed me off so much?"

"Sure." Tarlo remained cautious – he wasn't sure if Johann was opening up or preparing a villain's monologue that would precipitate some kind of drastic action.

"I spent months pushing for us to explore the DSL. Months. Told them all that it wasn't the true sea floor, but Mauve and her sycophants thought otherwise. Instead, they sent their little expeditions out in circles, always winding up back at the sandbar where you got picked up. Took almost half a year before they finally took me seriously and let me bring the Rock down. Lo and behold, I was right, as you saw. Five minutes later, we finally found proof of life – and boom, it's everywhere! No sooner had we returned to base, we get first news of your little expedition. Some little bastard named Tarlo has gotten all the credit for being the first man to discover life in outer space. I've been to Europa, Callisto, the Roids, was even lined up before the Kepler expedition went to shit. Twenty-five years of being second best. And even now, after all this time, I was still beaten to the punch by some kid."

Tarlo weighed up his next words carefully. "Not that I wish to be wise... but might your frustration be better directed at those who kept you from running your expedition so long?"

"It was, don't you worry. Eventually though, I calmed down. There was a lot of work to do, and when everything went south... but then you, of *all the people* in the galaxy, rock up, and next thing I see you're sitting next to me, chalking up more discoveries like it's just another day at the office?"

"I understand. For what it's worth, I'm sorry."

Johann snorted. "Enough of that. I'm just a crusty old man who doesn't like looking into twenty-year-old mirrors. Let's just move on."

Tarlo wasn't exactly sure if this meant they were friends now, but seeing an opportunity to move forward, nodded. "That works just fine for me."

The temperature in the shuttle continued to rise, and it wasn't until sweat gathered on his forehead that Tarlo realised it had nothing to do with their tentatively brokered peace.

"What's the thermos say?"

"Yeah, it's getting warmer. Water temp is about thirty-five degrees. Some regions of the seas here blow hotter. Usually we'd stay clear, but I'm getting a feeling we're heading in the right direction."

"I get that feeling too. This heat though, it isn't anything we need to worry about?"

"I don't know. This is about as hot as we've ever seen it. Hold on... there's something ahead." Johann pulled the vehicle to a halt.

"What, like, a lifeform?"

"No, they wouldn't come up on the radar like this. Well, not unless they were huge, like those monsters before. This is big enough to bounce a signal... but it's not moving... What in Sol?" Johann's voice choked up in surprise. "The hell is this?"

The fragile beams of the R16 headlights barely lit up the broader environment, but such was the positioning of their vehicle that they shined directly on a strange object looming in the dark. It was rectangular, stretching beyond vision above and below them, and bore an unmistakeable smooth, black surface that contrasted the colourless water around it. *Again, different kinds of black.*

"Swing us around, I want to see something," Tarlo said.

"Why?"

Tarlo knew vagueness would only provoke. "This looks like something I've seen before. Except, there were two of them. So, swing us around, please, I want to see if—"

The explanation clearly sufficed, as Johann yanked the vehicle into a full 360-degree turn. It wasn't until about 300-degrees that they saw it – another obelisk-like structure, standing parallel to the first, perhaps fifteen metres away. A cold shiver swept through Tarlo, mirrored in Johann's paleness.

"You've seen these before?"

"Yes. But first, you said half your expeditions got lost. Were you ever on one of those?"

Johann looked offended. "No. I actually know what I'm doing. But I read the reports."

"Do you recall mention of these structures? They marked the entrance to the cave... near the distress beacon."

"Nobody ever said anything about a cave, but yes, I know what you're talking about. You think... these could be the same two structures as what we see up there?"

"I do."

"Which would make them five, six kilometres long. And you're suggesting if we follow these up, we might reach the rally point?"

"I am. That, or some entirely new point on the map. But that would surprise me."

"Why's that?"

Tarlo hesitated. It was impossible to know how Johann would respond to his admission, and the last thing he needed was his companion deciding he was mentally unsound.

He chose his words carefully. "Well... back on Cahros, there was only one."

Johann stared at him, assessing. "One what?"

"One formation."

"Are you going to elaborate on that?"

"In a moment... I think we should begin our ascent."

Johann appraised the monitor again. "Hmm. The way above us seems clear. Might be as good a place as any to try resurfacing. But I want to hear more about what you know."

As they drifted slowly upwards – Johann was careful not to accelerate too earnestly – Tarlo did his best to share what he knew. While he omitted the part about how they'd used the formations to travel between worlds, he described the strange allure of the Blackrock, as well as the effects it had on standard machinery. When the navs of the R16 shorted out around a kilometre from the surface, Johann gave him a funny look.

"Just like you say. Maybe they were right in sending you down here with me."

"I volunteered."

"Huh, you did too. Idiot." Another strange look... was it respect?

The ascent continued without interruption, and Tarlo took notice of the total absence of any kind of wildlife. Just like on Cahros, it seemed that these formations were a home only to ghosts.

They had traversed half of the remaining distance, experiencing a lull that was as close to pleasantness as the situation would allow, when they were forced to another halt – only this time, it was due to a small object colliding with their windscreen. It did nothing to disrupt their momentum, but when it tumbled into eyeline, Tarlo gasped in shock.

It was an E12 helmet.

"Johann?" The ensuing silence was as heavy as the thousands of metres of water above them.

"Yes?" The helmet – thankfully empty – drifted below them and was shortly followed by a boot and two gloves.

"Why... what are they doing down here?"

Johann stared straight ahead, never blinking.

A large sheet of grey floated into view, followed by the slender nose of a shuttle-esque vehicle, similar to the one that had collected Tarlo from the formation. Then, a large, grey slab ghosted through their lights. *Moonsalt.* Tarlo's chest tightened as he realised the only place he could think of where such pieces could have fallen from.

Tuwia Skybase.

Tarlo's head split with fear and pain, and his vision went dark. What had happened while they were down here? Had the vertical migration of those great beasts continued all the way to the surface? To beyond? A bolt of pain ripped through his chest as he realised if, the skybase fell, so had everybody on it, including all their new hosts, Mai, and *Ashelyn...*

"I can't believe it. You seeing this too?" Johann said softly.

Nauseous bewilderment joined Tarlo's inner cocktail of panic. "Yeah..." He choked out.

"We've found them. I can't believe it."

"What...?" His throat was so dry, he wasn't getting enough air.

"Have you forgotten already, why we're even down here?"

Finally, Tarlo remembered how to breathe, but his head was still spinning as he stuttered, "So, you're saying this...?"

"Has to be the remains of Alvolito. How in Sol did they get here..." A double-layered bunk bed bounced off their window.

"But... how do we know this isn't Tuwia?"

"Sol, I didn't even think of that. But two reasons. That shuttle was X143, ours is X098. And we don't have double bunks."

Tarlo came perilously close to laughing, such was his relief. *Of all the things...*

"I still can't believe it. An ocean the size of a planet, and we've fucking found them." Johann grabbed Tarlo's tablet, propped it behind his monitor, and set it to record.

"Commencing report. We have identified legitimate evidence of remains of human settlement, most likely the lost settlement of Alvolito, which fell from the skies on eighteen, oh three, twenty-two." He proceeded to list everything they'd seen so far, before gently setting the tablet to mute.

"So, everybody who was onboard the skybase... You don't think we might...?"

"Find their bodies?" Johann grimaced. "No, thank every deity in history. The water is too cold, it's been too long and… well, you've seen the wildlife here. We'll see only the skeleton of their brief home. *Blissah cah taneh.*" Johann murmured the final sentence with a wave of his right hand above his heart.

Tarlo recognised this gesture, with a horrible tug at his heart. For a moment, the oceans around him morphed into a vicious sandstorm. In front of him stood a beautiful, tan-skinned woman. She smiled. *"Look how the heavens shine for me."* Then, the raging sands devoured her.

A *thunk* brought him back to the present as more flotsam swirled around them. Tarlo watched as furnishings, consoles, and building materials passed them by – the silent, scattered shells of misguided hope. After all the indescribable and deadly wonders he'd seen on the dive, things ending with this grim tour through the lives and deaths of another colony brought a taunting sense of foreboding. First, it had been Casarabe. Then Catal. Then Alvolito. *How long until Tuwia was next?*

He had seen so much but still understood so little. For all that the *Maleficus* were responsible for, their success could easily be explained as hubristic humans encountering a deadly species they were not prepared for. But what he, Ashelyn, Mai, and Terrus had borne witness to in the bowels of the Cahran formation suggested an even greater danger.

And now, these strange, colossal beings were rising from the depths of Alantia.

But why?

It was too much, too vast, and too confusing, and had happened altogether too quickly. Tarlo longed only for something peaceful and green, to bury his hands in the dirt again and just watch something grow. To listen to rain on the roof, and be able to step outside, onto *the ground*, and have no fear that something in the air or dirt or water would try to kill him.

But deep down, he knew he would never get the chance to do any of those things ever again.

12

SHIFTING SANDS

Catal, Cahros   CD: 09/04/2222
Jame

WHEN THE UCI returned to Cahros, they came in force. Gone were the days where eight soldiers were deemed enough to chaperone fifty colonists – now, it was the other way around: the *Nitimini*'s return brought an influx of forty-some troopers, whose gratuitous bravado was backed up by a lethal arsenal of flamethrowers, "war buggies", and new, heat-resistant E14 suits.

They were unleashed upon the sands around Catal, torching their way to depths of over twenty metres with voracious glee. New construction teams – into which Jame and the others had been drafted – were then tasked with constructing bunkers beneath the facility, developing a several-metre cushion between them and the masses of hungry, microscopic teeth below.

At first, Jame had relished in the retributory destruction of the tardigrades. For two years, he had been confined in the shell of Catal with just Han, Mon, Mury, and the four brave fleet reps who Binson had dropped off for company. To finally see some proper vengeance enacted on the fearsome little creatures was cathartic.

But in time, it wore off. No matter how many of the tardigrades died, it didn't bring back Jontie, Sel, Tarlo, or Terrus. The fact the creatures seemed infinite didn't help either – what satisfaction was there in trying to roll a rock up an infinite mountain?

During the long two years of waiting, they had learned many things. First, were the cycles. While feeding, the tardigrades – referred to by their new, trigger-happy "friends" as *Maleficus* – entered stuporous states, ignoring any kind of outside stimuli. The group had learned this when one of the Fleet Officers had fallen from an external roof, directly onto the killing fields... and survived. Unfortunately, when the creatures finished digesting, it turned out they were even more dangerous – which they learned when the same FO had wandered out onto the sands in a fit of deluded bravery, to prove a point that the "bugs weren't so bad". The sand beneath his feet actually *sank,* swallowing him whole. His terrified screams at the realisation of his folly were worse than any cries of agony.

Most pertinent was the early revelation that the predatory tardigrades had a reliable distaste for two things: intense heat and Moonsalt. Once Han and Mon finished restoring the solar arrays (complete with storm shielding, fashioned from repurposed remains of their watchtowers) there had been ample resources to divert towards ensuring the external walls and floors were always too hot for the creatures to attempt to chew through.

Han and Mon... had been really good about the whole thing. Somehow, they'd always believed the walls of Catal were enough, while Jame, Mai, and the others decided to take their chances and flee. When Jame was the only one to return, the pair had never so much as suggested that they "told him so". All that mattered was somehow, those who remained were finally safe.

Although the real challenge was just beginning.

Locked down for so long, Jame had little choice but to reflect on that fated twenty-four hours where everything fell apart. They'd been on the back foot from the start, fleeing a foe that had struck with fatal immediacy, whose capabilities they couldn't hope to understand.

It had been short-sightedness, not fear, that motivated his decision to leave base during the storm. Just as it had been simple, optimistic naivete, and ignorance that a threat so powerful could exist out here, that caused the deaths of forty-six of their friends. Over time, he'd come to accept that there was no way they *could* have known what they were up against, with there being no precedent in the history of human science for such creatures to exist.

Such was the consequence of blind exploration.

Had they not had the blood of so many friends on their tiny teeth, it would almost have been humorous how quickly the *Maleficus* shifted from mysterious, nigh-omnipotent beings to an entirely manageable, if dangerous natural force. They were just creatures, after all, and for all their freakish qualities, could be reliably halted by several inches of fused elements and a few hundred degrees of heat.

Thus transpired the longest two years of Jame's life – a period where he had more conversations with ghosts than humans. There was only so much they could distract themselves in the small gym and VR stations, and they were all hanging by a thread by the time the UCI returned.

The reinforcements were led by a hawk-nosed young captain named Ternal, who was quick to assert himself on Jame and the others – making a show of congratulating them on their "conquest of these unforgiving lands". When

Jame asked what the heads of the UCI thought about their ninety-six percent fatality rate, Ternal had rather callously stated "the *only* two purposes of the original expeditions were to discover life and establish a human presence on Cahros." Since then, he'd made a show of ordering them around on mundane tasks, as if they hadn't been sustaining the base on their own for two full years.

It was one such example of micromanagement that led Jame to his current position on the roof of the base, trying his best to look busy. He'd done enough to work up a sweat —the new E14 suits were meant to be excellent at keeping the heat out, but Jame found they did just as good a job of keeping it in, too. He always seemed to sweat more when the sun was out, even with the internal climate controls. Maybe he was just getting old.

Someone clambered onto the roof beside him, who he identified as Mury thanks to a splash of red paint on the helm. If that hadn't done it, the mild limp and heavy curses would have left him in no doubt.

Alongside the unfortunate fleet officer, Binson had also dropped off two medics. Between their expertise, a host of antibiotics, an ill-fitting prosthetic, and Mury's irrepressible willpower, they'd somehow managed to keep her alive and restore her to some sense of functionality. That said, the rusty rip-and-replace job they'd done on her leg never properly stuck, nor had her lungs fully recovered from the infection.

"Fucking don't know why I do this," she said, dusting her gloves symbolically. Assessing the solar grid was not strictly a two-person job, and Jame would have reminded anybody else of this fact. But not Mury.

"What's got you worked up today?" he said, gruff voice tinged with affection. He knew that she had only gone through the effort to get up here for the company, and *she* knew he would have figured that out.

"Where would you like me to start?"

"Definitely not from the top."

Mury snorted. "Always the foreman. Why are all sayings so stupid?"

"Because they were invented by idiots, not builders."

"The glue that holds the world together. Sol, I could use a lung tickler." Narcotics were banned from the colonies for obvious reasons, and barely a day went by without Mury lamenting the fact.

"I hear the Cahros air will give you quite a rush."

"Don't tempt me." Mury banged her right fist against her helmet before changing the subject. "It still doesn't feel right, you know."

"What?"

"All this setting the planet on fire."

"You think the bugs don't deserve it?"

"Not that. Although, honestly, I don't even know anymore. Just... how gung-ho everyone has been. We've been going insane cooped up here the last two years, and now it's all celebrations and medals."

Jame completed his rounds and wandered back over to her. The Cahran day had started about forty hours earlier, but it still looked like it was midmorning. Standing in front of the rising sun, Mury cast a vivid, elongated silhouette across the roof, distorted by the red-tinged solar panels dotting the area.

"That's how they do things – have you wading through carcasses by day, up on the podium by night."

"Just like Mars, right?"

"The resemblance is uncanny."

Mury paused and faced the horizon. Jame knew what was coming next.

"I miss them. All of them."

"Me too."

He assisted her with disembarking from the roof. Up until a couple of months ago, she would have put up a righteous protest, but she was getting better at accepting his help. She coughed viciously when she landed on the floor. "I'm still not sure whether I should hate you," she cursed.

"You never did, don't now, and never will."

"So smug. Remind me what I should be most grateful for, two years of solitary, the limp, or the crook lung?"

"You know full damn well you survived on your own merit and I am not to be blamed. All I did was change your pants every day until Binson dropped the doctor off. Oh, and a few days after, too."

"Some doctor he was."

"Some survivor you are." In this statement, Jame was sincere.

Mury sensed it. "At least you *did* something. You saved lives. All I did was lie there in a fever and almost die."

"I've met a lot of people, and not many of them would've fought off an infection like yours. And I'm not sure which lives you're talking about—"

"You saved mine, when I got hurt. And if we didn't have you around the last two years..."

Jame relented. If a serious infection couldn't knock her off, what chance did he have of winning this argument?

"But I'm not really worried about any of that anymore. It's just... how different things feel now. So many soldiers. This new crew brought what, one sci? And he's even more a soldier than Ternal."

Jame understood exactly what she meant, but decided to play devil's advocate, if only just to have something to talk about. "They pivoted. Maybe the funding prerogatives changed."

"That's what I'm worried about. When I signed up... when we all signed up, it was to be a part of something. Discovery, exploration, all of that. Now, it just feels like we're conquering."

Jame shrugged. "Exploring didn't work out too well for most of us, and the only example of life we identified was one that is unable to live in accordance with humans. What are we supposed to do?"

"We could've gone somewhere else."

"Ahh, but the terraforming..."

"Sol-a-shit. They haven't even properly salvaged Casarabe yet, and that's where all the gear was."

"I'm sure it's on their list," Jame said reasonably. "It makes sense to secure the home front first. We're lucky they didn't go *there* first, that would have made more sense for their big mission."

They made it back inside, and Mury popped her helm and gave him a tired smile, her grey-black hair sticking to her neck. "You've grown so soft, old man. Used to be you were the first to point out the contradiction of the powers that be."

Jame stripped out of his suit and placed it in a charging alcove. "For now, I'm just relieved to be moving forward again. I'm too old to be sitting on my arse for months at a time."

"Speaking of, what's your detail for the rest of today?"

They made their way to the mess area – an entirely new hab that hadn't existed before the soldiers arrived – and fingered through the dietary selections for the day. Mon had managed to keep the vegetable gardens alive, but breakfast foods were strictly of the artificial, paste-variety. Jame chose an oaty-whey.

"I'm meant to be overseeing the east wall. Like we're a Sol-damned military compound. You?" he said through a dusty mouthful.

Mury produced a cocoa-whey; a little perk of her injuries meant she received slightly more flavourful dietaries.

"Meant to be helping out with the new medbay. It's basically finished though. I'm sure they wouldn't notice if I was an hour or so late."

Jame knew what she was asking. They had been friends for a long time, having worked together prior to the Cahros deployment, but the sex had only started during the last few months. While their relationship fell short of anything romantic, the proximity and shared experiences had manifested in an arrangement that lay somewhere between comfort and companionship.

Jame shrugged. "Good a reason as any to be late for work. Just gotta be a bit quieter this time, not used to having so many people in the place."

Mury punched him on the shoulder. "Speak for yourself. The way that poor girl reacted, you'd think sex was illegal if you're over forty."

Jame rubbed his shoulder and winked. "Thank all the stars in the sky that it's not."

13

FAKE CAPTAINS AND REAL SALAD

Tuwia, Alantia   CD: 09/04/2222
Mai

AFTER LAYING RIGID and wide-eyed for a full minute, Bjora's breath returned. A spasmodic jerk came with it, and she shot upright, staring sightlessly at the wall behind Mai. Her face crinkled in terror, and she kicked her knees up against her chin, curling up at the head of the spartan medical bed. Mai stood, feeling useless, while the doctors rushed to Bjora's side. She became aware of a presence beside her – and turned with a start to see Elís had materialised, seemingly from thin air.

"Stat-rep! How long has she been like this?" Elís commanded.

With Ashelyn and Alesio still working to calm Bjora down, Mai realised the onus was on her to respond. "Just a minute or two. She came back to us, screaming Norwegian mayhem, then, well, you can see—"

"What did she say?"

"It was nonsense really, something about a *Jorgenmander*, or *cracking*..."

"*Jörmungandr*, and Kraken," Ashelyn said, somehow aware of their conversation despite Bjora's continued panic.

"She was referring to the old Scandinavian mythos. Put simply, they were sea monsters."

Mai's skin tingled.

"You're sure that's what she said?" Elís snapped. She stood taut as ever, but her fingers tapped anxiously at the holster on her hip.

"Yes."

"It would explain the rapid resurfacing. See something you weren't prepared for, panic, try to get out of there as fast as you can," Ashelyn surmised, stepping back from Bjora.

"But if that's what happened, then the others are headed straight back to the same place!" Mai exclaimed, turning to Elís. "We've got to get them out of there!"

"Enough." Elís raised a hand. "We follow protocol."

"Which is?"

"They are due to report in an hour. If we hear nothing, we go to the same place everyone always washes up – Bermuda. But, say they ran into trouble, they could surface anywhere. Sitting outside of Bermuda would cost as just as much time, especially with the dilation."

"But if they surface *at* Bermuda, they could be waiting for *us* for hours, thanks to that same phenomenon," Ashelyn argued. "If they're wounded, or in a similar state to these three, delayed intervention could be fatal." She kept her voice calm and controlled, but Mai noticed the strain in her brow.

"Either way, a wrong prediction will be costly," Elís said, looking conflicted.

"Maybe we could split the middle, hover just outside of dilation range of Bermuda. If we don't hear anything by the scheduled time, we take the gamble and fly in. As you said, all currents seem to lead to the same place," Ashelyn said. "And, I've had some experience navigating the rocks... I could come with you."

Alesio came forward. "I can attest that our new doctor knows how to place a priority on human life. And, given there are now two of us physicians here, one could easily be spared to go to with you to act as needed."

"I agree!" Mai said. Alesio shot her another smile.

Elís relented. "Alright then. Ashelyn, you and I will take the shuttle out as a precaution. The rest of you, keep monitoring things here. Mai, support the command centre and med teams as required." Everyone turned to their tasks, but Mai noticed a small smile on Ashelyn's face as she followed the imposing trooper out of the room, already shrugging the shoulders of her hazmat off.

With little else to do, Mai found herself hovering at the door.

"That does it. It's time to bring him back out. A surprisingly fast procedure, considering." Alesio was readying another of his endless supply of magic needles when Mai realised he was talking to her.

"Terrus, you mean? How long will that take? Won't it do some kind of damage, going in and out so fast?"

"The sooner the better, actually. Should take about an hour – it's a less physiologically complex process than going in, but he'll be just as groggy and achy on the other side. The cryocoma will have accelerated his recovery from the amputation – reduced blood flow, a quicker patch-up. That said, coming to terms with his new limitations will be a hell of a thing. It will be good for him to have a familiar face here."

"Okay, I'll stay." Mai had never had much to do with Terrus, in fact, had once found him a little too braggadocious for her tastes, but it at least was a purpose she could fulfil.

"You know, you're quite pretty," Alesio said as he worked. He kept his head down, attempting a casual mode of delivery.

Mai was taken aback. Sure, he was handsome by all conventional measures, but was now really the time?

"Ah, okay," was all she mustered. Her fringe was a mess, skin the worst it had looked in weeks, and she was sure she smelled terrible.

Alesio looked up, and again, Mai was surprised to see he looked suddenly rather anxious. "Sorry... it's just... there aren't many of us here to, you know. It's been a while."

Mai laughed. "Please don't take offence, it's just, not really my thing."

"If I'm not your type, I can... hold on, not your thing?"

This was the part of these conversations that, as a young person, Mai had dreaded. Now, she found them useful for protecting the often fragile egos of suitors.

"Sex. I have no interest. Never have. Don't blame yourself."

A look of realisation dawned on Alesio. "Oh, I'm sorry! But wow, that must be useful considering the life out here... you really are the perfect colonist!"

Mai was working out whether she should take offence when a muffled groan rumbled out from behind one of the curtains.

"That's Corbin. Check in on him, if you can, I've just got to finish with Terrus here," Alesio said casually, and a still-bemused Mai wandered over.

Corbin seemed about her age, but with sickly pale skin and just a few wisps of hair around his crown. Despite just awakening, his dark eyes conveyed alertness. When he spoke, it was with a surprisingly baritone voice.

"Have I been out so long we've had another batch come in?"

Mai laughed, impressed at his instant lucidity. "I am new here, so you're half right. But no, you haven't really been out all that long. How... how are you?" What was she supposed to ask?

"Feels like my brain is trying to pull itself out my ears. But the extended nap helped." Corbin pulled himself into a seated position and kneaded his temples.

"Some water might be a treat. You're not a doctor, are you?" Mai fumbled at the nearest hydro-dispenser and handed him some caps.

"Good evening, Captain! You're sounding well," Alesio called jovially from across the room. "So well, Elís might have to debrief you."

"Ahh Sol to that. Got any more seds?" The two seemed very familiar with one another, and their banter was a welcome tonic to the tension Mai was feeling.

"Yeah, but not for you." Alesio finished up with Terrus and came to stand beside Corbin's bed. "Good news is, it's going to be a while before Elís is back. But seriously, how are you feeling?"

"Tired, funnily enough. Like I just woke up after sleeping for far too long. What am I doing in the medbay?"

Alesio's smile wavered. "You were on an expedition…"

Corbin smacked his head. "Of course! Oh… I'm not sure I want to remember. Bjora? Arkans? Are they…?"

"Bjora is sleeping again now, but we have heard from her," Alesio said, wincing. "Arkans still has not come to."

"Shit." Corbin's eyes glazed over for a moment, before he shook his head and forced a smile. He took the caps that had been sitting loosely in Mai's hands. "Captain Lees hasn't tried to sleep with you yet, has he?"

Alesio blushed and turned away. "You mean him?" Mai said, giving her best impression of a dismissive shrug. Corbin laughed, and Mai allowed herself a small smirk.

"Don't act like you're any better," Alesio mustered in response.

Corbin laughed merrily. "I'll take that hit. You, wherever you're from, did you bring any gentlemen with you?"

"She did, matter of fact. Though they're both far too young for you, and one is a little worse for wear."

Corbin made a *tsk* sound, but upon noticing Terrus across the room, his demeanour changed again, to one of genuine concern. "What happened?"

Alesio gestured to Mai.

"He was wounded after coming into contact with Black-rock. The stuff you might have run into at the sandbar where you were rescued," Mai said.

Corbin's brow furrowed. "Those rocks damn near got us killed. Threw out all our systems."

Alesio placed a small recording device by the bedside. "As mentioned, it's your lucky day, Corbs, as Elís is actually out of office. But we do still need to get your statement of what happened down there."

"Alright. Is our companion here allowed to be privy to such a report?"

"My name is Mai. And I don't know, actually."

Alesio shrugged. "Everyone knows a bit of everything at this point, I don't see the harm."

"Okay. Well, get me something to chew on, and let's get this over with." Alesio left them for a minute, returning with a small pack of what looked like salad. Mai salivated at the sight. It had been nearly seven months since she'd eaten fresh food.

"That's the stuff," Corbin said between mouthfuls.

He ate slowly, as if trying to delay the inevitable. Once finished, he brushed himself off and took a deep breath. "Now, as you know, we were out patrolling the pelagic zone of most likely match for the location of... you know... Had catalogued a couple of species, perhaps less than usual, but nothing out the ordinary. Then, out of nowhere, we lose navs, visibility, everything. Ark wanted to keep looking, but Bjora knew immediately something was up. If it wasn't for her, we'd all be dead as dinosaurs. Our sensors went completely stupid, started telling us the sea floor was rising, that there were gigantic cliffs all around us, and then, we were smashed by some kind of current, propelled us all the way to the surface. Pretty sure Bjora was the only one conscious at the time, enough to activate the beacon. Speaking of, if you already spoke to her, I'm sure she would've said all this already."

"Negative. She was highly distressed. The only legible words were those of mythological sea creatures, like the Kraken?"

Corbin looked troubled but shook his head. "The readings we were getting… No creature can be that big. My guess is some kind of geothermal event, or even tectonic."

"Anything else worth adding?"

"No. Except I don't think we should go down there anymore. Not until we're reinforced, at least. Unless…?"

"Mai is one of but four colonists to join us," Alesio said, switching off the recording device. "And her journey is one I'm still trying to make sense of."

"You and me both, Doc," Mai said. She was tempted to share a little about what she'd been through, but this didn't seem the time or the place. "But let's wait for everyone to get back first. Hopefully the captain here is right, and their biggest threat are just rogue current patterns."

The two men gave her a look, before bursting out laughing.

"What?"

"I'm no captain, chew," Corbin said with a wink. "It's just a cute thing we like to call each other when Elís isn't around."

Between his funny-shaped head, deep voice, and self-effacing manner, something about Corbin was effortlessly likeable. Mai shot him a smile and raised a weary arm in mock salute. "Noted, sir. Seeing as we're doing away with rank, how about you fix me some of that salad?"

14

OMNIA MORSAE

The Seas, Alantia   CD: 10/04/2222
Tarlo

THE CLOSER TO the surface they got, the more freely Tarlo and Johann spoke. Tarlo shared details of his first experiences out in the Gobi, cataloguing new breeds of locusts and centipedes, while Johann divulged about his time on Europa, as part of the "First Failing" – what expedition members had retroactively dubbed an ambitious early-century search for an ocean theorised to exist on the key Jupiterian satellite. This failing had led to the abandonment of hope of finding life in Sol, and later, the development of the Martellus Index.

Also key to their discussion was Johann's use of the phrase *"Blissah cah taneh"*. Johann explained that it was a farewell prayer, part of the sub-language developed by the *Meteora,* a population of people who'd occupied a flotilla-base in the asteroid belt for multiple generations. While Johann was not born of their society, he had spent several years working among them. Tarlo brought himself to ask if Johann knew of Vel – the brave, spiritual soldier who lost her life on Cahros – but Johann denied any association.

Despite their conversation, Tarlo never really relaxed. Whenever he breathed in too deeply, the scent of death assaulted his lungs, reminding him of Mawie's fate. How could they talk of their careers while a body lay behind them? *Won't make a damned difference what we talk about, she's still dead,* Johann probably would have said.

While it would be a lie to describe Johann as warm, he had just enough in common with a figure of Tarlo's past to bring forth more painful reminders. Tarlo knew there was little chance Jame could have survived that last trip into the desert, and the weight of yet another person dying in his stead was one he didn't want to bear.

Such morbid thoughts still assailed him when they finally crested above the surface of the Alantian ocean, barely fifty metres from the great black pillars. They were greeted by the bright light of the planet's two moons, and a star-speckled sky that resembled Earth's a lot more than the one on Cahros had. As for the pillars, they had been imposing enough already, but now Tarlo knew they extended *kilometres* below the ocean's surface, they seemed to exude a deep, timeless power. He wondered just how far those rocks burrowed into the bowels of this planet.

The surface of the ocean was a uniform grey-blue but for the dapple of moon and starlight. From a distance, the small, unbroken waves could have been desert dunes. There was something lonely about the visage; after all that they'd seen in the central oceanic zone – and beneath – it was almost... sad to think that none of these animals would ever glimpse the sky.

"Thank Sol," Johann said with a cough. "Would you look at that."

He gestured vaguely back towards the Blackrock formation, where Tarlo was surprised to see the lights of the Tuwian rescue shuttle, perched on the edge of a small sandbar. Comms were still faulty, so they pulled the R16 alongside the shuttle to greet their unexpected escorts.

"What are you doing here?" Johann was first to shout across the divide. He cracked the R16 open, treating Tarlo to a blast of wind and sea spray. The gust shook their little bubble vigorously, sending a stark reminder that directly beneath them lay several kilometres of water, darkness, and forces unknowable. Tarlo stood, but his legs felt very shaky.

"We got a tip from Bjora, gave us reason to believe you might be in trouble," Elís said, businesslike as ever. "I can see only two of you, was Mawie injured?"

They were close enough for Johann's expression to tell the tale.

"Oh. What happened? Were you breached in any way?"

"Don't be a fool, boss. If something compromised the shuttle, we'd have all folded into nothing. It was... blunt force trauma. We've a lot to report."

"Okay. Is she with you now?"

Johann nodded, but the darkness denied Elís the sight.

"Johann, is she with you?" she said again, strained.

"She's fucking dead at our feet."

"What about the Rock? Everything still working?"

"Yes."

"Oh... Listen, I know you won't want to hear this, but given your vehicle is still operational, our best course of action is to escort you back to Tuwia. We can't leave the R16 or Mawie behind."

Tarlo's stomach sank, and his body tensed in expectation of an explosive reaction from the man beside him.

But none came.

Wordlessly, Johann slumped back to his seat, a defeated look on his face.

Elís took this acknowledgement. "Follow us back to base. Our navs are out, but I know the way well enough by moonlight."

Tarlo didn't doubt her, after all, she'd already picked him up from here once before. He peered past her, catching a glimpse of Ashelyn perched on the roof of the shuttle behind Elís. She was suited but for her helm, and the breeze tussled long strands of black across her face. She nodded to him, but the shadows denied him a glimpse of her face.

The R16 wasn't well suited to hovering through the air, so they followed the shuttle from just below sea level. Since they'd allowed fresh air into the sub, the smell of blood and bodily fluids had somehow gotten worse – exacerbating the maddening feeling of entrapment – and Tarlo grew desperate for the journey to end.

At last, they came to Tuwia. Given its height, it was difficult to see at first, but as they rose higher, a great shadow spread across the sky. The skybase loomed with a sullen grace, silver-white lights illuminating its underside and promising a safety that Tarlo still could not feel.

Johann demonstrated calm skill once again when it came to the precision task of docking, but once the R16 was safely stowed, he leapt out with deceptive haste. Alesio, Zhang, and a devastated-looking Viola were waiting for them. A long, dark bag hung limply from their hands. Tarlo turned away from the R16, vowing never to set foot in it again, and gasped in the sweet, tangy Alantian air. He couldn't watch while the others wrapped Mawie's body, nor could he walk away, so he ghosted towards the far side of the docking platform, losing his gaze in the larger moon. It was huge, perhaps ten times larger than Earth's, and its closer proximity clearly explained the at-times vigorous currents and tides of a planet with no land masses. He wondered if its surface bore the same grey dust, minerals, and gravitational composition to enable the construction of Moonsalt. As he gazed, it seemed to grow even larger, and his pulse raced as he imagined the celestial body hurtling into Alantia, creating planetwide tsunamis ten kilometres high – or worse, crushing the planet into pieces.

He wasn't sure how long Ashelyn had been standing beside him before he noticed her.

"Elís tells me it's called *Hvitgarde*. The White Guard," she murmured.

Tarlo made a small noise. He tried to speak, but the words caught in his throat, and a world of weariness crushed his shoulders.

"Maybe give me some warning before the next time you galivant off somewhere." she said, her own voice barely above a whisper.

Tarlo flinched. The last thing he wanted was her ire. "Ash..."

She snuck a cold hand into his, and barely audibly, whispered, "I'm glad you're back."

A tear of relief formed at the corner of Tarlo's right eye. "I wanted to mean... I mean, I meant to say, thank you, for last night. And everything else."

Ashelyn flashed him a small smile and gave his hand a little squeeze. "Come on. We'd best join them."

She held his hand all the way to the command centre, where he left her at the door. Unlike in Cahros, where meetings tended to be held with all colonists present, there appeared to be a clear chain of command here, so only Mauve and Elís attended the debriefing – denying even Mai and Ashelyn entry.

Tarlo and Johann took turns recounting the events of their journey. Mauve appeared concerned, even frightened, hearing their descriptions of the gigantic, leviathan-like creatures, but Elís chose to focus on the fallen facility, and the Blackrock. "So it really is a grand kind of magnet. All the tides lead to the same place."

"I can't believe it. A planet sized ocean, and we've actually found where they ended up," Mauve added.

"Yes," Elís said. "Though it was nowhere near where we presumed, and only through luck – or the properties of these rocks – that we ended up doing so. And what's more, at the cost of another life. Whatever these creatures are, through their intention or otherwise, they are deeply threatening. I'm initiating a stand-down order. No further missions into the deep will be taking place."

Tarlo was a little surprised. Despite his inner promise to refrain from another such journey, he had been left with a burning feeling that this colossal migration they'd been caught in was not something they could just turn a blind eye to.

He wasn't the only one surprised. "But now that we've found them, with another trip we could learn what happened to them, and indeed, if we are in any—" Mauve said, but Elís made a sharp gesture to cut her off.

"Curiosity is no justification for sacrifice. No more expeditions. We will review the footage we have, and that will have to suffice."

Mauve's brow furrowed, but she accepted the command with silence.

"Now," Elís continued. "We see you've made some discoveries on this trip, and Mauve will ensure they are going into the catalogue. Do you have anything else to report?"

Tarlo was driven to speak. "Something about all this, it just doesn't feel like we can ignore it. I feel horrible about what happened to Mawie, but... we need to learn more about these creatures. You've been here for two years, but their depth was so consistent that you thought they were the seabed. If they are moving now... Something has changed."

"He's right, you know," Johann said. "No animal leaves its home without good reason."

"Be that as it may, we cannot risk personnel, or our vehicles," Elís insisted. "I'm amazed the R16 wasn't damaged, considering the force you were hit with from the things... flippers? Legs?"

"We have plenty of drones we can still deploy," Johann said. "We should drop them at the point we found those creatures and get some images of their true size. And, if possible, trajectory. From what we gather, they haven't moved far since we saw them."

"Moving those limbs would require *massive* amounts of energy. They probably aren't going anywhere fast," Tarlo agreed.

Elís relented. "You are right, we would be failing ourselves if we didn't monitor them at all. Things that size could pose a threat to Tuwia, even from deep below. Especially if they have some form of... electrical, elemental power, as you say."

Johann gave her a terse nod.

"If that is all... we're going to have a service. For Mawie. Tarlo, you and your friends are welcome – encouraged – to join us. Thank you both, and well done." Elís and Mauve left the room, and after a few mumbled words, so did Johann. Tarlo stood in the quiet, at a loss where to go. So many things were happening, his head and stomach hurt, and he just wanted to sit down in the quiet somewhere and try to make sense of it all. There was something about those gigantic entities that seemed... familiar, maybe not in their size and shape, but their *energy*.

After a few deep breaths, he wobbled through the corridors until he found everyone in the mess area, where the dining tables had been cleared and the lights were dimmed. Perhaps a dozen people were spread through the room, and at its centre stood Alesio and Viola. Absently, Tarlo wondered why so few were present – he'd only met a few residents so far but had assumed everyone else was busy or resting. Was this really the entire population of Tuwia? And by extension, Alantia?

Mawie's body had been wrapped, concealing her shattered face, but her hands were free and placed on her chest. Alesio stepped forward, presenting the most remarkable of souvenirs, a genuine wax candle, by her head. He placed one hand on his heart and took her top hand in the other.

"In tribute to Mawie Bolo, one of our own from the start. Join the ranks of those whose lives were lost that we might learn more about this world and continue our purpose. Thank you, and rest well." He stepped back and joined the morose crowd.

Viola stepped forward, tears strewn across her face, and uttered a poem between cracked sobs. "Words mean little, what's done is done. The passing of time can only numb. *Omnia morsae*, but why today? I'll remember you, my little one." Gently, she took Mawie's hand and kissed it, taking a knee beside her body. It was the first time Tarlo had heard her speak more than a few words, but their heartbreaking beauty almost brought him to tears as well.

All stood silent and still. After exactly ten minutes, Viola rose again, the lights flickered back on, and Alesio and Zhang removed Mawie's body from the room.

Most of the colonists, barring Viola and Elís, stayed in the room for a time afterwards. Mai joined Tarlo and Ashelyn by the window.

"That was kind of nice," Mai said. "Not that she... obviously... but, to come together, to say something."

"It was a hell of a lot more than what we were ever able to do," Ashelyn said.

"Well, we could do something," Tarlo said. "What do you both say, we get Alesio to find us one of those candles, and go up to the roof and... have our own moment. For everyone."

Mai tilted her head approvingly. "I would like that."

"Me too. But, not yet," Ashelyn said. "Not without Terrus."

Tarlo felt a flush of self-loathing. How could he forget? "You're right. After what he's been through, and what he's done for me... Of course. How is he? I shouldn't have even—"

"It's okay, Tarlo. And, well, we managed to convince them it was safest to remove the arm entirely. The spread seems to have been contained. Alesio has taken him out of cryocoma too. He might even wake up soon."

Tarlo smiled. Terrus had such a powerful, positive personality, and Tarlo still hadn't gotten the chance to properly thank him for saving his life.

"What say you, we go see him?" Mai said, and the three of them left the mess area. It was dark in the corridors between rooms, but the walls between the mess hall and the medbay were decorated with something Tarlo had not seen for months – photographs.

Rendered on the thin, digital screens were smiling faces, recognisable as the colonists of Tuwia. In some, they stood proudly, showing off their work on the windmills, the R16s, and the atmosphere generators, while others displayed "daily life" shots – Alesio and Corbin playing chess, Mawie and Viola holding hands, Johann arm wrestling with a man Tarlo didn't recognise.

As they ambled through the corridor, Tarlo took the chance to fill Ashelyn and Mai in on everything that had transpired beneath the waves. Once, he might have spent hours talking about the brilliant and bizarre lifeforms he'd seen, speculating on their many traits and adaptations, but now, his descriptions of the gigantic *Kraken-esque* creatures were just another desensitised detail, as was the discomfort of what happened to Mawie. There was, however, one thing he kept coming back to: the ghostlike entity that hid in the deepest of deeps. It's haunting image, shrieking scream...

Now that he was out and dry, most of what he'd seen beneath the waves was beginning to blur together in a cocktail of reds, silver, green, and blue. There had been a flow to the ecosystem, with its predators and prey in their death-defying dances. But not with that thing. Its presence still scraped through his mind in a way that felt wrong, that felt... *otherworldly.*

Ashelyn's eyes displayed a flicker of understanding while he spoke of it, but Mai was most interested in the Blackrock.

"It seems to function almost identically to what we found on Cahros – that strange *pull* feeling, the proximal distortion of all our systems. But somehow, once again, it's been your saviour," she observed.

They arrived at the medbay. It was bright and clammy, and smelled of a headache-inducing mix of disinfectant and various body odours. Ashelyn and Tarlo took a seat beside the prone Terrus, while Mai perched by the exit door, eying the other patients warily.

"I have been thinking about everything," Ashelyn said. "These two sets of formations existing, almost identical, despite thousands of light-years between them."

"It's like convergent evolution," Mai said. "But with rocks, not creatures. And with entirely opposite planetary conditions."

"Which means... they were most likely *placed*. Right?" Ashelyn said.

Mai shrugged. "The scientist in me insists that we know so little, and without means of testing, even hypothesising is pointless."

"From what I could tell from the... visions, those entities that Tarlo and I kept seeing on Cahros... it was like they created or at least harnessed the Blackrock as part of their civilisation," Ashelyn said. "So, if the Blackrock is here... does that mean *they* were here too?"

"If they were once, they certainly aren't now," Mai said grimly.

"What does that mean for us? Are we... following in their footsteps?" Tarlo said. "I think we can all agree that on Cahros, they were trying to warn us about something, likely the tardigrades. But if after that, they consciously sent us here, that must have been for a reason?"

"It all seems too outrageous to have been random," Mai agreed. "How and why would such strange technology exist if not for some purpose?"

"Maybe. Or maybe, they just had these rocks set up to enable their own advanced form of transport. Maybe this is just the next stop on the line, so to speak. Maybe they colonised hundreds of planets, and it's just a coincidence that the path led here next," Ashelyn said.

"We're in a strange place where both chaos and purpose-driven theory seem equally unlikely and nothing really seems all that plausible," Tarlo surmised. "We could ponder this for hours and still get nowhere."

"Whatever grand plan this is or isn't, do you think there's room for a day off?" Mai sighed.

Tarlo shook his head. He was tired, drained, and surprisingly hungry, but he knew there were deeper revelations to be had – and maybe not so much time left to have them. "We've been through so much already, but it would feel wrong to turn our backs. I can't tell you why, but I just *know* we've stumbled on something important here." His mind drifted to the five planets he'd seen in his own vision. "And maybe not just for these colonies."

"So you're saying...?" Ashelyn said, unsure.

Mai anticipated his next remark, though she clearly wasn't enamoured with the idea. She pursed her lips. "We have to go back to the Blackrock."

"There is some bad news on that front. Elís has locked down further expeditions, citing safety concerns," Tarlo said.

"Well, she's not wrong in those concerns. Do you think we can convince her?" Mai asked.

Ashelyn scoffed. "No chance. Having spent a little more time with her on the trip to collect Tarlo, I can tell you, she was already pissed. Cold as she may seem, she does not take the idea of risking her people lightly."

Mai smiled. "Reminds me of someone else I know."

The smallest blush crept across Ashelyn's cheeks.

"After what they've done to take us in... we shouldn't break the rules so willingly. Perhaps the chance will arise sooner than we think. For now, we should rest up, and give Terrus some time to—"

A groan erupted from their until-then sleeping companion, causing Tarlo to jump in fright.

Terrus, not yet fully conscious, was trying to lift himself up. Unfortunately, the arm he attempted to spring himself up with was no longer attached to his body, and he nearly rolled clean from the bed. Ashelyn was ready for this, and steadied him quickly, receiving several mouthfuls of phlegmy coughs in exchange for her aid. Unflinching, she rested him back into bed, and his eyelids fluttered open.

"Heard your name, did you?" Mai said, but her words fell on deaf ears.

Terrus's eyes widened in terror. He tried to speak but only coughed again. Once more, he tried to lift his left arm to cover his mouth and panicked even further upon realising he couldn't.

Ashelyn took charge, placing her hands firmly on his cheeks and looking into his eyes. Tarlo was impressed by her strength, which nullified the trooper's thrashing. She spoke with the same gentle voice Tarlo had heard her use before, when comforting the injured.

"You're okay. You're alive. You're safe." She repeated the phrases several times, and eventually, Terrus began to calm.

"You were wounded, and we've got you in the medbay. Take it easy, we're going to get you some caps. Don't try to move your left arm, okay?"

Over the next ten minutes, Ashelyn gradually nursed Terrus back to full consciousness, feeding him some hydro caps and repeating several slow, calm phrases. Eventually, she broke the news to him about his arm, but it seemed his comprehension of the fact was still not entirely clear.

"Is Carlyle here? Or Jontie?"

"Not right now. You should get some more rest, Terrus. We'll be here when you wake up." Terrus eventually obliged, and though he said no more, his distress must have followed him into unconsciousness, as he continued to spasm and groan in his sleep.

After a week from hell, watching his saviour reduced to anguished twitching was torment. Abruptly, Tarlo stood. He had to get out.

He fled to his dorm and closed himself off from the world. If anyone knocked, he would not answer. The idea of facing up to anybody was too much, and he had nothing more to give.

He lay on his bed, hammered by wave after wave of guilt.

If you knew how to defend yourself, Terrus would be fine.

If you acted sooner, you could have saved Mawie, Vel, and Sol knows who else.

If you were smarter, you would know what to do.

If you were stronger.

If you were better.

15
PHANTOM COMFORTS

TUWIA, ALANTIA   CD: 13/04/2222
TERRUS

DESPITE THE UNIVERSAL climate control, Tuwia base always seemed colder in the early hours of morning. Since returning to the land of the conscious, Terrus had fallen into a routine of exercising at this time. There were fewer pitying eyes to worry about.

It wasn't like he was getting much sleep anyway.

Never in his life had he experienced insomnia like this. For starters, he'd always hated sleeping on his right side. Throw in the paranoia of reopening his new wound, lingering fears that the infection would spread beyond his ghost limb, and the deathly hangover of his rapid in-and-out cryocoma, and he was lucky to be getting a few hours a night.

The hours of wakefulness weren't much better. Every time he took a deep breath, he felt like there were hooks in his lungs and he was inhaling a giant mouthful of dust. A delayed side effect of the coma, so he'd been told. But Doctor Alesio didn't know what Terrus had been breathing in before he got here.

Surprisingly, running seemed to help. And with nobody else using these facilities at 0325 in the morning, he was free to enjoy them in his own way.

As if all the cardio in the world could somehow grow his arm back.

Terrus still hadn't really had any time to think about what he'd been through. It felt like every time he blinked, he found himself in a drastically new environment. From leaving his friends at the rock formation on Cahros, being exposed directly to the planet's deadly air during his lonely sojourn to Casarabe, acquiring his Blackrock wound from that little coward bastard Yerald, falling through that weird portal and now, waking up feeling several decades older, it had been a hell of a week.

Poor Tarlo, he still looked about ready to cry whenever they ran into each other. That didn't help, though Terrus didn't hold it against him. Terrus had just been doing his job, and if he was going to lose an arm for anyone on the former colony, Tarlo probably would have been... in the top ten candidates worth doing it for.

The weights bench caught his eye, and he gave it a look of longing. He could still use the individual bells of course, but he had always loved the press. *Just one of the little things that you miss.*

A sharp pain surged through Terrus's missing left wrist. *Damned phantom limb.* Prior to his amputation, Terrus had thought that "phantom limb" was far too cool a name to waste on such a pathetic-sounding ailment. He'd been right.

An hour of sweating and grunting later, and he had just about exhausted himself enough to consider trying to get some more sleep. He wiped down the cardio station and started to tiptoe back out of the mess hall when a tall, bouncing shadow stopped him in his tracks. He considered taking his chances and making a break for it, but an arc of pain clamped at both of his calves at once. *Cramps.* He resigned himself to his fate – another awkward conversation.

The shadow shrunk to the size of a regular human, and Terrus tensed as a medium-built man slid through to the mess hall. Noticing Terrus, he stopped dead, and silence hung in the air.

"Johann, right?" Terrus croaked.

His new companion cleared his throat. "The same. Terrus?"

Terrus nodded. Johann looked him up and down, before shrugging and sitting at one of the benches. Instead of tucking his legs under the table, he sat backwards, sticking his elbows back to prop himself up. In his right hand, Terrus noticed a bottle of clear liquid.

"Bit early in the morning for that, isn't it?"

Johann gestured to him to take a seat beside him.

"Or maybe it's too late in the evening."

He didn't seem at all drunk. Terrus couldn't even smell it on his breath.

Johann passed him the bottle. A sniff revealed it to be odourless, but a taste suggested it was rather potent.

"What brings you to this fine establishment at such an hour?" Terrus asked. "The wait staff are a little busy, but I can take your order."

Johann gave a single snort. "Silence and peace, if you still serve that."

"I'm afraid we're all out of silence today." The liquor burned his chest pleasantly, almost like it was searing away the dust and muck that perpetually lingered. They passed the bottle back and forth as the conversation continued.

"Just my luck. How are you finding the place?"

"Quiet, which I can't complain about. You?"

"Shit."

"Really? You all seem really close."

"We are."

"So, what's shit about it?"

"Pfft. Live in a fishbowl for two years, forgotten about, while looking at the same twelve faces every day, and tell me how you like it."

"Point taken. Is there really so few of you?"

"Yeah. Lost a few people at the start, others left with the second expedition. The place was terraformed, life had been found, and the novelty had well and truly worn off."

"In that case, why did you stay?"

"Those of us left here... we're the types who finish what we start. Beneath that, I guess we hoped they'd reinvest, send another, proper batch out."

"But still no word?"

Johann smacked his lips. "Not a whisper. Just the sound of wind on Moonsalt, every day."

Terrus had never thought about this. The plan had been the same on Cahros – get the base built, then send most of the workers home. He had never really considered what that would actually mean for those who stayed behind.

"I heard a bit about your last dive. Sounded pretty... I don't know. How you been holding up?"

"Same answer. I liked it better when they let us out of the place. But now, can't say I want to go back down either."

"Do you think we're safe up here?"

Johann shrugged. "All I know is, if what I saw down there feels like fucking with us... consider us severely fucked."

"Not really anywhere we can go, is there?"

"Nope. Sitting ducks. Or swifts, maybe."

"Swifts?"

"The bird that never lands. Like us. Well, close enough to never... it doesn't matter."

"Is there someone you can talk to? Elís, Alesio...?"

"To say what? There's nothing any of them can do." Johann finished off the bottle and leaned forward, elbows on knees, shadows playing across his lined features. Looking at him, Terrus felt a deep sadness. The death rates on these expeditions were awful, but was this the toll of survival?

"Thanks for the drink. I hope today is a better day." Terrus patted Johann on the shoulder on his way past, but the man did not react, lost in his thoughts and misery.

Terrus shuffled back to his room via a quick shower. He still hadn't been given a schedule yet, as he was meant to be "focusing on his recovery", and even that was starting to get to him. He was a soldier, defined by his routine, his physicality, and by always having someone to protect, and right now he had none of those.

Things with the other survivors from Cahros still felt strange, too. Terrus's closest companions from his time in the UCI, as far as he knew, were all dead. He'd never really gotten on with either Mai or Ashelyn – both were too reserved and seemed to look down on him. He liked Tarlo fine, but theirs wasn't the same as the connection he'd shared with Jontie, Carlyle, or Velentini... But they were the only ones in the universe who had been through what he had, minus the physical trauma. *In war, you don't get to choose who makes it out. Savour everyone you get the chance to walk beside.*

Terrus smiled; the words of his old trainer would never leave him. "Thanks, Remi."

Their idea to hold a vigil was something, at least. Not only was it a way to acknowledge their lost friends, but maybe it would provide a chance to connect again.

His phantom elbow was itching again, and it took all his discipline not to rip the bandages free. His scheduled daily dressing change with Alesio was still too far away.

Terrus took a deep breath. That was enough woe. The sun would be rising soon, today would be his first day eating real, solid food, and with the vigil planned for that evening, there was something other than horizontal discomfort to look forward to. Maybe it was because he'd consumed *just* the right amount of alcohol, but Terrus realised he didn't relate to Johann, despite all the horrors he'd endured.

Right now, he was just glad to be alive.

16
VIGIL

Tuwia, Alantia   CD: 13/04/2222
Tarlo

SHORTLY AFTER DAWN on their fourth day at Tuwia, Arkans – the final member of the first, fated dive – was pronounced dead. There were few tears when Corbin led the gathering later that morning, but it was clear that the loss was a bitter blow. Little by little, life by life, Tuwia was losing its soul.

Looking down on Arkans's covered head, Tarlo saw a series of different faces. Spectres of those he lost on Cahros were joined in the rotation now by Mawie, whose kind visage he was already forgetting. All he saw were the cracks in her skull, the refuse leaking across her face...

It was always during the quiet moments that his scars reared their blood-splattered heads. When he was walking alone through the dim Tuwian corridors, the smiling photos of colonists morphed into contorted, spasmic grins. When a stern wind accosted the facility, he always braced for the screeching of a shattered watchtower. His heart still raced whenever he saw a little, orange light.

The difficult nights continued as Tarlo ruminated over his ongoing, miraculous avoidance of death. Was his continued existence some grand, tortuous play by a vindictive god? Was it simple, dumb luck that deserved no further scrutiny? Or was it something scarier than them both, that he might still be alive due to holding some grand purpose or destiny that he had not yet realised?

He knew one thing, though: he was no hero.

At some stage each evening, Ashelyn had joined him beneath the covers, a cool shadow in the night. Tarlo did not yet know what this covenant they shared was; they'd done nothing as conventionally lustful as make love, or even kiss, but their actions suggested a deepening bond, exemplified through closer-than-close proximities, shared body warmth, and hand holding. Even those little touches were enough to ignite him, sending charges from the tips of his fingers to the space between his shoulder blades. Once, she'd leaned against him, and they pressed their foreheads together – in that moment, the only things in the universe were the two of them and their gentle, shared breaths.

They rarely spoke during moments like that. Tarlo gained an idea that Ashelyn preferred the quiet and calm, and once, she shared with him how distressing the constant lights and noises of everyday life were for her. He learned that her abruptness was never deliberate, but a response to these constant, bombarding stimuli, and the stress that came with expecting too much of herself. She never mentioned it, but he knew she carried the weight of everything that happened on Cahros, a physician who had been unable to tend to her patients. She still blamed herself for it all too, for the one innocuous decision that had awakened the threats below.

But in these moments together, there were no bright lights. No noises. No failures. In these moments, surrounded by the greys of Tuwia and the skies of Alantia, they found safety in one another.

During the daytime, Tarlo worked with Mai in the command centre, where they spent most of their time observing the oceans for any sign of movement or change. As far as they could tell, the upper DSL still rested at the same depth during the day, which suggested the colossal entities of the depths were yet to breach it. Still, Tarlo worried. After a suggestion from Mai, probes were also deployed to the atmosphere to measure temperature and weather patterns, to assess if there was some natural cause for this migration, while the deep-sea scouts were being prepared by Johann and some of the engineers. Tarlo didn't see much of him, but a subtle nod in passing was enough to suggest they maintained some level of rapport.

Ashelyn worked with Alesio in the medbay, and advised that although Bjora was conscious, she remained a shell of a person, never speaking, and reacting with terror whenever approached.

The general atmosphere around the colony was grim, and this was exemplified most clearly through the changes in how Mauve presented. Since Mawie's vigil, Tarlo had barely seen her, and on the occasions where he had run into her, she'd been a shell of her former jovial self.

It was only Elís who showed up at the daily musters now. An hour after the gathering for Arkans dispersed, she put word out for the Cahros four to meet her in the command centre.

"Thank you all for joining me, and for the efforts you've made to fit in so far. The more time we've spent together, the more I've come to understand the unique challenges you've faced so far. And... there's something I wanted to ask you."

"What is it?" Terrus asked.

"We have alluded to this before, but as time has worn on, our relationship with the heads at the UCI has become considerably more strained. We sent word after losing Alvolito, over a month ago now, and yesterday, we heard back for the first time... we've been given a firm directive to salvage as much as we can from the remains of the settlement, regardless of the risk."

Mai gasped. "They said what?"

"Yes."

"And you said?"

"Nothing, yet. Listen... I haven't taken this to any of the others here. With Arkans this morning... besides, I know them so well, and what they'd all say, how they'd react. But I wanted to ask you all, did you ever experience anything like this?"

"We were only on Cahros a week," Ashelyn said. "But once we were down there, they were loath to pick us back up. They maintained strict quarantines even after we told them we were losing people, said the safety of their ships was more important than our lives."

"What about you?" Elís pointed towards Mai. "You worked with them? Understand, I don't say this to attack you, but you mentioned having insight into the longer-term planning that took place. Is such a directive congruent to the organisation you knew?"

Mai lowered her eyes and whispered something under her breath.

"Sci?" Elís prompted.

Mai straightened her shoulders out and took a breath. "Yes, it's congruent. Although I was never UCI. The ECP, where we worked on the Martellus Index, was a branch, formed from old scientific bodies and gobbled up by the umbrella corporation that superseded the UCI. Anyway... no, none of this should be a surprise. The UCI's priorities were always proving to the world that they could colonise others, and the public goodwill they could get from capturing the imagination with something like the discovery of life."

"I have a question," Ashelyn interjected. "Do you plan to follow their directive?"

For the first time ever, Elís relaxed her posture, leaning on the oaken briefing table and massaging her jaw.

"I've always been a hierarchy woman. Follow orders, stick to the script..."

Tarlo winced. Had she brought them in here to tell them they were going to be her guinea pigs? Was she going to send *them* back—

"But not this time."

He let out a relieved sigh.

"You were willing to risk lives to find them in the first place," Mai challenged. "Why not now?"

Elís stood upright, shooting Mai a fiery look. "That is not the same. The search we undertook was to honour those we lost, to learn about what danger *we* might be in. As soon as we discovered those creatures, I grounded everyone."

Mai nodded and gave her a look of approval. "Power to you, Sergeant. In their transmission, did the UCI give you any indication of when, or if they're coming back?"

"No."

"Typical."

"I've noticed the mood around the facility," Ashelyn said. "It has been dark, to say the least. Given what happened at Alvolito, have there been concerns the same thing might happen here?"

"In a word? Our people are terrified. Even more so since the discovery of those creatures. But you don't need me to explain that we are devoid of alternative options. Without support from land, sea, or space, there can be no evacuation plan. Such is life on the frontier."

Tarlo felt cold. The way Elís put it, they may as well have been floating on a sky-mine.

"What are you... we, going to do now?" he asked.

"For now, all we can do is monitor the seas. You advised these... creatures can instigate some kind of underwater electric discharge – lightning – which seems incredibly dangerous. We detected and received no reports of anything like this before we lost contact with Alvolito, but I still wonder if these creatures were somehow responsible for what happened over there. If they were... we must be ready to act quickly. I will consider what preparations can be made."

"If they come for us, I don't know if there are *any* preparations we can make," Tarlo said. "I don't think there's technology in the universe that could stop something like this."

Elís looked at him, her face blank. "Then I will consider how we might safely evacuate."

"I have a question," Mai said, then, without waiting for a response. "Is it true that you had people... leave, when the second expedition arrived? Why did they go?" Mai asked.

Elís's jaw tightened. "Yes. Turns out, the more advanced things become and the fewer threats you are presented with, the fewer people you are assessed to need to keep things running. They stayed long enough to upgrade our facilities – our 'reward' – but when they left, we numbered only fifteen. It was about the same for Alvolito." Elís tugged at her hair, which for once, flowed free from the constraints of her uniform bun. "You know, Alvolito was named after a Latin word for 'fly'."

Tarlo shifted uncomfortably, unsure where this was going.

"What about Tuwia?" e asked.

Elís turned to him, her eyes glazed. "Named for an old settlement on Earth, the second highest human settlement, by altitude."

"We had the same idea. Catal was named for one of the first settlements in human history," Ashelyn said.

"It's funny, the things that we bring with us. If that is all, I have a call to make." A small, defiant smile tickled at the edge of her lips.

Tarlo spent the rest of the day in a reflective state. Since their arrival, some of the Tuwians, namely Alesio and Corbin, had been welcoming, but most of the others kept their distance. He was starting to understand why. The people here were trying to manage their own fear and grief – not just for the friends, but for the dream they'd been promised.

He had grown so used to constant danger and action that he was finding it harder and harder to relax at all – apart from those precious, quiet moments with Ashelyn at the end of each day. As it was, he still woke up through the night, pursued by nightmares where his flesh withered away and dark, bird-like figures danced in the shadows. Since the dive, these spectres had been joined by that freakish, ghostly entity from the depths, whose hideous scream always shattered him into wakefulness.

He worked a later shift that day, tinkering around, mostly alone. When Viola came in to relieve him at 2000hrs, an awkward nod was their only communication. She never said it, but he was sure she blamed him for what happened to Mawie.

And who was he to deny her that?

Dinner was carrots and kale, flavoured by a spiced tartare condiment he'd found in another dispenser beside the paste stations. After mess, he wandered over to the hydroponics garden and put all his attention into replanting spinaches, taking far more care than was necessary to ensure they were perfectly aligned and given millimetre-perfect soil coverage. By burying his hands in the dirt, he was as close to the "ground" as he'd ever get on this planet.

When the wall-screen read 2100, he made his way back to the quiet mess hall. Terrus, Mai, and Ashelyn were all waiting for him, laden with the supplies needed, and they headed outside.

Both moons shone brightly, and the wind was mercifully sparse.

"Should we...?" Mai said, gesturing to the harnesses, but Terrus shot her a trademark grin.

"We'll be fine, the platform is the safest spot here anyway!" With that, he turned and ran for one of Tuwia's two watchtowers. Despite his impairment, he made short work of the ladder, curling his feet around each rung and holding himself in place with impressive core strength. Tarlo smiled. It was nice to see a glimpse of the Terrus he'd once known.

Mai shook her head and made a point of still grabbing a harness, but Tarlo and Ashelyn shared a little look. The more time they spent together, the more they seemed to understand one another without the need to speak, and in her eyes he saw a challenge.

"Forecast is still calm, right?" he said, and darted towards the ladder.

"Atta boy, Tarloooo!" came Terrus's hoots from above, already at the top. The rungs were icy against his hands, but otherwise, the climb was easy, and the cool air refreshing. Now that his system had adjusted, it was truly delightful to be able to breathe again, and the air here carried a lightness, a sweetness unlike anything he'd tasted back on Earth. There, it was always thick and heavy, even out in the desert – the result of centuries of pollutants.

Ashelyn followed him up in short order, while Mai made a point of taking her time.

"Wasn't expecting that from you, Doc. I know Tarlo is quite the daredevil these days, it must be rubbing off."

Ashelyn's eyes glinted in the moonlight, their emerald lustre unmistakable even in the blue and grey of the night. Tarlo's breath caught as a flush of hormones released in his chest.

"Maybe you just don't know me well enough," Ashelyn said, deadpan. Tarlo sensed she was teasing.

The viewing platform was roughly four metres squared, providing a clear view of the world below. Not that there was much to see, with the dark waters of Alantia spreading in all directions.

"It's so similar, in a way," Mai said.

"To what?" Terrus asked.

"Cahros. Just where once it was orange, it's now blue. But otherwise, just as smooth, just as empty... just as deadly."

"There is something linking these planets, of that much I am for sure," Ashelyn agreed. "But that is not a mystery for tonight." She stood beside Tarlo, and her hand brushed against his. Another spark, another flood.

"Who would like to go first?" Mai said, lighting the candle. It had a long, thin, cream-coloured body, and wouldn't have looked out of place in a medieval bedroom. The four of them turned inwards, and an eery silence fell. They'd agreed that it would be best for each of them to have their say, one at a time, but had forgotten to organise any kind of order.

"I'll do it," Terrus said eventually. Maybe it was his impetuous nature, or maybe he just didn't like the silence.

"To everyone back on Cahros... The last I saw most of you, it was a happy occasion. An exciting one. The Sunfall. Jontie had just roused us with one of his speeches, and me and the others were heading out to explore the great unknown." His right arm gripped the railings fiercely, giving away the tension behind his relaxed delivery.

"I don't really know much about what happened next. The planet got a hold of us, I suppose. I remember feeling so unlucky that I was the one who wasn't to go inside that cave... but from what we now know, that is the only reason I'm still here. From there, I somehow scouted what felt like half the Cahran desert, alone. I thought I was going to die out there too. As if that wasn't enough, I had a dose of the planet's actual *air*, walked through a ghost city, and drove all the way back to those cursed rocks, only for that bastard to nearly take me out. I feel like I should've died twenty times, given what everyone else went through. Yet here I am. And here I will remain, no matter how many more limbs I might lose. For them, I'll live on."

Terrus looked rather heroic, standing there in the moonlight, determination in his brown eyes and hair cascading around his face.

Tarlo wondered if, in another life, something might have ever happened between them. But Terrus had only ever treated him as a friend, and now, that was the best thing they could be.

And, of course, there was Ashelyn.

"Well said, Terrus. We're glad to have you with us," Mai said, treating him to a look of admiration Tarlo hadn't seen before. "I might go next."

Terrus smiled and nodded.

"It was my decision for the survivors to head out into the storm. Even if it truly was an act of... sabotage, that caused their end, it was me who enabled... that man to take their lives." Quiet tears trickled down her cheeks, but her tone did not waver. She spoke again of Yerald, who, in a deteriorating state of panic and hate, had crippled some of the fleeing group so that they might be targeted first. At least, Tarlo was sure it had been him.

"Not a moment goes by where I don't think of Sestry, who in their last moments, ensured my safety. A person who, until then, had been a stranger. Sestry, wherever you are now, thank you." She paused for a few moments, gazing out at the rising moons.

"And then, there's Jame. We had our disagreements, you grumpy old man, but you held things together, you helped me find a way to... fight back. And at the end of it all, you took the D6 out to the desert and tried to call for help. I hope they picked you up, even if they couldn't catch us."

"And if those little freaks got to you, I'm sure you gave them the worst indigestion of their lives," Terrus added with only the slightest of laughs.

Mai gave a little laugh as well, before finalising her dedication. "To all of you who did not make it, I promise you this. I will find out what is going on. And none of this will be in vain." She looked ten years older, but the grey light revealed a look of steely determination.

Tarlo realised it was his turn to speak. Despite everything going through his mind, words abandoned him. The slender candleflame wavered as a gust of wind came through, bringing with it a cool change. The flickering light caused distortions in the shadows of his friends, and for a moment, he saw three shadowy figures looming behind them. Beakish hands raised, looming like ghoulish, legless spectres that—

Ashelyn's hand was even colder than the air around, but her gentle touch grounded him.

The words returned.

"When I first left Earth, all I knew was hope. I had dreams of seeing things that nobody before me had seen. Of discovering something wonderful, something that would make my mother and sister proud. Sol, I miss them. I can't tell you all how many times in the last week that I've thought about my mother's little home, our childhood paintings on the wall. Or how many times I think that it should have been me who died, was left behind, or lost a *fucking* arm." Terrus reflexively stroked his left shoulder and winced, before shrugging as if to say, "don't worry about it".

"But here I am. I could talk for weeks about how wrong it feels that I'm alive in the first place, but you know what's worse? I'm glad that I am. I'm glad that I didn't meet the fate of so many, and I'm glad that none of you did, either." His warring emotions took turns taking centre stage, coming out in intermittent bitterness, sorrow, and angst. Another gust of wind raked them, and they huddled together a little closer. Tarlo felt the meagre warmth of the candle against his hands, and the residual heat of their skin.

"We've stumbled onto something big, we all know that. And, by still being here, we owe it to the fallen to get to the bottom of all this."

Mai and Terrus nodded enthusiastically, but Ashelyn stiffened and kept her eyes firmly on the candle. The winds increased, threatening to extinguish the candle at any moment.

"There's nothing I can add to what you've all said, except that I will see this through to the end, and you can count on me," she said. Her voice was flat, but Tarlo sensed a deep well of turmoil beneath her calm, cold exterior.

"But the fact will always remain, that it was my actions that set all of this into motion." Her angular features were worn, and her dazzling eyes sunk in deep bags, and for the first time Tarlo saw the weariness that she held.

Every once in a while, somebody says something that stays with you forever, not due to the words they use, but the way you feel every piece of their heart breaking as they say them.

Ashelyn's final words that night were an example of such a time.

"I'm... so... so sorry."

At last, the candle blew out, and its dark, grey whisps spiralled into the night sky, taking the souls of the departed with them.

PART THREE

UNRAVEL

17
THE SWARM

ALL THE SMOG in the world couldn't shield the plains of the Gobi from the fierce blasts of Sol's rays. Elsie had been out here all morning, and a combination of sand and sweat now clung to every area of exposed skin on her body. Her thin cotton garments were caked with grit, and all she wanted to do in that moment was strip her clothes and take a shower.

Thankfully, her shift was over, and she was almost back to the relative cool of Gürragchaa Base. Arriving at the door, she batted a sand-beetle from her cheek and absently wondered what she would have to do to get her hands on one of those new E14s. Hell, even an old E12 would do. The rusty metal door was jammed shut, as usual, an insult to a very hot, sweaty injury.

Eventually, Temüülen let her in, grinning in that way of his.

"Shut up. You wish you could look this good after a sixer." She pushed at his chest playfully.

"Sixer? I do nine, at least," he said in his guttural voice, before laughing and striding out into the sun. Elsie smiled and made her way to her quarters.

Once, she would have said having the chance to work on the frontier of entomology and eco-restoration was the thing that made the brutal hours all worthwhile, but most of that sheen wore off after six months of digging and sitting. In truth, the real reason she'd stayed out here for over two and a half years was the people. Temü, Livi, and Zhi-wei were her favourites, but she got on with all her companions better than any team she'd ever been a part of.

When Elsie first arrived, they told her she was replacing a shy, thoughtful young man who had surprised everybody when he announced he'd been selected for one of the big interstellar expeditions. Several months later, when news had filtered through that same man had been the first to discover life in outer space, there had been a great celebration in Gürragchaa. Their expedition lead, Andriy, had taken personal credit, claiming he'd taught the young upstart everything he knew during his time here, and had Andriy been thirty years younger, it would be *he* whose name the world now knew.

But those brave pioneers weren't the only ones having all the fun. Biodiversity in the region was skyrocketing, and every day brought new discoveries. The yearly count was sitting at *243* species, and just last week, Temü had brought in an arachnid skin the size of his forearm. It had been displayed proudly in the lab ever since.

Elsie smiled as she walked past the framed face of Jügderdemidiin Gürragchaa. Over two hundred and fifty years ago, he'd been the first Mongolian man in outer space. Now, just as he supposedly had in life, he dominated the room, watching sternly over the entryway to his eponymous research base deep in the deserts of his homeland.

"Elsie, wait up!" It was Livi, excited and breathless.

"Hey beebs, what is it?"

"It's the *Rachnoscorpius!* No point explaining, just come!"

"Calm down, Livi, I haven't even wiped my—"

"It can wait! Come on! Can't let Andriy have all the fun!" Livi grabbed her arm, oblivious to her stink, and escorted her to glass viewing window outside the lab.

Green sanitary benches flanked the far side of the room, and a single, metallic table lay in the centre. Previously, the splayed remains of the shed skin lay on the table, but now, the room was empty.

Elsie rolled her eyes; this was just the kind of shit Livi would pull after she'd been out all morning. "Great prank, beeb. Can I go shower now?"

But Livi was silent. Elsie turned to face her, and she'd gone white as fresh Moonsalt.

"Come on then, what have you done with it?" Elsie jibed, but Livi's chattering teeth was her only response. Elsie brought her attention back to the room, stepping right up against the glass. An uncomfortable wedge formed in her stomach, but she fought it off.

"You said Andriy was in here? He must have taken the skin with him somewhere. He's set you up, darling." Despite her insistence, something didn't seem right. For all his banter, Andriy had *never* been one to mess around with specimens, alive, dead, or otherwise.

"Come on then, let's go find him." Elsie half-expected him to be standing behind them, gigantic grin on his face and a withered jumble of spiky spider-legs in his hands like a spooky puppet.

But the room was empty.

"Who else is around?" Elsie said, finally drawing a response from Livi.

"Yasmine should be in comms. The rest are all out and about. Elsie, wait!" Elsie was at the doorway when the alarm in her friend's tone pulled her to a halt.

"What is it?"

"What I wanted to show you... the *Rachnoscorpius.* It isn't just a skin."

"Come on, you've had your—"

"*Listen to me.* We were messing around with it before, and I pretended to feed it some water. Andriy looked ready to send me back to Spain for tampering, but then it started twitching!"

"Stop it!"

"No, I'm serious!" Elsie could tell that she was – the fear in Livi's eyes was genuine. Besides, she'd always been a terrible actor.

"Okay, well, he's probably still having us on. Taking it for a walk or something. Let's go find him!" Livi gave her a dubious look but followed her out of the viewing area.

"Let's go to comms first. Beat him at his own game." Elsie tried to give her a reassuring grin.

They made it to the small comms centre without incident. Inside, Yasmine was a flurry of movements and words.

"I don't care what you've found, Jaxyn, a storm is a storm and not even a UCI suit will protect you from that much sand. Everybody is coming right back indoors, now!" Yasmine flicked a few switches. "Temü, that means you too! Inside, and I won't hear another word of it." Another *click.* "Fucking heroes. As if we haven't been through this a hundred times before."

It was only then Yasmine noticed them. "Sol, you two look like the living dead! I'd love to ask, but we've got a Cat-4 cooking up here."

"Huh," Elsie said, distracted. *Guess Temü won't be doing his nine hours today.*

"Yeah, so stay put, alright? Have you guys seen Andriy? I thought he was meant to be in the lab."

"He's done a runner, or so he'd have us think. Guess he didn't think we could just check the cams for him." Elsie laughed, striding up beside Yasmine.

The cams displayed clear images, albeit infected with that night-vision-green hue typical of low-budget gear. At first, the base looked abandoned, and Elsie trailed her eyes across the dozen screens, looking for a sign of movement.

"There!" Yasmine said, jabbing a finger at one of the central monitors. "Although, what the fuck is he doing?" She punched the base-wide intercom. "Ohhh fearless leader, would you kindly stop fucking about and get to the situation room? We've got a Cat-4 brewing and everything needs to be secured."

When Elsie finally saw him, the last of her false bravado fell away. Andriy was standing on the far side of the room, facing the wall. If that wasn't strange enough, his usual hunch had been replaced by a militarily taut rigidness.

"No..." Livi whispered, gripping Elsie's hand.

"The hell is he doing?" Yasmine sounded more annoyed than concerned as she pushed between them. "Do you think the speakers are busted? Wait... what the hell is that?"

Elsie and Livi leaned over Yasmine's shoulder and peered into the small, rounded square. At first, it looked like the air around Andriy was shimmering, but after a second, she realised that it was *Andriy* who was quivering. Otherwise, he was stock still, head angled slightly towards the ground.

"Shit. You had the sample, right? The *Rachno*?" Yasmine said, her tone suddenly sharp.

Livi nodded.

"Should we go get him?" Elsie asked.

"Negative. I can't believe I missed him leaving the lab – fucking storm. Argh, okay, we're locking him down until Zhi-wei gets here." Yasmine mashed another button, and the screen displaying Andriy darkened as the door to his room engaged remotely.

For a moment, Elsie thought she saw a small, dark object flash out the door right as it closed, but she dismissed it as distortion in the feed. A far more pressing matter demanded her attention: Andriy was moving.

Elsie breathed in to speak, but the air caught in her throat – the others were looking too, also shocked into silence.

It started with a spasm. Andriy's right shoulder jerked backwards, as if yanked by some invisible, clumsy puppeteer, and the movement twisted his torso around so he now faced the camera.

Only, he did not have a face. The green filter distorted what must have been the dark crimson of bloodied tissue, upon which writhed countless thick tentacles. They twisted and twirled, slithering through widening holes in his face, blood dripping from their exposed tails. Nauseating horror gripped Elsie even tighter than Livi's hand, and she realised they were not tentacles, but *leeches,* feasting on their still-live prey with determined glee.

One of Andriy's eyeballs still hung by a thread, and the thickest worm forced its way into his ear canal, causing another shudder. It had almost disappeared completely inside Andriy's head by the time he went rigid and collapsed, crushing several of the leeches with the impact.

So transfixed were the trio on the grisly scene, none of them noticed the small creature scuttling into the room behind them. None of them noticed it take up a position behind Yasmine, ready its venomous pincers, and plunge them into her Achilles'.

But there was no missing her agonised scream.

Without thinking, Elsie took a step towards Yasmine. Driven by adrenaline, she delivered a kick with force and timing that would shame a professional fighter. The creature went flying into the far wall of the room with a satisfying *splat.*

The only problem was it left its mandibles behind. Yasmine screamed again, her face reddened and puffed.

"Sol save us," Livi gasped, rooted to the spot.

"We need Zhi. Where are they?" Elsie said, her skin prickling. She took another look at the thing she'd pelted against the wall, and realised the body looked familiar. It was the *Rachnoscorpius,* only without the long, wormlike legs. *Wormlike legs...*

Reflex took over again, and Elsie activated the alarm. A calm, droning voice echoed through the facility – *"Code Olive, bio-threat, initiate quarantine. Code Olive, bio-threat, initiate quarantine."*

Yasmine tried to say something, but a stream of foamy, light brown bile erupted from her mouth, coating the console and splattering across Livi's face. Livi screamed in disgust and shock, and Elsie's world descended into a series of flashing images.

The first was of Yasmine's clenched fist, swinging in panic, about to connect with her temple.

Then the consoles sizzled as the bile leaked into the circuitry.

The lights flickered red as the alarms kicked in.

Then the punch landed, sending her staggering into the far door. A flash of white, a tearing pain in her skull, and then a flush of heat. Then two hands on her arm as Livi grabbed her and pulled her from the room, slamming the door shut as Yasmine's terrified screams continued.

Code Olive, bio-threat, initiate quarantine.

"Els, we have to get out of here," Livi said, her voice quavering.

"What about Yas?" Elsie slurred. "The storm—"

"Yes. We need to go somewhere they can't find us. To hide." Livi sounded different, almost trancelike.

"And seek? Who's it?" Elsie said, allowing Livi to escort her through the base.

It wasn't until they made it to the outside of the base that Elsie returned to lucidity, just in time to see her friend sink to the ground, back against the door and head in hands.

"I was just trying to joke around," Livi whispered.

Code Olive, bio-threat, initiate quarantine. Now they were outside, the announcement was a little muffled.

A buzz on Elsie's hip reminded her she still bore all her gear, and she absently lifted her portable talker.

"G-Base, this is Jaxyn," an easygoing voice keyed into comms, some contrast to the chaos around them.

"I've got Temü now, we're not gonna make it in time before the storm hits. We've got somewhere to hole up though, so don't worry about us." Despite the chaos of the last few minutes, it was reassuring to hear their voices. What had happened to Yasmine and Andriy was... brutal, but there had only been one *Rachno,* and the worm-things had now been quarantined.

"Still going to get my nine hours in!" a deep voice chirped in her ear as Temü affirmed his existence. A semblance of calm had almost returned to Elsie when Temü uttered his final words.

"Make sure you shut the windows back there. Wait. This... no storm. Jax, we—"

The talker went dead.

A distant hum played at the corner of Elsie's ears while she helped Livi back up. *Probably the concussion.*

"We have to get help."

"From who? The others are all out, they're—"

"No, from Dalanzadgad. We need someone to get us out of here."

"They should have been alerted when we triggered the alarms, right?" Livi said. The humming had grown louder, but a vicious headshake seemed to clear it up a little.

"Okay, our best chance is to go back inside. I know they're scary, but they're just bugs, right? We can't survive a Cat-4 storm."

"Yeah, you're right. I'm sorry, I shouldn't have brought us out here. I was just... scared. We ready?" Livi clapped her shoulder and they turned as one to face the door. Elsie grabbed the handle, but it wouldn't budge.

"Elsie... what are you doing?" Livi's tone sounded urgent again, and that damned humming was back, louder than ever.

"It's the door! It's jammed again."

"Just get it open!" Livi was growing frantic.

"I'm trying, *fuck it*, why are you in such a hurry?" A deepening shadow fell upon the door, and Elsie hesitated, but Livi tapped her on the shoulder again.

"Just, don't worry." The din grew louder.

"And don't turn around. Here, let me." Livi came up beside her, and they both wrenched at the door with all their strength. The skin in Elsie's fingers tore and the blood only made things more slippery, but she sensed Livi's urgency and kept on pulling.

Livi shouted something, but it was lost as the noise behind them reached a thunder.

Finally, with a great squeal of hinges, the door swung open, sending the two staggering backwards.

...initiate quarantine.

The dark hallway beckoned, silent and ominous. It seemed there was nothing in there, but still, Elsie hesitated.

It was that hesitation that would cost her life.

Rather than run for safety, she turned towards Livi, just in time to see a sheer wall of hand-sized insects smash into her. Livi might have screamed, but Elsie heard nothing other than that world shattering *hum* as a million legs and wings vibrated all at once.

The creatures feasted, and in only a few, short seconds, Livi's clean-picked skeleton hung in the air, suspended only by the momentum of the swarm.

It fell to the ground in a clatter.

The mass turned on Elsie.

A thousand points of pain lit up her body, so fast and so acute that she immediately lost consciousness. Elsie didn't feel the sting of a hundred piercing mouths, nor did she feel the acidic pressure of half as many proboscises as they plunged into her flesh, drawing all the nutrients forth with insatiable hunger. She felt neither the last impulse of thought, the last beat of her heart, nor the thud as what remained of her slammed into the ground.

Code Olive, bio-threat, initiate quarantine.

Three hours later, the swarm had cleared and once again the hot sun bathed Gürragchaa Base. From a high enough bird's-eye, one might not have noticed anything unusual at all. But anyone on ground level would agree: all the sunlight in the world wouldn't be enough to brighten the deathly miasma that had descended upon this place.

18
WHISKY AND DESPAIR

THE FOURTH SHOT of whisky was the first to go down without too much of a fight. Demi still winced, but the pleasant fire in her throat quickly overcame the bitter swill on her tongue, and she sank into the growing, fuzzy warmth of the liquor's embrace. One day soon, she'd quit that Sol-forsaken job. Hell, maybe even in a few drams' time.

She waved her wristband over the table-code on her booth. The dirty little screen flashed: *Would you like to order again?* Another flick. *Thank you. Please drink responsibly.* Demi snorted and slumped back into her seat. She'd drink as responsibly as the situation called for.

Just as the server laid the next shot in front of her, her wristband lit up. *This is a reminder of your appointment with Brownleaf Wellbeing tomorrow. Please be advised that cancellations within 24 hours will still be charged.*

Demi snorted again, wondering how much money those clinics made from people forgetting their appointments. She wouldn't miss it though, even if she had to ride there on a cloud of whisky-vapour; the last two years had given her enough "inspiration" for a lifetime of therapy.

The fifth shot went down even better than the fourth and was accompanied by another message.

You doing much?

No matter how far away they were, Maven always seemed able to smell the alcohol on Demi's breath, to sense the softening of her resolve. Even when it had been over two years since they'd last been together.

Demi swiped right, deleting the message. A rogue thought punched through her liquor-weakened mental walls. *What would Tarlo say?* For a blissful second, she imagined his pursed lips and slight disapproving look, which quickly melted into a kindly shrug – *whatever makes you happy, makes me happy.*

Then she remembered he was gone. Immortalised in the tactless name of a stupid bug that cared only about sinking its microscopic teeth into anything stupid enough to go near it. That's what all of this had been – a stupid waste of money and life. A publicity stunt to tame the masses and dump excess profits that could've been better spent in literal *millions* of places closer to home.

Tarlo, in his infinite optimism, had still seen something in all of this. When he left, Demi had known she probably wouldn't see him again, but it had been one thing to know he was up there, living out his dreams.

It was another to think he'd died for them.

Whenever their mother, Karee, brought him up, she spoke of Tarlo in present tense. As though he was still out there, just wandering around somewhere in the oxygen-less desert. Demi had screamed at her so many times just to let it go, to stop rubbing this blind, stupid faith in her face, but Karee never once bit back. She only ever looked at Demi calmly, stating, "He's okay, I can feel it. He's just lost."

Demi figured Karee was the one who should be visiting the Brownleaf Clinic every second Saturday.

Despite the enduring hell of grief, she had reached a point she could at least do her job without crying, screaming, or drinking herself to sleep every night – that was, until the latest news broke. Four stations in the Gobi, the frontier of evolutionary research, all dark in an eight-hour window. Another two in the Arctic, and six in the Sahara. The same story every time, a plague of predatory locusts, or wasps, or centipedes. Twelve stations, all part of the most positive, Earth-based ecological news of the last century, gone. The announcers had tried to frame it somehow as a noble sacrifice, and a sure-fire sign – and casualty – of "ecological stabilisation", but Demi knew all about the spin game.

If she didn't do it for a living, the professional gaslighting might have actually worked on her too. If it hadn't been the very base that Tarlo once lived and worked in, maybe she wouldn't have been so destabilised by the news and could have stepped back and seen it for whatever positive sign it supposedly was. Maybe she could have convinced herself that everything was going to be okay. Another snort escaped her nose – loud and obtrusive, but what did it matter? For once, she didn't even care that she was sitting here, drinking alone, making noises to nobody.

There was another message which came through that morning, that she hadn't deleted.

I heard about what went down in the desert. Thinking about you, D. Always. Demi brushed a half-formed tear from the corner of her left eye. Flo deserved so much more than anything she'd ever be able to provide.

She downed her failures with the sixth shot, and it tasted wonderful.

Another flash from her wrist. Demi looked down, and the messaged letters waved and flowed over each other to form the words: *I miss you.*

Sights and sounds flashed through Demi's mind, of tattoos, tangled legs, lip biting, and neck kissing. Maven had always known *exactly* which spots to touch, and when. Like most drugs, the comedown was never worth it...

But who the hell was going to stop her? The last connection she'd had to her brother had been severed, she was drunk, and as far as she was concerned, the world was ending.

Demi raised her wrist to her eyeline and carefully constructed the most careless of messages.

Be there soon.

19
TRUST

Tuwia, Alantia   CD: 22/04/2222

Tarlo

TWENTY-FOUR DAYS after their first conversation, Tarlo and Ashelyn first made love.

Their initial attempt was clumsy, awkward, and largely unsuccessful. Throes of lust gave way to a shared nervousness when their naked skin touched, and Ashelyn, usually so assured, retracted in momentary panic.

"It's okay," Tarlo breathed, stroking her hair behind her ears and planting a light kiss on her cheeks.

Two hours later, she returned the gesture in more pointed fashion – and this time, it was Tarlo who faltered. For a moment, they both lay with a clear inch of space between them, unsure how to make their bodies fit together and scared that they might embarrass themselves, or worse, put the other in any kind of discomfort. Then, they laughed, a nervous, high-pitched giggle that melted into tender gasps and whispered moans. All throughout, Ashelyn's hands never stopped moving, and at their climax, her lips met his, and she gripped him as though she were clinging to life itself.

When Tarlo awoke, his first sight was of Ashelyn's bright green eyes. A wave of hormones rushed through his chest – and further down – but her blissful smile calmed him.

"How long have you been awake?" he croaked, feeling more than a little dehydrated.

"I'm not sure. I've been trying to work out how long we've known each other." The glint in her eyes diminished as she furrowed her brow.

"By our standards, or the universe's? As the universe would say it's over two—"

"Ours," she said quickly. "Ours is all that matters."

"Well, we didn't really speak until we landed on Cahros."

"But I saw you before then."

Tarlo blushed. Yes, he recalled the first time he saw Ashelyn during the early days of UCI training but he never would have thought she noticed him too.

"It was week three," she continued, "I think a Friday. You were ever-so-gently arguing with someone about how evolution could occur in real time, and that if something new were to be discovered on Earth now, it was likely it had only recently come into existence."

Tarlo had forgotten this conversation, but he remembered the concept. Earth had gone through so much environmental transition in the last century that the nature of evolution *itself* had changed too – it had gotten faster.

"But the first time we spoke... don't remind me," Tarlo said, wincing.

"You'd just embarked on the most graceful of landings," Ashelyn's face remained completely straight, but for the slightest wrinkle in her cheeks.

Tarlo kissed her. "You really were watching over me from the start, weren't you?"

Ashelyn nodded quietly.

"And here I was, thinking it was chance that we kept running into each other. The jump, the trip out to the formation. You saved me twice down there, didn't you?"

Ashelyn nodded again. "I don't know what it was you saw while we were in those caves, but my vision had never been clearer. The first time, you'd almost removed your helmet clean off when I got to you. The second... was when Yerald..." She snapped her eyes shut, and said in the quietest voice, "I never thought I'd kill someone."

And there it was, confirmed out of her own mouth. That thing he'd been assailed by in the caves was no eldritch monster, but the man who'd lost his mind, lost his way, in the wake of their universal crisis.

Tarlo didn't have the words to comfort her, so instead, he held her. As her skin pressed against his, he marvelled at its eternal coldness. She was an overcast sky, bleak and secretive, whose dazzling personality was hinted at only when she opened her eyes. Maybe one day the release would come, and she'd rain for him.

He wracked his brain for something to offer but was disturbed by the two words that kept returning to his mind. *Thank you*. Thank you, for taking a life, that his might continue? What had he become, that he'd witnessed a murder and felt only gratitude?

A survivor.

"The way I see it, you're strong," he eventually whispered. As he breathed life to the words, a new sense of conviction took hold. "You protected me, even if it meant doing... that. You always protected me. Thank you."

Ashelyn didn't reply, but her shoulders relaxed and breathing slowed. A minute later, he realised that, for the very first time, she had fallen asleep first. The significance was not lost on him. She was always so alert, guarded, and protective – she had to be the one maintaining vigil, ensuring the horizon was clear.

Tarlo ignored the discomfort in his left shoulder, or any impulses to roll over to his preferred side. The night was not yet over, and for now, there could be quiet. He drifted to a deep sleep with a single thought in his mind:

What a beautiful thing it is, to be trusted so completely.

20
A LIGHT IN THE SKY

Catal, Cahros   CD: 22/04/2222
Jame

THE DEATH TOLL the UCI had exacted on the *Maleficus* was now estimated to be in the billions, but the UCI soldiers were yet to gain a single metre of clean ground. For a while, Jame had been amused, and almost reassured that the toughest and most gung-ho of the UCI had achieved little more than his scratchy band of luckless colonists. It gave their losses more meaning, in a way. But as time passed without meaningful gain, tensions increased. Everyone was beginning to tire of the endless holding pattern.

Catal was almost unrecognisable from the square-horse-shoe it had once been. Now, it was an imposing fortress, complete with walls, bunkers and towers. To Jame, it felt colder, greyer, and emptier than ever. Terraforming had come to a halt, as had R&D, and his work comprised the same patches, maintenance, and surveys, day after day.

In short, this just wasn't what he'd signed up for.

In the face of such boredom, his mind kept returning to the fates of his friends who he'd last seen at the Huronium formation in the south-east. Tarlo, Terrus, Mai, and Ashelyn, perhaps the four most useful members of the colony that had once been. Balanced out, of course, by Yerald, the least useful member of any colony since the first man had wandered down from his tree. While everyone clearly thought it reasonable to presume they were killed by the *Maleficus* or resource failure, Jame wasn't so sure. He had *been* to that place, and there was no sand there. No sand meant no tardigrades. As for resources, they'd had plenty before they disappeared without a trace. Unless there lay some greater threat inside those caves...

Given it had been two years, Jame was under no illusions that any of them would still be alive, but it bothered him to think that their losses were unobserved, and the manner of their passing was still a mystery. Gnawing away at him most were his thoughts of the two younger men, Tarlo and Terrus. Both of them were good lads, in their own ways, and he'd always felt a sense of protectiveness over them. That's why he'd gone out to send that last distress call, after all. But with how everything played out, it just felt like he'd abandoned them.

He was playing pool with Mondes when Elhanto came rushing in with news.

"Did you hear about the sighting!" he said excitedly. Mondes frowned in confusion and Jame gave him a stern look. He didn't like being out of the loop.

"You know who you're talking to? We don't hear about shit," Jame grumbled, hesitant to admit his curiosity was piqued.

"On the front lines, they's thinking they saw something on the other side of the dark zone." The dark zone was the uncreative term allocated to the region of sand spanning a five-kilometre radius around the formation, where navs and systems had a regular habit of not working as they should. The troops had little interest in that area, and rather than investigate, had cordoned it off while they focused on bigger – and smaller – problems closer to home.

"So? It's still a no-travel zone," Jame said.

"That's just the thing Ternal wants to talk to you about!"

Jame tried to act nonchalant, but his next shot flew straight past the yellow he was aiming for, pocketing a black and ending the game.

Han and Mon were really good about it.

Jame made a show of massaging his shoulder. "Our conversations always go so well. Just me?"

"Aye, sir. I think you'll want to hear him out. He's in the BCC."

"Okay then. Wish me luck." He left Han and Mon with a couple of handshakes and a joke about Ternal's head, before trudging out towards the command centre. This part of the base hadn't changed much. At times like this, during the night-time circadian cycles, the corridors were almost comforting; dimly lit reminders of the home he'd once built. Resolute, un-breached, and eternally unchanging.

Ternal stood with his hands splayed over the oaken table, barking out orders. He was one of the younger officers Jame had met, but he seemed determined to compensate for this through sheer volume and lack of compromise. At his flank stood two corporals who may have been clones: carbon copies in crew cuts.

"Talwyn, just the chew I was looking for," Ternal said. Jame hated how they always insisted on using surnames. But he loved how much it pissed them off when he *didn't*.

"Ternal. How's the war going?"

The young captain scowled. "This is an occupation, not a war."

Jame's eyes narrowed. Ternal used the word "occupation" as though it were somehow nobler.

"A war would suggest our foes are active participants, I suppose. Can't have that," Jame replied. When it came to winding Ternal up, he just couldn't resist.

"I didn't summon you here to educate you on the necessity of military intervention. Not that I should need to, given what happened when this was a civilian expedition."

Jame grimaced. He'd brought that one on himself

Ternal didn't bask in his victory of words for long, brow furrowing as he almost spat, "The *Maleficus* species continue to show resilience. For every million we burn, an ostensible ten million more fill their place. We are getting no closer to any sense of progress."

"Keeping them out of here no longer a valid achievement?" Jame retorted.

Ternal looked at him coldly. "I have my directives, chew."

Jame shrugged. "Han told me your guys have seen something new, at least."

One of the corporals cleared his throat, but Ternal shook his head. The four original survivors had been granted a kind of immunity from military procedure, so there were no grounds for Jame to be reprimanded for insubordination. Nearly two years, and some of the stiffs *still* didn't get that.

"You bet. I wanted to get your thoughts on this." Ternal summoned Jame to his side and flicked his wrist at one of the monitors using the motion-activated tab on his wrist – one of the many little upgrades the second wave had brought with them.

The hanging monitor flickered for a moment, before clearing up to display footage that Jame inferred had been gathered from the front-facing cam of one of the burners – flamethrower-sporting military buggies. The coordinates at the bottom of the screen were recognisable; they were just outside the dark zone.

"What were you doing all the way out there? I thought we hadn't cleared them past our doorstep," Jame said, narrow-eyed.

"You're right, we haven't. That doesn't stop us scouting out ahead though. The burners give us an idea of where they're concentrated. But that's not the point. Check the skies."

Jame had already noticed the phenomenon to which Ternal referred. The feed displayed the endless dark skies of Cahros, free from the cloud cover that dominated the early night-time sandstorms – but something was different. Instead of the usual, dazzling starscape, a shimmering, orange light flowed through the skies.

"Reports onsite confirm this was no lens flare or distortion," Ternal said – not that Jame would have asked. He'd seen enough of that place to know what it was capable of. "It would be easy to lump this in as some kind of *aurora* but given the nature of that region of the planet, it makes me uneasy. I know it is likely no joy for you to reminisce on such things, but I wanted to ask you, have you seen anything like this before?"

It was obvious that Ternal was referring to the period before he and his merry gang had arrived on Cahros. One that he and Jame had nearly come to blows over when

Ternal callously referred to some of the decisions made by the early colonists as "rash and ignorant".

"You've worked on your tact, I see," Jame said. "But no, we've never seen anything like this. To be fair, things went to shit while we still had cloud cover, and after that, we were holed up inside until you got here."

"Yes, but there's been several of these long nights, and we've never caught such a sight before. Some of the soldiers reported some other... observations as well."

"Such as?"

Ternal hesitated. He was a literal person who always struggled when it came to anything that couldn't be solved with a weapon of some kind. "They reported... feelings. Like they were being tugged, or pushed, towards the zone."

"We've talked about this before. What did your sci call it?" Jame said.

"Cellulo-magnesis. But that was just a blanket term for the theory, not an explanation. See, we've been doing these little scouting expeditions for quite a while now, but this is the first time anyone has made those reports since, well, since your people did. And it has come right at the same time as these orange auroras. I just wanted your take on it."

Jame pondered for a moment. "Maybe its waking back up."

"What do you mean?"

Jame shrugged. "I don't pretend to know how these things work, but I've always seen it like a volcano. Since that first month or so, it's been dormant. Based on what you're saying, maybe it's waking back up."

Ternal adopted a look of alarmed confusion, but upon realising his subordinates noticing this, quickly snapped back into gear.

"Well, then we'll draw back another five kilometres. Whatever is going on in there, it's not our priority. Kozo, make it happen." One of the corporals nodded and moved to a console on the far side of the room.

"We'll also set up a daily patrol of those borders – keep an eye on if anything changes. Same protocol though, scorch and burn the ground before you roll over it. Garde, that ones on you. In the meantime, business as usual, nobody leaves the building unless assigned. Talwyn, you're dismissed."

Jame loitered just long enough to communicate his insolence before heading out. Instead of going back to the rec, he went straight to his dorm. They were still set up to accommodate twelve, but due to the 24-hour military deployment schedule, rarely slept more than three at a time. Tonight was unlucky, and he counted at least five sources of snoring or heavy breathing before he made it to his bunk at the back of the room.

He probably wouldn't have been able to sleep anyway. Something about those floating streams of orange light burrowed into his brain, leaving him with a strangely warm feeling that he didn't want to let go of by drifting off. It was a similar feeling to what he used to get whenever he thought of his younger friends, towards who he'd felt almost... paternal.

Four hours later, he'd made his decision.

Jame was going to heed the call.

He made it as far as the vehicle bay when he realised he couldn't leave without saying goodbye. Han, Mon, and Mury had lost so many people, the least he could do was give them an explanation, even if it might risk blowing his cover.

He needn't have worried – they were already waiting for him inside the darkened hangar.

"Call it a hunch." Mury winked. "You know, I just can't believe you went this long without trying to break out." Interestingly, she was partially clad in an E12, wearing all but a helmet.

"Me neither," Mon said, shaking his head. "I owe Han a full work duty now. I said it would happen twelve months ago."

Jame was a little taken aback. "You were placing bets on me?"

"Shhhh. If we're made, then all bets will be off," Mury said.

"I…" So focused had he been on his ideals of adventure, Jame wasn't at all prepared for the emotion of the moment. What was he thinking, leaving the only three people he *knew* were alive? And to do what, exactly? Go starve, freeze, or worse down in the depths?

But the desire to leave was entrenched now, like an itch beneath his skin, a tugging at the edges of his mind.

"It's okay. We feel the call too," Mury said calmly.

The surprise must have shown on Jame's face.

"Don't worry, we won't be making a burden of us'selves," Mon said. "You know us – our place is here. With each other." Jame understood. Han and Mon weren't scared of dying; they were scared of losing each other.

He gave them both another firm handshake, accompanied by a shoulder clasp. "We're the ones who built this place. The only ones. Don't let them forget it." They nodded, and Mon blinked rapidly, as if fighting tears. And that was their part in the farewell over – they had always been men of few words.

When he reached Mury, he was startled by the steely look in her eyes as she said, "I don't think you'll find me so hard to shake."

"Mury... I'm almost certainly going to kick it out there, why jump on the sinking—"

"I know how much they mean to you." Her voice had a peculiar layering to it, almost as though there were two of her. Jame shot Han and Mon a glance, but they didn't seem to notice.

"And as much as I hate to admit it," Mury continued, sounding normal again, "you mean something to me. The idea of staying here without you makes my skin crawl."

Jame turned away, fighting a flash of frustration.

"Don't be an idiot, Ree. You want to have come back from all the shit you've been through, just to throw it away out here on me?"

"You don't get to make that decision for me. I was stubborn enough to fight through infection, amputation, and prosthesis, what chance do you think you have?"

"You know what happened the last time people followed me out of this place."

Mury's grey-tinged fringe swayed over her forehead as she shook her head gently. "Maybe you can follow me, then."

"I'm not kidding. Don't do this."

"Nor am I. Now if you don't get your suit on, Ternal will be up for his 6 am piss soon and put us on house arrest."

Jame thought about turning around right then and there... but then what? He'd continue going through the motions, bickering with Ternal until the day the flamethrowers ran out of fuel and the tardigrades evolved the ability to digest Moonsalt?

Mury took his silence for the acceptance that it was and threw him a pair of boots.

"Now, just one questions remains. Which car do we steal?"

21
A DEPARTURE

Catal, Cahros   CD: 22/04/2222
Jame

THE RIGID MILITARY protocols in place meant that there was no way of truly "sneaking" out of Catal. Instead, Han and Mon made themselves useful by convincing the young squaddie monitoring the command centre that Jame and Mury were heading out for their daily repairs two hours early. By the time the lad realised they'd surged beyond the perimeter, it was too late to send anyone in pursuit.

Ternal was roused, and, once he'd lambasted the squaddie (one of the few people on base younger than he) had done his best to raise them on comms. Jame would have happily kept them turned off, but Mury convinced him to hear him out. It was well she did.

"I'm not going to chase you, you know," Ternal said drily.

"What, you got a burner waiting for us?"

Ternal's staccato laugh rang through their cab.

"You don't need me to tell you how many ways you can die out there that don't require I lift a finger."

They hadn't been so bold to take a burner – that would have really pissed Ternal off – instead commandeering one of the new B9s. A large upgrade on the old BBF buggies, the B9 came equipped with a second seat, expanded life support capacity, and a faster top speed.

"You know, this actually solves a few problems for me," Ternal continued. "See, I really do want to know what is going on over there but didn't want to go against orders or risk the personnel or collateral. As much as your expertise has been valuable thus far… I'm sure you'd agree we reached a point of diminishing returns."

"So basically, if your men died, that would be unacceptable, but if we kick it, who cares?" Jame shook his head.

"I do not wish you death, Talwyn. You're getting what you want."

Jame pursed his lips. *He's got me there.*

"Thank you, Captain. We'll ensure we update you when we get back," Mury said.

A pause. Did anybody think they'd be returning?

"I do ask that you document as much as possible. Keep the cams running at all times. Ad Aeterno."

"You got it. See you on the other side."

Ternal didn't try to raise them again. Initially, Jame felt relieved, a sense of expeditious freedom washing over him. It felt *good* seeing the sand fly beneath his wheels, leaving behind the ghosts of Catal and the frustration of inaction. It reminded him of the first few days after they landed, surrounded by possibility and potential. He floored the accelerator, sending mists of sand flying behind them as they surged away into the night.

As Cahros slipped away beneath them, Jame and Mury talked. Sometimes conversationally, sometimes deeply, but never about what might lie ahead. It was for the scientists to hypothesise.

A few hours later, they crossed into the dark zone. At first, they suffered no noticeable effects, but this changed when the vehicle's main console let out a shriek.

"Bigger buggy, same problems," Jame mused.

"Would you believe it? Right on Cahran midnight, too," Mury said.

"Spooky."

"Do you think we'll see Exsar rise again?" Mury gazed through the glassy dome of the B9, moist-eyed. They had gotten into the habit of climbing onto the Catalan roof at the first coming of the sun – ever since that first, horrific night had ended. The splendour of Exsar's first coming had never lessened.

Jame joined her in contemplation, surveying the world around them. Oblivious to their mechanical problems, the stars above shone with defiant radiance, sparkling against the navy blanket of space. From one particularly dark region of the sky, faint, orange tendrils of light curled, flickering with a tentative beauty. He wanted to stare at them, to get lost in their shimmers, but they also triggered a primal fear, a reminder of the untameable power to this place. They beckoned, but to where?

There could only be one place.

"We'd best not stay still for long." Mury brought him back to the present. "Can't have the Tardis catching up." The UCI still hadn't figured out where they all kept coming from, and, considering none of them had fed for two years, why they continued to wake up, but there continued to be reports of rogue colonies stirring out in the sands, especially where there had been heavy traffic.

"That would be embarrassing, wouldn't it." Jame's forced grin hurt his jaw.

Jame had witnessed the stuporous effect of the formation firsthand without ever really feeling it himself. As they edged towards the formation, he felt a mix of concern and amusement watching Mury's head droop repeatedly.

When their navs stopped working, Jame didn't even slow down, so convinced was he that the orange lights in the sky would lead them to the formation. The wasteland was featureless and timeless, but when he squinted, he could make out a dark outline, somehow denser and blacker than the sky, that ended directly beneath those ethereal orange streams.

Jame's eyes had started to lilt when the two Blackrock pillars seemingly sprung from the ground, transitioning from vague specks against the horizon to huge, looming towers in what felt like a few seconds. Their vehicle shuddered and swerved as the surface transitioned from sand to pebble, restoring their alertness in the process.

Jame brought the B9 to a halt. Here in the monoliths' shadow, there was no sky, no sun, no stars.

"The end of all things is at hand. Therefore, be serious, therefore be watchful," Mury chanted. Jame had been around long enough to remember the old faiths that existed before the Last Great War. He'd never heard them from Mury, though.

"Just the way I remember it," he said, easing the B9 back into gear before adding, "Don't let Ternal hear you talk like that."

"Shit, I don't know where that even came from. I never practiced," Mury replied, sounding anxious.

"Relax, I don't care, Ree."

"No, it's not that. It was something my grandmother used to say, before the seizures. Like she knew there was a great darkness ahead of her. Just reminded me of it, is all."

"I can see why. But don't worry, the greatest thing we have to fear here is each other."

Mury snapped her head towards him, looking for the punchline, but he kept his eyes on the darkness ahead. Their headlights did so little to pierce the gloom.

"It fucks with you, is all," he said eventually. "But I've told you all that."

"Jame... what are we doing here?" Mury had never really been one to show – or feel – fear, but the vulnerability in her voice was clear.

"I... I actually don't know. It was something about those lights in the sky. I knew they were a sign."

"Of what?"

"I'm hoping now we're here, we'll find out."

He edged the B9 slowly through the base of the formation, eventually arriving at a familiar site. A large, van-like carrier vehicle was parked at the edge of the clearing, beyond which lay a collection of defunct devices.

"Suit ready?" Jame asked, and when Mury nodded, he popped the cockpit of the B9 and leapt out. Mury tailed him hesitantly as he made his way through the site, attempting to draw life from the various apparatuses without luck. Two years on a place with a very light atmosphere or wind should have kept things in reasonable condition, but most of the gear looked like it had been there for decades. Indeed, some of the smaller consoles shattered at only a slight touch, and others seemed to have already eroded away.

"Were these... ours?"

Jame nodded, the beam from his helm-torch casting a strobe-like effect on the campsite.

Everything around them was either black or grey, devoid of colour or life. "It's like we've stepped into an old movie," Mury said.

"Yeah. A weird, boring one."

Fuzzy memories tugged at the edge of Jame's consciousness, of riding, hunched and weary, with five other survivors. Of a last game of *Shōgi,* played with trembling hands and misty eyes. Of a lonely trip to the desert, only to learn that no rescue was coming.

The oncoming sandstorm had been only thirty seconds away from him when Jame decided he wanted to live. All this time later, he still didn't know exactly what motivated that decision. On the surface, he might have attributed it to some concoction of stubbornness, anger, and frustration, but deep down, he knew that wasn't all there was to it.

As it always did whenever he thought about this, his mind wandered back to his missing friends. The kindly Sel, who had fallen, but whose memory did not deserve to die with him. The lively Terrus and caring Tarlo. The young doctor, Ashelyn, with her insistence on always looking like she knew what she was doing – but a core devotion to protecting those around her. And Mai, who had fucked up just as much as he had but soldiered on anyway.

Jame reached the edge of the camp and dropped to his haunches, trailing his gloves through the rocks until he latched onto a large stone. The impulses in his suit told him it was cold, almost freezing. He stood back up and threw it into the shadows. The total silence of the place amplified the piercing *clangs* as it bounced off various rocky surfaces. He couldn't see where it went, but it almost sounded as if it were *falling*.

Then he saw the footprints.

There were five sets. Some were clearly defined, others dragged and smudged, but they all led in the same direction. Jame followed them, his vis-torch finally illuminating the great cave entrance down which his stone had fallen.

THEY AREN'T HERE.

The impulse crashed through his mind of its own accord, seizing control of his consciousness and imprinting itself on the insides of his eyes.

Jame staggered, but the words disappeared as quickly as they came.

He barely noticed Mury come up beside him. "What have we here?" she said with sudden confidence, and before he could react, she jogged on past him.

"Wait!" A sudden alarm gripped him as he tried to follow her, but an otherworldly heaviness descended upon his boots. With a heave, Jame managed his first step, then another, but the weight on his legs only increased.

He tried to call out, but the words caught in his throat, and he felt as though he was stuck in a nightmare, powerless to exercise control over his surroundings.

Mury reached the entrance to the cave, a chasmic hole in the ground that stretched between the Blackrock monuments, and turned to face him. His torchlight reflected off her visor, bestowing an inhuman brightness upon her eyes as she waved her arms excitedly.

Jame calmed a little, managing to close half of the distance between them.

He was looking directly at Mury when something appeared in the space above her left shoulder, a little way behind her.

It began as a glint in the darkness. A glint that, once observed, surged forward at speed before coming to a halt right behind her.

It was a face.

A *human* face.

Excitement gave way to confusion, which gave way to dread as Jame realised there was something wrong with what he was seeing. There were no people here. There couldn't be. As if cued by his doubt, the helmet began to shimmer, as if it were a projection on a screen.

A new threat caught his attention: a set of claws.

Black, beakish, and viciously sharp, they slowly extended around Mury's waist. Jame had time to cry out once before they plunged into her stomach, ripped her from her feet, and dragged her down into the depths.

22
COLOSSAL

Tuwia, Alantia   CD: 22/04/2222

Terrus

"SO LET ME get this right," Terrus bellowed, wind stinging his cheeks. "There was a whole other floating settlement here. It disappeared a couple of weeks before we catapulted out of nowhere, and is now at the bottom of the ocean. Meanwhile, we are witnessing some kind of cosmic, unfathomably gigantic creatures that shoot Sol-damned *lightning* making a vertical migration? Have I missed anything?"

The staircase shook, and he did his best to make his cross-armed lurch for the handrail look natural.

"A few things, actually," Mai shouted back up at him. "But I think those are the key themes."

"And what do they think happened to the other base? Flying fish? Sabotage?"

Mai shook her head. "More likely the same as what happened to us on Cahros, minus the tardigrades."

"Hubris?"

"Ha, but no. Weather. Elís says the leading theory was it went down due to a misfire in their boosters – either thanks to a freak accident, or due to a weather anomaly triggered by the terraforming."

Terrus was no scientist, but something about that seemed far too simple. "What, so they get a bad storm over there and fall apart? Why wouldn't the same thing have happened here?"

"Altitude, apparently. Alvolito was a kilometre or so higher. When they supercharged the atmospheric oxygen, it led to some pretty serious lightning storms."

"So, put up a shield? Wouldn't they have thought of that before parking it up there?"

Mai gave him a look. "You know what, Terrus? I completely agree, it makes zero sense. If you ask me, Elís, and everyone here, is just as worried that it might be something to do with those creatures below. Why do you think we're down here right now, packing up the shuttle?"

The platform beneath his feet suddenly felt even more thin and shaky. Terrus did not like heights, and he definitely didn't like the idea of floating around on a planet without a *ground*. And now, he had to come to terms with this idea that they might just... fall from the sky at any minute?

Any more news like this, and he'd wish he was back on Cahros.

Mai helped him loosen his harness enough to be able to traverse the deployment bay platform, and he gave her a bashful nod of thanks. As long as he stayed away from the edges, he could almost convince himself they were just standing in a regular base on the regular ground. Yes, it was *totally* normal for the ground to shake like this every time the wind blew a little strong.

"You know, if I lost an arm back home, I'd be the centre of attention for at *least* a week. How is everything I do so quickly outshadowed?" he moaned. He and Mai had spent enough time together over the last week for Terrus to be confident she understood his protestations to be insincere, but he still wondered if this was a joke too far. People here had died, after all.

"Do you mean overshadowed?" Mai said with a smirk, and he breathed a small sigh of relief.

"Forgive me, none of these damned planets come with anything that can even cast a shadow, I'm forgetting what the concept even is. How do shadows work, again?" he mumbled, still a little concerned he'd been too facetious.

"You seem to have forgotten how *you* work, too. Where is the man who loudly insisted in front of everyone that he be the one who loads the shuttles?" Mai said.

"Ahh, prompt taken. I'll carry your bags, my lady," Terrus said, flourishing his good arm before hoisting the strap of a supply kit over his shoulder.

Mai shrugged at his faux chivalry, and took up position by the shuttle, letting him mule the gear over while she took care of the precision task of placing each item safely inside.

"They've got some nice stuff, I'll give them that," Terrus grunted, passing her a metal box labelled *oxyGen*. "What is this?"

Mai studied it for a moment. "Doesn't the pun give it away? It's a portable generator. Can be used alongside *this*," – she pointed at a larger, black box – "to charge our suits and keep us breathing."

"Man, I could have used one of these on Cahros."

"Couldn't we all?"

"Still… if the skybase somehow goes down, what do they expect us to do? Nowhere to land, nowhere to go, what's the point of recharging?"

"You don't need me to explain it to you, do I?"

"No," Terrus sighed. "I get it. It calms people down, thinking there's a way out. A plan."

Mai pointed her index finger and thumb at him and flicked her wrist upwards.

"But we're all smart here, right? So, who are we actually fooling?"

"Doesn't matter how smart you are, you know what they say about idle hands and idle minds."

"I don't, actually."

"Huh. Prewar term, religious origins. Basically, boredom is bad."

"I never took you to be a Theologian."

"I just know everything." Mai twitched her left eye, and so unnatural was the gesture, it took Terrus a second to realise it was intended as a wink.

"Except what happened over at Alvo."

"Yeah. And a million other things. But what I do know is this: we need to stay ready."

"Why, because this thing only seats six?" Terrus laughed, but Mai wasn't smiling. He felt a chill, remembering what she'd said about the last time she'd been in charge during a survival situation.

He was sure she'd done all that she could...

Right?

He powered through the rest of the task, unable to suppress the relieved sigh as he dumped the last first-aid pack in Mai's arms. She pretended not to notice his white-knuckled grip on the handrail as she tightened his harness again, and he did his best to mask the pain in his chest as they climbed the stairs once more. Alesio passed them halfway up, on his way to perform mandatory checks on the supplies they'd just loaded.

"How are you?" he asked.

"Jolly. Swell. Vivacious," Terrus grinned.

The handsome doctor patted him on the shoulder, and Terrus detected a citrusy scent coming from his chest. *Stop it, he doesn't swing your way.*

"No more physical exercise today, okay? And that includes the gym. Cryocoma symptoms last at least two weeks."

Terrus made a face but nodded. "Yes, Captain," – he and Mai had picked up the nicknames Alesio and Corbin gave one another – "I trust you'll find everything down there in order."

"They'll be waiting for us in the command centre," Mai said pointedly, and Terrus hustled after her. Elís hadn't been keen on the four of them attending all briefings together, but to Terrus's appreciation, Ashelyn had insisted. He was tired of being the last to know everything.

Today, the BCC was crowded. Elís, as usual, had point, and at least six others were in the room, including Tarlo and Ashelyn. Terrus noticed immediately something different about them – they seemed... closer.

He crept – as much as someone of his stature could creep – beside Tarlo and gave him a nudge. "You two were late for breakfast. Did it finally happen?" Ashelyn glared at him, while Tarlo found something of great interest to study on his shoes.

Mai joined Elís at the head of the table, and the sergeant wasted no time commencing her briefing.

"As you all know, we've been working over the past days to put together a running hypothesis of the situation here. None of you need me to tell you… it's not good."

Terrus could have laughed. Whenever she did her briefings, Elís inadvertently caricatured every hard-ass military persona he'd ever seen, with her clasped hands, foreboding expressions, and dramatic platitudes.

"I don't mean to give you all a history lesson, but for the benefit of those who are new, a quick recap. When we were first deployed here, we found no signs of life for a significant period of time. Directives came for us to switch our focus towards terraforming, and terraforming only. We accelerated in our efforts to cool the atmosphere – which in turn, led to global changes in the currents and water temperature. This, we anticipated. What we did not anticipate, was the biodiversity of Alantia being discovered with the DSL revelations."

"Revelations indeed. Basic marine biology," Johann scoffed.

"Be that as it may…" Mai jumped in. Terrus suppressed another inappropriate laugh. *May. Mai.* He was a mess. "It is with high confidence we can attribute these environmental changes to the mass migrations we've witnessed, including… the stirring of these other, larger entities."

Mai looked right at him as she continued, a glint in her eyes. "As we have discussed, the local species have been displaced from their initial environment. Given their size and capabilities, this can only be a bad thing, and not just for us. To sustain itself, a single animal that size would need to consume *tonnes* of food daily. If they do not return to their place of origin, we are looking at an immediate ecosystem collapse. Furthermore, their capabilities are still unknown, and they may represent a genuine threat to the safety of Tuwia, and the human presence here on Alantia."

What was left of Terrus's giddiness faded. He hadn't been involved in these working groups, but he could see why they'd taken so little time to come to these conclusions. *This just in: Huge monsters rise from the deep dark scary depths of the ocean. Bad news for the rest of world.*

"We have already put a stop to all atmospheric manipulation, but it is not a case where we can simply reverse the work we've done. At this stage, we can only hope for a gradual temperature increase in the seas, and that these creatures decide the deeps are a tenable place to return to. With a stabilisation of conditions, it is possible."

"Fat chance that happens any time soon," Johann grumbled.

Elís ignored him. "There is more."

"Good, or bad?" Terrus called.

Elís turned her bright blue eyes on him. "If you are someone who appreciates clarity, then it's good. Corbin has finished putting together the composite scans from the one-use probes we deployed. He is confident we will have a faithful image of these creatures."

"So, we'll know exactly what we're up against?"

"As much as we can from outlines and photo-imaging."

Mai came to stand by them as Elís readied the monitor, whispering, "I haven't seen these either."

"Each probe has a scan range of approximately forty metres squared," Elís said. "We deployed a dozen probes, each roughly sixty metres apart. Their combined reach would have been – accounting for current fluctuation and general pathing interference – between seven-hundred-and-eighty and one thousand metres." Terrus and the others watched the monitor intently.

The tracing developed in real time, with a white outline flashing against the light-blue background. Each time the screen refreshed, the diagram grew another inch.

"Given this extraordinary mapping distance, I'm sure you would expect we'd capture the outlines of at least a few of these creatures. We got only one."

"Meaning, they have scattered?" Mai asked.

Elís shook her head. "Words do not do it justice, and I'm loath to descend to superlative, but these things... are truly massive."

The white outline continued to grow, and a four-word message popped up beneath it:

Estimated Total Size: Calculating.

"The reason we detected only one entity? It filled the entire radius of the scan."

The message updated, and a number flashed on the screen. A few people in the room gasped, and Terrus was beset by a feeling of fragile insignificance that erected every hair on his body.

"The largest animal in Earth's history, *Sibbald's Rorqual,* was thirty metres long." Mai's voice had dropped to little beyond a whisper, but somehow Elís still heard her.

"This is not Earth. And these things... are over twenty times larger than anything that we've ever known to exist."

23
THE LAST, SLOW SWIM

Tuwia, Alantia   CD: 22/04/2222
Tarlo

UNTIL NOW, TARLO had maintained a small hope that his experience at the bottom of the ocean had been something he'd dreamed up, dazed and confused – it wouldn't have been the first time since the expedition began that he'd seen things that simply *couldn't* be real. That ideal faded fast as he watched the image compile, coinciding with a deepening pain in his stomach and shiver in his spine. He dropped his eyes, hoping nobody would notice what a mess he was.

He needn't have feared – the screen had them captivated. A collective murmur signified the render was complete, and he forced himself to look up at it again.

A stocky, tubular body that took up most of its mass. A dozen double jointed limbs. A frontal region that resembled the orifice of a worm.

Despite its immense size, this thing was familiar. Almost identical, in fact, to something he'd seen before.

A tardigrade.

It was only the cold, strong grip of Ashelyn's hand that kept him on his feet.

Mai was the only one to muster any kind of speech.

"No... not... again..."

Fearful silence gripped everyone in the room. They all knew about the *Maleficus* on Cahros, and the dangers they'd posed. And they were microscopic.

What could they do if they were the size of a village?

"What are the fucking chances..." Terrus said, hand coursing through his long, brown hair.

"No, this cannot be chance," Ashelyn replied, voice low.

Still, Tarlo said nothing. The giddied rush of his night with Ashelyn was already a distant memory, lost in a cold shell of dread and inevitability.

YOU THOUGHT YOU COULD JUST LEAVE?

The six-word sentence shattered his mind as though it came from another, external place. But nobody had spoken.

"Your reactions are... notable," Elís mustered, perturbed.

Tarlo noticed Mauve perched by the communications station. At first, he was happy to see finally see her again, but her horrified look of realisation was quickly sobering. "These creatures..." She gasped. "They are built with the same basic anatomical outline as the predators they found on Cahros. *Tarlosius Maleficus.*"

The name brought bile into Tarlo's mouth and a dizzying flush inside his skull. Somewhere, he lost Ashelyn's hand, as she moved with Mai towards the front of the room. It was Terrus who steadied him.

"Mauve speaks rightly," Mai echoed. She seemed the most composed of the Cahran group. "These creatures share a similar bodily structure to those we met on Cahros."

"Is this not just an outline?" Ashelyn interjected. "A poorly assembled collage of photographs taken by dead probes? Sure, they look similar to tardigrades, but how many magnitudes of difference in size – not to mention planet, climate, locale, everything!"

Mai shrugged. "You are right, this is not sufficient to make an accurate identification. However, the profile fits in more than just their physical appearance. Their survivability – being able to withstand the unfathomable pressure at the bottom of the ocean. The near immortality to grow to such a size... a case of deep-sea gigantism? Biologists across history have made far bolder assertions with far less information."

"Yes." Tarlo found his words, returning to an old comfort – Earthan biological references. "It happens all the time back home, that species will vary drastically in size based on their environment. The largest dogs are fifty times greater than the smallest. Insects too. Whales, as well. This is only exaggerated when it comes to the gigantism, which is obviously on show here. Still... tardigrades in their small form exist at the bottom of the oceans already. And this is a size scale of millions, billions? With such size, these creatures would need to sustain themselves with incredible amounts of food... unless they were able to enter extended periods of hibernation. But forgetting all that... something tells me these truly are tardigrades – whether or not they are related to those we found before."

"It's something," Johann said. "To know what we're up against."

"Do we have to be against them?" Mai said, a thoughtful look on her face.

"We better hope not. But still, the more we know, the better."

"Of course. While we were scanning, was there any indication of further movement?"

"No," Johann replied. "The scans wouldn't have been completed. Likely, the probes would've been crushed in the process, too."

"Well that is something. It is a totally new habitat for them, and at a size like that, it's fathomable than any kind of movement is exhausting," Mai said.

"Yes, but if they are migrating, it's unlikely they will stay still much longer. Animals don't tend to take the scenic route during a migration like this."

"We have altered the weather for two years..." Mauve said despairingly. "We have scanned the seas for two years. Why now? Why *them*?" Her eyes were sunken, and her hair seemed to have lost its red hue – she was a total shadow of the cheery, bubbly person who'd greeted them at the formation.

"Ecological changes take time," Mai said. "And we've probably just reached the tipping point for their comfort levels."

"But these are tardigrades! They've existed everywhere, for millennia, and have countless iterations! Why would they worry about a few degrees?"

"There are other reasons they could be moving. Feeding, for one. Even if they can sleep for decades, eventually, they must eat. Could this just be a coincidence?" Johann said.

Mai shrugged. "Sure, if that will help you sleep tonight."

Johann glared at her.

"There is another option. A behavioural explanation," Ashelyn said.

"What?" Johann replied, but somehow, Tarlo knew exactly what she was referring to, even though they'd never spoken of it before. The thought had taken root in his mind at the bottom of the ocean, while he thought of the *Maleficus*. As brutal as their attacks had been, they only started after *human* intervention on the planet.

"An ecological defence system," he stated, feeling hollow. All eyes fell on him. "Evolved, or placed, to protect their planets from threats. And we are that threat."

"There is no evidence that they are even aware of us," Elís replied, the haste of her words belying that she was not immune to the growing fear in the room.

"No. To them, we are ants," Johann said.

"Our impact on the planet is far greater than that of any insect," Mai said. For a moment, everyone fell silent.

"We should name them," the words escaped Tarlo's mouth unbidden.

"We've barely classified them, and you think we should—" Mai began, but Tarlo cut her off, with more vigour this time.

"That didn't stop the UCI giving *my* name away. Whatever happens to us now, I would deny them that."

"Tarlo is right," Johann said. "And I'm sick of calling them *things,* or *them*. It would help in conversation, at the very least."

"What do you suggest then, Tarlo?" Elís said, but Tarlo shook his head.

"Johann. I think I owe you this one."

Johann gave him a long look. "I've named many creatures before this. Don't see why I should—"

"If these creatures are what we believe, they will be placed alongside the... *Maleficus*... for all time to come." The respect he felt towards these creatures surprised Tarlo. Despite everything, he felt a strange connection to them. Just as he had during one brief moment of clarity on Catal, where he'd been dipping his hands into the orange death, drawing forth a sample...

"*Postremus tardinata*," Johann eventually said. "The last, slow swim."

"May both of those things ring true," Ashelyn said. "But we must turn our focus away from what little we know of what they are, and towards what they are capable of."

"It would seem to me that we are pretty well fucked – providing they know we exist. For all their wonders, no deep-sea creature can fly, and it's unlikely they even possess a concept of the world outside the water. That said, their destructive, electro-generative powers cannot be understated," Johann said.

A gust of wind lambasted Alantia with a force that could be felt even in the confines of the stabilised interior. Tarlo's eyes drifted out the window, in search of a white sun, but he found only dark clouds that brimmed with a rising fury.

"You forget something, Johann," Mai said in a small voice. "Their size."

"That has been covered," Elís snapped.

"No, not in how I mean. Their mass... means they could have brains the size of a starship. There is no knowing what level of intelligence these things are capable of. Even the tiny ones on Catal seemed to operate via a hive mind; they coordinated their first attack to be so lethal..."

"Sol help us," Mauve wailed.

"The power these things hold is not just a threat, it is incomprehensible," Mai concluded. "They may as well... be gods."

"We are entirely at their mercy," Elís said, lifelessly.

From his corner, Johann cursed. "Looks like it's about to get worse."

The cold tension in the room reached a snapping point as a series of thuds heralded Corbin bursting into the room.

"Corbin? What is it?" Elís said, alarmed.

It was obvious from his dilated pupils and sweat-stained forehead that he was in a state of panic. He tried to stammer a few words, but they were incomprehensible.

"You were reviewing the footage of the last dive, weren't you?" Elís prompted.

"Yes..." Corbin finally managed.

"And?"

"*Alvolito!*"

"What about it?"

"The Moonsalt, the divers must have missed it. There were signs, of damage!"

"What kind?"

Another gust of wind blasted the facility, whose groans and screeches were evocative of an abandoned, wounded animal.

A thunderous *boom* heralded his next sentence, and a collective, cold shudder spasmed through everyone in the room.

"Burns. As if... they were struck by lightning."

"This doesn't necessarily change anything!" Mauve protested, her strained words tumbling through the tense silence of the room.

"Mauve's right," Elís said. "It still supports the atmospheric anomaly theory." She, too, seemed unconvinced.

Tarlo glanced over at Johann, who had grown pale.

"No... it doesn't," Corbin said, his voice barely above a whisper. The winds howled once again as all eyes turned to him. "The area that was damaged... it's a certain variant of Moonsalt. The heavier variety, only used in the outermost layer of padding."

"So? The whole base is padded with—"

"Not quite," Corbin continued, expressionless. "The top of the bases used a duller, lighter variant. The part that was damaged... could only have been attached to the bottom of the facility. Barring an extraordinary feat of it somehow flipping and being struck on the way down..."

"Alvolito was hit from beneath," Johann finished.

ALL IS EPHEMERAL.

Tarlo's ankles wobbled as he envisioned the facility plummeting from the sky and into the ocean. He saw water and foam and shattered glass and limbs fly around him, before all was swallowed into the welcoming grasp of a great and terrible hand. He felt it close around them with suffocating hunger and drag them to deepest, darkest depths of these waters, where their souls would be trapped for eternity.

Elís turned on Mai and spoke sharply. "The shuttle, is it prepared?"

"Everything is ready," Mai replied, voice lined with high-pitched panic. "But to go where? To fly aimlessly through the skies, waiting for the charge on the shuttle to wink out?" *And send us to those huge, clutching hands in the dark.* "There is no help above, no other base, not even a patch of land to try to land on."

"I have been thinking about this. I'm afraid we have one recourse." Elís took a deep breath. "The Blackrock."

"That is, if it truly does possess the capabilities you spoke of," Mauve added, her words tinged with uncertainty rather than spite.

"Everything we said was true!" Tarlo exclaimed, "But we can't tell you if it will work again, or if it does, where it will send us."

"We could always stay here, try our luck. Maybe the *Postremus* are not here for us..."

"Tarlo and Johann captured footage of what these things are capable of," Elís said. "Whether they mean us harm or not, we have mounting evidence they are a mortal threat to Tuwia. We will leave now – and should the threat pass, we can always return. Staying in hope leaves us at their mercy. If the worst happens to Tuwia, we make for Bermuda. The possibility of survival trumps the certainty of death."

Tarlo drifted towards the viewing port on the far side of the comms centre and gazed out at the seas below. For now, they remained docile.

"An apt decision," Ashelyn said.

"The way I see it, the decision has been made for us." Elís's crisp commands brought a sense of order to the room, but there was a lack of impetus as the colonists began to shuffle forth. Perhaps it was the uncertainty of the threat, or the simple resigned hesitation that they must leave their home behind.

A cry from the corner of the room changed all that.

"Large scale motion detected!" It was Johann, who had been perched by one of the consoles throughout the meeting.

"What is it?"

"The sensors... think the sea floor is rising. The *Postremus* are coming."

The last, slow swim had begun.

24
THEY ARE INFINITE

JAME WAS NOT going to lose someone again. His torchlight flickered against dusty cave walls as he skidded through the chasm, charging nigh-blindly in the direction from which the faint echoes of Mury's cries came. Fixated on the tender sounds, he didn't even notice the array of greens, pinks, and turquoises proliferating in the air above him. He couldn't feel the confusing enmeshment of entities clawing at his feet, and he didn't see the remains of an old E12 suit, pinned against the cave walls in Vitruvian fashion.

He was getting closer. The cries grew louder, and a flickering white light played on the rocks ahead of him, illuminating suggestions of monstrous, exaggerated shadows. *Just a little further.* Jame's lungs and calves burned as a sudden exhaustion fell upon him, but he pushed on, sliding around the bend. Strange images itched at the corner of his mind, refusing his attempts to suppress them – hellish Martian landscapes and storms of crimson dust. Plagues of winged abominations soared above piles of bones and debris, heralded some cursed new age.

He found Mury curled in a ball at the foot of a slab of Blackrock. Paying their surroundings no heed, Jame dropped to his knees and patted her down, starting with the area around her stomach and waist where he'd seen those claws pierce her.

Strangely, he found no breaches. Not even a scratch in the lining of her suit.

"The fuck…" he murmured, flipping her to see the back of her helm. A blissful green light.

"That's no way to handle a lady." Mury's voice was weak, but full of her typical cheek. The cavern around them brightened with her words.

Jame rested her on her back and sunk to his haunches, smiling in relief. "Thank Sol, Ree. What the hell was that?"

"It was warm."

Her discordant response elicited a confused laugh. "That's all you have to say?"

"Honestly, yes. I felt like an osprey riding an updraft towards the sun."

Mury sat up and took Jame's hand. "I've never seen you move so fast, not even the first time you saved my ass."

Jame shook aside his misgivings and gave her hand a squeeze. She was safe, and that was what mattered.

"Just try not to fly away on me again," he said. "Anyway, where the hell are we?"

The pair helped one another to their feet and scanned the cavern, their vis-torches shimmering across its dark, shiny walls. While still maintaining its ruggedness, there was a sense of geometry to the chamber, as though it had been partially carved into a rough rectangle.

"The walls!" Mury gasped, making her way to the nearest outcrop. "Turn off your torch!"

Jame was sceptical, but trusted Mury enough to comply. The ensuing darkness was total, and he instinctively dropped back into a crouch.

"Give it a moment," Mury whispered.

A few seconds later, Jame became aware of dozens, maybe hundreds, of faint orange lights speckled across the cavern, providing a gentle ambiance to the space.

"Look!" Mury ran her hand over a smooth band of rock, drawing Jame's attention to something dark on the surface.

Carvings.

With their artificial lights off, they noticed how the little orange glows accentuated a continuous series of divots and crevices in the walls.

"They're symbols. Writing!" Excitedly, Mury skirted the chamber, tracing her gloves along the carvings. Jame slowly trailed her, peering at the indentations in the rock.

"They go all around. Sol, this place is like a library!" she exclaimed.

"If only we could understand what they say," Jame replied. He tapped the side of his helmet – the closest thing to a head scratch while suited up.

Mury pulled up when she reached a sheer wall, smooth and black, devoid of the little orange lights. Slowly, she extended a hand towards the surface.

"Don't touch it!" Jame hissed, drawing up beside her and grabbing her shoulders. "That looks like *Huronium*. Blackrock."

"The new element..." Mury breathed.

"The deadly element." They'd read the reports of the Casarabe expedition, where explorers had died just from touching the stuff.

"I repeat, do *not* touch it," Jame said through gritted teeth.

"Oh, but I want to," Mury said playfully, and Jame began to feel his own compulsion to raise his arm and lean against the tantalisingly smooth surface.

"But let's finish our circuit first," Mury said, leading Jame away from the strip of Blackrock. Together, they identified four other streams of symbols, each accompanied by its own sliver of Blackrock. One of the strips of Blackrock was different to the others, completely devoid of its sheen.

"What do you think?" Jame said.

"It's almost like the others have a kind of... power to them," Mury said, looking around. Their eyes were well adjusted to the dim orange light now, so they could easily make out the far side of the room. "But this one... it's like it's been spent."

Jame nodded. He couldn't have come up with that himself, but as she said the words, they felt *true*.

They reconvened in the centre of the room, by the Blackrock slab where he'd first found Mury.

"So, what now?" he said.

"Three options, right? We turn around and go back, we wait for another hallucination, or... we touch something?"

Jame imagined the cheeky grin on her face. Despite the voices in his mind screaming *danger,* there was something about this room that set him at ease...

Mury made her way back to the first strip of rock they'd found. He didn't stop her.

She stretched out her right hand...

Laid it on the shiny surface...

And fell right through it.

The rock shimmered, its outlines lighting up with a dark purple glow, and a great pressure dragged Jame towards it, as though he were being flushed out of an airlock. Still swallowed in the heavy calmness of this place, he allowed it to pull him in. A brief falling sensation was cut short as he was spit out onto his knees.

He flicked his helmet torch back on and looked to his left and right, expecting to find a laughing Mury.

But he was alone.

Jame pulled himself to his feet and stumbled forward. His suit informed him all systems were green, but his vis-torch would not stop flickering in and out.

The room went dark, and the feeling of safety vanished.

There were no gentle orange glows here.

Just as his eyes were getting accustomed to the blackness, the torch snapped back to life, nearly blinding him. It settled into a pattern of activating and deactivating every ten seconds as he gingerly felt his way through the passage, eyes and ears peeled for any sign of Mury.

The ground beneath him was compact, like compressed dirt, and his boots occasionally scraped over rocky surfaces. A strange, cloying smell wormed its way into his helmet, ignoring the suit's air filter, and he became aware of an odd dripping sound that seeped directly into his right ear.

It was after another ten seconds of darkness that his torchlight flickered back on to a reveal a startling sight – a body. They lay facedown, as though they'd been crawling, and had dug a message in the rough, dark sand around their outstretched right arm.

I'm sorry.

After restoring his bearings, Jame edged slowly towards them. Using the tip of his boot, he prodded at their shoulder, heaving them onto their back. The movement, hesitant as it was, managed to dislodge the helmet from their head, which shattered to dust on the ground, revealing a face Jame couldn't help but recognise.

"You son of a bitch."

Despite running out of air years earlier – or months – the seals on the helmet must have preserved them from the expected erosion or decompression. Sure, their lips were pulled upwards, eyeballs were shrunken, and features sallow, but the shape of their head was unmistakeable. It was Yerald.

Had Jame been aware of the full extent of Yerald's self-serving betrayals, in his sabotage of their fellow colonists and attacking of Tarlo and Terrus, he likely would have stomped the head into dust. Instead, he settled with a harsh kick before moving on.

The discovery of the next body elicited a significantly stronger reaction. It was in a far worse state, missing both legs and an arm. In fact, their entire suit was gone, and their remains were barely recognisable. It was only when he noticed a string of brown beads wrapped tightly around the wrist of their remaining hand when he knew.

Sel.

He'd given her that little oaken bracelet just before she'd departed Catal during that fatal Sunfall.

Jame clenched his fist, and was milliseconds away from unleashing a maddened, despairing punch against the rocky walls of the cave. Just in time, he realised such a move would likely tear a hole in his gloves, so brought his hand down in a fierce slap onto his quadricep instead. He felt no pain, but his leg automatically buckled as the suit restabilised. He fell forwards, planting his hands either side of the brown, desiccated wrist. After a few breathless shudders, he tugged at the bracelet and stowed it in his hip pouch.

It wasn't news to him that she'd met her end here, in the bowels of this forsaken place.

But until now, his last memory had been of her smiling face and playful touch. Now, that had been replaced by a grisly, crumbling visage that would haunt his dreams for as long as he'd live.

"You deserved better," he whispered, staggering back to his feet and continuing his journey in the dark.

It could have been an age that Jame spent striding through the bowels of Cahros, but he felt no pangs of thirst, hunger, or fatigue. As his bold pilgrimage wore on, he forgot his purpose, his present or past. Eventually, he forgot himself.

He might have been standing in the blue-lit chamber for hours before something clutched at his arm. Mutely, he turned, and was surprised to see somebody who looked just like him. Grey-suited, with the trademark black foot-ball-dome helm on their head.

They didn't speak, but they gestured to the wall beside them. The rock was a uniform dark brown, but tendrils of that sleek, obsidian substance weaved through it. After a moment, Jame noticed a pattern to the spirals – a picture. Two hideously long limbs – arms – that ended in beak-like claws, joined to a large body through some kind of webbing, a shrouded head over bulky shoulders. Beneath the large figure was a collection of symbols, a language unknown to humans, but whose individual lettering vaguely resembled *words*.

ᚷᛖᚠᚠᛟᚱ

Gerfor.

Whatever this creature was, had it somehow harnessed the Blackrock into a sculpture of its likeness, and then used the element to paint these walls?

His companion gestured towards another piece of... art, which sent surges of reflexive hate through his core. It was *Tarlosius Maleficus*, rendered in exquisite detail. And it wasn't alone – dozens, hundreds, thousands more of them were etched everywhere along the wall.

A voice screamed inside Jame's mind, devoid of language, but somehow, utterly clear in meaning.

THEY WERE HERE BEFORE.
THEY WILL BE HERE AFTER.
THEY ARE INFINITE.

Was this place... talking to him?

He had no time to process the mind-shattering message before a cataclysmic shudder gripped the cavern, creating an illusion that the creatures were moving, racing all around the walls. A low hum drew Jame's attention to the centre of the chamber, where four rectangular slabs of indigo protruded from the ground. The shaking grew even more intense, and rocks began to crumble around them as a dreadful, continuous *boom* echoed through the depths of Cahros.

Mury appeared before him, pressing her helmet against his, and her determined eyes burned through his stupor. "Come on, we need to leave!"

"How?" he mouthed, beset by a sudden panic as he looked around. He couldn't see the entrance anywhere, and the walls continued to shake with even greater violence.

The decision was made for them. A large portion of the cave ceiling cracked, slamming into the ground ahead of them. The impact shattered the world, causing a great rift in the rocks ahead. There was nothing to hold onto, nowhere to brace, and Jame only had time to grab Mury's arm before they were both sent hurtling into the abyss.

25
AS IT ALWAYS WAS

Catal, Cahros
Elhanto (Han)

CD: 22/04/2222

IT WAS PURE coincidence that led to Elhanto's presence in the command centre when the first emergency transmission came in. Jame and Mury had been out of comms range for over an hour, but he had loitered in the BCC to update his daily work issue – and procrastinate actioning it. He had just about exhausted his welcome when he was startled by the warble of the comms station.

"Come in, HQ. Yan here, patrol one," a shaky voice said.

"What is it?" Ternal was there in a flash. He maintained a straight face, but Elhanto noted the tension in his jaw.

"Do you have cams back there?" Yan spluttered. "It's the sky, it's—"

"Hold on, squaddie," Ternal said, bringing the feeds up to the main display above the oaken meeting table.

Han gasped. The orange auroras had spilled beyond the region of space above the dark zone, illuminating the dead skies. But their beauty was deceiving, for beneath them, in line with the bright streaks of light, the sands seethed. The typically ultra-flat Cahran surface undulated into wide dunes, which streaked towards the patrol at speed.

"The sands! They're alive!" Yan said, and a combination of shouting and static warped into the command centre.

The shifting dunes shuddered into the station bearing the broadcast cam, sending it hurtling into the air.

"We've lost you, patrol, give me a status!" Ternal barked. From their various alarmed noises, it seemed they were still alive – for now.

The camera slammed back into the ground, facedown, and Ternal grunted in frustration. He waved his hand at the display, switching to the smaller, lower-res cam that was attached to their burner.

"Patrol, give me a status!"

A calmer, deeper voice replied. "Bohrs here, patrol lead. We're attempting to make a retreat... but the sands are moving faster than we are. Anticipated impact point in ten... five...two..." A crash and a blur as the vehicle was tipped, landing on its side.

"Fuel cannister for the weapons has been damaged," Bohrs reported.

"Sol, get out of there!" Ternal exclaimed. "If that thing's breached it's going to—"

The vehicle rumbled. The two squaddies leapt free from it just as the conflagration burst forth, melting the camera lens and leaving Han and Ternal in the dark.

"Status?" Ternal called again.

"Alive. But sir, we're out on the sand. It's..."

Ternal looked grave. "We will send someone out to get you. Hang tight."

"Belay that, sir. The sand beneath our boots is moving like waves, compromise is inevitable." A series of shuffles and grunts followed. "And sir... Yan reports orange lights on the rear of my helm."

Han's heart sunk. He and the other "originals" had often laughed at the military's attempts to subdue the *Maleficus,* but this was different. Two men had just been thrust into the mouth of the maelstrom, and he was here to listen to their last moments. Just as he had from this same place, over two years ago...

"Bohrs. How you feeling?"

"Fine, sir."

Ternal took a sharp breath. "You're a damned brave man."

"Nothing to do about it now, sir."

"Bohrs? Describe everything that happens. Everything you feel."

"Understood, sir."

"Yan?"

"Yes, sir?"

"Describe everything you see."

Bohrs's stoic calmness seemed to have spread to the younger trooper. "Understood."

The seconds passed in agonising silence. If anything, the lack of visuals made it worse – the inevitable horror of their demise was coming, and while Han knew exactly what it would look like, not knowing when it would hit left every second laced with peril.

Five minutes passed.

"Talk to me, Squaddies. Status!" Ternal was clearly compensating for his nerves with bluster.

Bohrs's voice was contrastingly calm. "Nothing sir, I feel fine. We'll update you, don't worry."

Ternal bristled and began to pace the room with manic angst. Han shrunk by the corner, bracing himself. More than anything, he wished Mon would find him in that moment, to comfort him with his gentle, quiet warmth.

Another five minutes passed when Bohrs finally spoke again. "Nothing has changed, sir. No numbness, no pain. I feel normal. Maybe they aren't hungry to—" his words cut short, and two separate cries rang through the BCC.

Ternal froze, and a cold sick feeling spread through Han's body as Yan began to panic.

"Bohrs dropped! He's down, unresponsive, fuck, Ternal, I don't want to die! Don't leave me out here alone!"

Ternal had gone white, but he said nothing.

"Ternal? Command? Is anybody there?" Yan's wails tore at Han's heart, but he didn't dare to try to push past the captain.

"Fuck, fuck, fuck, you can't just leave me here! Who the fuck, who's out here! Where are you? You can't fucking do this to me!" A *thunking* sound, that might have been a foot kicking something...

Or a body dropping.

"Oh Sol, save me! Is anybody listening?" The harsh screams faded, and Yan's voice fell into a whisper. "I don't want to die alone. Please, somebody."

Han couldn't take it anymore. He shouldered past Ternal, who was still rooted to the spot, and leaned onto the comms station.

"You aren't alone, squaddie," his voice was hoarse, tainted with pity.

"Who... who is there?"

"Han. It's alright, Yan, someone is here."

"They're going to rip me apart, Han. Just like they did Bohrs. They're inside me right now, I know it."

Han shivered.

"We were so stupid to ever think we could tame this place."

"We were."

"Han?"

"Yes, squaddie."

"You should know… the waves have not stopped. They're getting bigger, actually."

Han's stomach dropped as he realised what Yan was going to say next.

"They're coming right for you."

A hideous sound scraped through the comms, somewhere between a wail, a gurgle, and a screech, finishing with another *thump*.

Then all was silent.

"Thank you, Yan. Rest now." The sentiment felt disgustingly hollow.

Han turned towards Ternal. Usually a tall man, he now looked smaller and younger than ever.

"What do we do, Captain?" Han said, the words choking in his throat. Even as he asked them, he knew the answer.

But it seemed Ternal didn't. The captain still stood mute.

"Sol-damn it, Captain, we need to ready ourselves!" Han strode across the room and grabbed Ternal's shoulders.

"Everyone here *needs* you."

Ternal's eyes flashed, and he returned to himself.

"You're right." The captain straightened himself up and marched over to the primary console. He slammed both hands onto the keyboard and activated the internal intercom.

"All members of Catal, suit up and rally at the V-Bay immediately. Repeat, all colonists and troops – drop, stop, and suit up, NOW! We are under attack." Ternal activated the alarm system and turned to Han as grating klaxons blared.

"As a civilian, you are under no obligation to fight. Should you will it, I release you and Mondes from Catal. You are free to take one of the B9s and flee."

Han just laughed. "Don't be stupid. We've had three chances to leave this place now, it's not happening. We stand with you."

Ternal pursed his lips and nodded in respect.

"In that case, suit yourselves up and meet at the rally point."

Han nodded once and fled the room. Between the harsh alarms and the rustle of nervous movement, Catal was suddenly alive with anxious energy, but he had a mind for only one thing. *Mon, where are you?*

A flurry of broad-shouldered men and women coursed past him in the opposite direction, and Han's vision blurred with rising panic. Come what may, but he couldn't do any of this without—

A warm, strong hand grasped his left bicep and pulled him out of the traffic. Han's nose was flooded with a sweet, tangy musk that felt like home.

"What is it, Han?" Mon's dark eyes appraised him, but Han couldn't meet them.

"So, it's finally happening," Mon said, pulling Han into an embrace. Every nerve on Han's skin came to life at the touch, and he realised this might be the last time they ever embraced like this. He ran his hands through Mon's course, dark hair and planted a rough kiss on his forehead.

"That won't do it," Mon chuckled, yanking his hair so their lips met, hard.

"It's the sands," Han gasped when they pulled away. "They're coming for us. Just like in your dreams."

Mon nodded solemnly. "We've held the line as long as we could, Han. It is time to face the end."

They were the last to make it to the V-Bay, just in time for the beginning of Ternal's briefing.

"This looks bad, chews, there's no other way around saying it. We've got waves of sand, which we know to be compromised, on a collision course with the facility, seems to be inspired by the anomalous lights in the sky. You've all been assigned your groups. Bravo and Charlie, you're on perimeter. You will be the first to face this world's fury. Use the burners. Delta, you'll be in the basement. Rearguard action. Rig the whole area to go up in sparks when breached, close the door behind you, all the way up. Alpha will remain here with me, first responders to any breaches."

His eyes rested on Han and Mon. "Civvies, stay with us, or pick a place to watch the fireworks."

"Sir," one of the women in Bravo called, "Why so worried? We've been blasting sand ever since we got here – and kicking its dusty ass." A couple of sniggers rippled through the crowd.

Ternal frowned. "This is a new threat, never has the land itself mobilised like this. Until now, we've been cooking flat ground, at our leisure. Footage shows these dunes are rising in at up to two metres, and moving faster than even the top speed of the B9s."

The squaddie who'd spoken up blanched. "Then what the fuck are our pea shooters going to do? We need some fucking scorched ground!"

Ternal nodded. "We all know there's no air support, no evac, no retreat. When these things hit, I don't know if we can even fight them. But we will stand together. If we are breached, it might not get all of us. Hold firm, and hold strong. Ad Aeterno."

The muster in the V-Bay now felt like a funeral. Ternal's speech was unconvincing, but everyone present knew they had no choice but to follow his orders. Where else was there to go?

"Come, Han, I know where we need to be," Mon said, leading him from the room. "Let us share one last moment under the light of the stars."

They activated their suits and clambered to the roof of the facility, taking a seat on one of the batteries. Han felt a wave of strange nostalgia, realising this was the only battery that had survived since they'd first built Catal, all those years ago.

"Some journey it's been," he mused, taking Mon's gloved hand.

"We signed up for adventure. Can't say we didn't get one."

Han looked out upon the dark horizon and saw the faintest orange tint. It could have been the rising sun, but he knew that was still dozens of hours away.

"It's like the planet itself has decided to be rid of us. Why didn't it do this earlier?"

"I think it was waiting for somethin'. Or some'un."

"Better not tell Jame that, can't have him thinking it was *him* keeping us safe."

They two laughed and sat quietly, watching the orange bolts in the sky edge towards them. Below, two squads of troopers peeled out from Catal, manning the various burners and turrets they had installed, and a nervous quiet descended upon the facility.

Han had lived a long enough life, he thought, and had seen every conceivable attitude towards death in the people he'd worked with across the frontiers. Few really wanted to die, even the spiritual types, but for him, he'd never placed too much weight on it. So much of life in places like this was dictated by chance, and his one comfort had been taking the decision into his own hands – staying in Catal, committing to the place he'd, for better or worse, dedicated his life to maintaining. There had always been comfort in knowing this was the place he'd die.

But he still felt a little cold.

"Interstellar broadcast has been prepared. One day, everybody will know what happened here." Ternal's words were a dirge, and Han was sure they provided little comfort to the various energetic, hopeful people who'd committed themselves to trying to salvage this planet.

"Cahros was never ours to have or to hold," Han whispered.

"Aye. Shame we couldn't hold on for just a little longer," Mon said.

"Why?"

"I'm not sure I'm ready to stop being with you. Two years doesn't feel like enough time."

Han's lips trembled. "I'm not sure twenty would have been, either."

A rumble echoed from beyond the bright floodlights of Catal, accompanied by an almost-soothing, wavelike noise – the sound of tonnes of sand cascading from these mobile dunes.

Dazzling magmatic streaks brightened the skies above them, signifying the arrival of their doom. The perimeter lit up as the squaddies activated their flamethrowers, but the wall of sand was unimpeded. It crashed into their barricades, swallowing the pyres of red-heat the same way it did everything else on this planet. In seconds, the defenders were enveloped, their deaths eerily silent, suppressed by the walls of sand.

Irrepressible, the wave coursed on, bringing one of the watchtowers down with it. The fallen tower slammed into the eastern flank of the facility, crushing through the roof with a great *whoosh* as the base depressurised. Stray flecks of sand flew through the air between Han and Mon, and panicked cries rung through the comms. Han flicked his wrist, cutting them mercifully short as he disconnected from the feed.

There was no need to continue listening.

The great wall of sand crashed into Catal, breaching the damaged habs to flood the rooms within. Han tried not to think about those inside, the "Alpha" squad whose deaths were prolonged those few extra seconds before they, too, were swallowed. Same with those in Delta, who by now would be buried beneath them all.

For a moment, everything went silent. The waves of sand had ceased as they soaked up their prey, and Han and Mon shared a glance. Once more, they were the last ones here, accompanied only by hubris and death. Once more, they were the last to bear full witness to the power of this place.

Then, Catal began to sink. Slowly, at first, as the sand beneath them hollowed out, but then with greater speed as the base filled with orange death. The mounds of sand around the facility rose, closer and closer.

Han clutched Mon's hand and drew him close, and they shared one last embrace as the sands tumbled over them, burying them with all that they had accomplished.

Moments later, it was over.

The sands smoothed, just as they always had, and not a single sign of Catal or humanity remained. The lights in the skies flickered out, and the gloom descended on the empty, deadly Cahros deserts evermore.

26
ASCENSION

Tuwia, Alantia   CD: 22/04/2222
Mai

"EVAC, NOW," ELÍS bellowed. Everybody started moving at once, and a flurry of feet and legs emptied the command centre.

A nauseous sense of deja vu swept over Mai as she wondered what kind of difference it would have made if someone like Elís had been there at Catal, leading in her place. Faced with crisis, Mai had effectively told her fellows to "do what they like", while improvising a plan that had led to most of their deaths.

The lack of responsibility was a liberation that triggered a sense of clarity about what she needed to do now. Instead of allowing herself to be swallowed by the tide of bodies, she ran for the comms console. Nobody was left to notice her raise a heavy hand to input a series of commands.

Mai took a final, deep breath, and broadcast the message.

That our story can be told.

Then she turned and fled with all the rest.

Outside, it was still bright, and warm as it ever got on Tuwia, though a heavy wind sluiced through the humid air. For the first time since arriving, Mai ignored the harness at the staircase, taking three stairs at a time as sweat and fear began to blur her vision. She leapt off the final stair, but a great gust of wind rocked her, causing her to land with a terrible twist to her ankle. She fell, cracking the side of her temple against a metal ledge. Her head *clanged* and her vision went white, and she barely noticed a strong arm grab her collar and drag her the rest of the way to the shuttle.

When she came to, she was looking at a red-faced Terrus and a white-faced Elís, seated in the shuttle they had first been rescued in.

But nobody else had made it.

"Where in Sol is everyone?" Elís shouted. "Mai was meant to be the last out!"

"Mauve and Alesio went back to make sure they got everyone," Terrus replied, but in her daze, Mai was distracted by what she saw through the downward-pointing shuttle cockpit.

The Alantian oceans were stirring.

She watched in stunned horror as the seas grew darker than they'd been even in the dead of night, heralding the arrival of an impossible presence. Devoid of identifiable features, it was a gigantic black mass stretching as far as she could see.

A maelstrom formed at the epicentre of the amorphous being. Its growing magnitude muted the cacophonies of panic and confusion around Mai, leaving them in a state of suspended silence as their shuttle hung precariously from its dock. An unknown pressure sucked the air from her lungs, and it felt like her skull was shrinking against her brain, and the discomfort reached its most acute right as the swirling sea-storm finally calmed.

But the awakening was only just beginning.

A great *boom* rippled out from the colossal entity; a noise so deep, so total, it vibrated what felt like every cell in her body.

A few moments later, came the waves.

The first crested from the east. Initially, it seemed small and unthreatening, but as it drew nearer, Mai realised it was almost half the height of the skybase. A gust of wind lambasted them right as it slid beneath them, and shivering panic gripped her as she contemplated what might come next.

A shout from Terrus brought a brief relief. "There!"

Her eyes followed his pointed finger to the top of the staircase, down which Alesio was marshalling several colonists.

When all I did was save myself.

A searing brightness interrupted the evacuation, and the air crackled with a fierce, electric heat. Mai's skin prickled with phantom sparks.

"Lightning!" Terrus exclaimed, but a hoarse scream from Elís drowned him out as she slammed the release to close the rear entrance of the shuttle.

"The magnets, they're going to dis—"

Then they were in freefall, and Mai's stomach felt like it was being ripped from her body. Grey skies flashed around them as her strength to withstand the g-force failed her, and she slammed into a supply pack, seeing black.

Mai didn't know if it was the actions of the fast-thinking Elís, or the shuttle's inbuilt stabilisers, but they came to a halt a few feet above the water, their descent controlled just well enough to avoid whiplash snapping their necks.

Ears ringing and fighting to keep down the bile, Mai clambered back to an upright position. They were suspended at hovering height, and fear surged through Mai's body at the realisation there was essentially nothing separating them from the ocean... or the *Postremus*. She couldn't bring herself to look down, but she noticed how dark it was here, as though whatever floated just beneath them was *absorbing* all light.

Directly above, Tuwia still floated perilously, and Mai tried not to think of the people they'd left behind. *The shuttle was supposed to hold SIX.*

Beyond Tuwia, the skies were that same, uncaring grey, while the seas of the horizon were tinged with a peculiar aqua colour. Convulsive shivers overcame her as Terrus and Elís wearily pulled themselves up.

Another *boom* ravaged the universe, heralding the next assault of the elements. Would it be whirlpools, waves, lightning, or storms? Would it be all of them?

Whatever she did, whatever she thought, Mai would not look down.

"Go back... we have to... go back," Elís croaked, hand pressed against a crease of blood on her forehead. "But first, buckle."

Mai complied while Terrus used his good arm to swing himself to his feet, bounding towards the front of the shuttle.

The roar of cascading water filled the air, and the world went dark.

But she would not look down.

"I'll take us back up. Wait, how the hell do I fly this—"

Terrus's words were cut short by the impact of the largest wave yet, which overwhelmed the shuttle in an instant. Moments later, they were underwater and upside down, careening backwards in the clutches of the tsunami. Before losing consciousness in the dizzying spiral, Mai's last thoughts were surprisingly hopeful, as she wondered who would be the first to read the message she'd sent forth into the beyond.

27
FALLEN

Tuwia, Alantia   CD: 22/04/2222
Tarlo

THREE MINUTES EARLIER.

THE TIDE OF fleeing colonists swept past Tarlo, leaving him alone and disoriented in the hallway outside the command centre. His vision narrowed, and the hammering of his heart between his ears and temples dulled the chaotic sounds around him. Despite the imminent danger, he could not move. The mere thought of going back inside the R16 to which he'd been assigned squeezed the air from his lungs and made leaden bricks of his feet. *Ashelyn. Where is Ashelyn?*

He couldn't go back down there again, with the darkness crushing him, the scent of blood everywhere, surrounded by those ghostly...

A firm grip on his right bicep wrenched him from his delirium, just as it had all those days ago, when he had watched helplessly as dozens were consumed by the sands of Cahros.

Ashelyn didn't speak as she weaved through the shaking hallways of Tuwia, outside, and down the first of the two flights of silver stairs. Ahead of them, Alesio escorted a group towards the shuttle, which was poised and waiting for them.

A blinding flash of light rocked the world, sending painful red streaks through Tarlo's eyes. When he forced them back open, his stomach dropped. The shuttle was gone.

Alesio's group came to a halt in the deployment bay.

A flurry of voices drew Tarlo's attention above him, and he saw Mauve leading another two colonists from Tuwia, gesturing they run towards Tarlo and Ashelyn on the stairs.

A deep groan echoed from beyond them, coming from the watchtower where Tarlo and the others had held their vigil. Tarlo watched helplessly as the foundations snapped and the tower began to fall. It crunched into the side of the living area, smashing in half, flinging several chunks of Moonsalt free.

Straight at Mauve and her companions.

They saw it the same time he did, and the same desperate, horrified expression plastered across their faces as the dark shadow crept across them. There was no time to speak, act, or move.

Tarlo jammed his eyes shut right as the remains of the tower crushed the three colonists with enough force to tip the whole facility, flinging him and Ashelyn down the stairs. It was fortune that kept them from hurtling over the safety rails, though another colonist, Viola, was not so lucky. She slammed into the rails right beside Tarlo with a vicious crack that rendered her body limp. He met her eyes, widened with pain and terror, and he raised his arm to help—

But she disappeared overboard before he could reach her.

Having absorbed the worst of the impact, the skybase righted itself enough for Tarlo and Ashelyn to struggle to their feet. He stole one last glance at the platform above. All that remained of Mauve was a limp, pale hand poking out from the rubble.

Ashelyn gripped his arm and escorted him towards the others. Now they'd made it to the illusionary sanctuary of the docking bay, the roaring elements had quietened enough for the colonists to at least hear each other speak.

"Is this everyone?" Alesio said, eyebrows creased in concern.

"I don't know. But with the shuttle gone… there's too many," Johann said. He was right – each R16 could safely fit three people and was seriously pushing it at four.

There were nine colonists still here.

Another earth-shattering *boom* reverberated from below, shuddering through the deployment bay as another huge wave crested beneath them.

"We've no idea how long before the next charge hits," Ashelyn breathed, only loud enough for Tarlo to hear.

"But what right have we over anybody else here?" he whispered, squeezing her hand with a gentle kind of despair.

"Corbin, take Ashelyn, Tarlo, and Johann and get in," Alesio said, gesturing to the far-side R16.

But Corbin only laughed. "You're a fucking idiot if you think I'm leaving without you."

"How do we choose, then?"

"Go by initial allocations. That's Bjora, Viola, Belsevic, and Zhang for this. Johann, Danniel, Ashelyn, and Tarlo for the other."

The first four people mentioned bundled into the R16 and prepared to detach from the bay. All of them were panicked, but Bjora – being perhaps the only one other than Tarlo or Johann to truly comprehend the power beneath them – was ghost-white and dead-eyed. Tarlo could have sworn he saw her mouth *"It ends"* just as their R16 detached from its swivel-dock.

"Danniel didn't make it. That's why I'm saying you should be one—" Alesio grabbed Corbin's arm, but Corbin pushed him back, a tear in his eye.

"I'm not leaving if it means you stay behind, damn you. We can wait for the shuttle to return. If it doesn't... we're captains, aren't we? What's that meant to mean?"

Alesio gripped him tightly. "Down with the ship. Like captains, as brothers."

Tarlo didn't know what to say – these men were effectively strangers, and they easily could have overpowered he and Ashelyn to claim the seats for their own. And yet, it seemed the thought had not once occurred to them.

He could have vomited for his guilt.

Ashelyn was first into the R16, and she took a place in the driver's seat.

Tarlo paused, awkwardly, to allow Johann into the vehicle first, but Johann had his own idea, shoving him roughly into one of the back seats.

This gesture saved Tarlo's life.

And forfeited his own.

A second bolt of lightning coursed from below, ripping through the first R16 that was halfway through its descent. For all its tenacious qualities, the little globe was unable to withstand tens of thousands of degrees of heat and energy, and it, along with the four Tuwian colonists within, perished in an instant.

The bolt continued its inevitable charge, thundering into the facility. The solid stream of electricity surged close enough to Corbin to catch him in its hateful blitz, blackening half his body and killing him just as quickly. The bolt coursed right through the heart of the skybase, ripping it in half with extreme force.

This time, there was no way it would right itself. The lights flickered out, and the technological wonder fell from the sky.

At eye level, the floor beneath Alesio and Johann disappeared, sending them plummeting to the black seas below. Again, Tarlo could only watch as another two small, hapless people were swallowed by the void.

Then their R16 detached. They fell for only a second before ramming into the head of another giant wave. Tarlo clung to his seat as they were taken by the momentous blue.

He looked to the piece of the sky where Tuwia had once serenely floated… but it was completely empty, as though it were never there.

If any fragment of humanity survived the intentions of these vengeful monsters, there would be none here to ever find them.

And so, just as it had been with Catal, Casarabe, and Alvolito, the colony of Tuwia was condemned to become another memory, another mistake – and Alantia another planet fed by the blood of those whose deaths were a mere footnote to a millennium of folly.

PART FOUR
UNDONE

28
THE RISING DARK

New London, Earth   CD: 22/04/2222
Demi

WE AT BROWNLEAF Wellbeing were sorry to miss you today. Due to late/missed cancellations, an appointment fee will still be charged. To schedule a new time, please contact us on 020 419.

Demi groaned as her wrist buzzed, emitting a crisp, loud *ping* that could have split her head in two. Maven's room was always dark – she had those auto-shutters on the windows – so the sleep-in had been inevitable. Not that they were really to blame; the sun had probably already risen by the time they finally went to sleep.

Fighting the beginning of an icepick headache, Demi sat up, activating the blue light on her band with a twist of her wrist. A pair of thin wine glasses rested on the coffee table at the room's centre, beside three empty bottles of dark red, and clothes were strewn about on the floor. Otherwise, the room was immaculately clean, and the wall-mounted burner ensured a refreshing, woody smell overpowered the less-enamouring scents of alcohol, sweat, and sex.

A slight snore turned her attention to the woman beside her, whose face was hidden beneath a mess of black curls. Light sheets accentuated the generous curves of her body, and a defiant pang of lust punched through Demi's growing nausea.

It was a surprise to see Maven still here. Usually, after nights like these, she was a ghost by the time Demi awoke, unreachable and uncontactable until the next time she felt like pulling the strings.

And it worked again. Guilt tugged at her stomach. *Skipping therapy AND sleeping with your ex? Bravo, Demi, Bravo.* This kind of immaturity would be fine if she was still in her early twenties, but Sol, she was nearly thirty now. How did she get off, acting like this?

But oh, how she had gotten off...

A second horrible ping pierced her brain.

De, where are you? Demi sighed, about the only thing she had energy for. It wasn't like her mother to be needy about things like this. Regardless, there was no chance she'd be answering that question.

"Shut up," Maven groaned, rolling over to reveal the smooth cocoa skin of her back.

Demi fell back into the plush mattress and closed her eyes. She knew she should leave, but their humble flat had nothing on this penthouse, and damn it if Maven didn't have *taste*.

Thoughts swam through her mind in unfinished sentences, and her dry mouth contended with a growing pressure on her bladder, but Demi only sank further into the sheets. She'd have to go back to work tomorrow, to deal with the sneering suits and the increasingly ludicrous demand to keep that corporate smile plastered on while everyone pretended everything was going great.

Her wrist pinged again, and she flinched as Maven repeated her earlier reprimand with some new expletives.

I'm sorry De, just saw something on my feed, about the stuff I know you've had going on at work. I thought you might know something about it. Chat to you later X

Demi would have rolled her eyes if the gesture didn't hurt so much. Karee had a habit of treating her like a translator for each and every current affair in the world.

She lay in a half-stupor for several more minutes, working up the strength to get up. If Maven hadn't left, was that because she wanted her to stay? Or did that mean it was Demi's cue to leave instead? Sol, her head hurt too much for this.

A fourth ping screamed out, and Demi winced. This time, Maven made no sound, but it was clear she had no intention of getting up or engaging. Demi's eyes drifted towards the bar, where she noticed a slick, black device. *Is that a Brevista?* Drawing into her deepest wells of courage, she kept moving. The coffee machine would wake up half the building, and she was anxious enough already.

Time to go. With a deep breath and a guilty, lingering glance at Maven's exposed body, Demi departed. It wasn't until she had tiptoed to the door that she actually checked her band.

It was Flo.

Did you see the clip? Scary. I hope you're okay. Call me if you ever need.

Demi edged out into the hallway and leaned back against the outside of Maven's door. Maven's upscale interior decorating was positively humble compared to the rest of this building. In a past era, it had been a high-rise hotel, and the over-wealthy custodians seemed intent on reminding everyone of this. Polished golden architraves framed each door, and lush carpets stretched towards an elevator that completed its rounds without a single shudder. Demi shuffled down the hall, breathing a sigh of relief that nobody encountered her looking like this, and slumped against the golden handrail. The whisky-wine combination from the previous night assaulted the back of her throat as the elevator launched downwards, and she glued her eyes to the wall-screen in a desperate attempt at distraction from her rebelling body.

The screen displayed the standard pod-talk fare, where over-decorated suits discussed the state of the world, but there was an unusual grimness to them today. Demi strained her ears to pick up the dulcet voice of the masculine half of today's hosting pair.

"We'll play that for you one more time now, while we wait for our next guest to weigh in."

The screen transitioned sharply from the warm hues of their chat couches to a low-res, high-vantage recording. The footage was shaky and unclear, as if being transmitted via a weak signal, but looked like it was being broadcast from a low-flying drone.

Despite the blurriness, the vista being broadcast was unmistakeable. A vast land of snow flashed by, pristine and white beneath a pale sun, with blue-grey shadows bathing the dark sides of the dunes. Occasionally, the land thinned out into great ice sheets, whose beautiful crystal-blue sheen belied a fragility born from years of planetary heating.

There was only one place on Earth this could be.

Antarctica. The final pole.

The drone crested over a final mountain, revealing a huge crater that swept all the way to the edges of the frame.

Alarm and confusion flooded through Demi at the sight – there were no such craters in Antarctica, and the only thing that could create something like this was some kind of extraterrestrial object. A meteor.

But to make a crater that size, such an impact would have been astronomical, and they'd all be buried under a mountain of debris by now, if the planet-spanning earthquakes hadn't crushed them first.

So how had this happened?

The final frame of footage froze on the screen, and Demi choked on her next breath.

Two gigantic pillars of rock rose from the centre of the crater, their black glisten splitting the Earth. Even with the blurry visuals, their fearsome power was unmistakeable, burning into her mind where it would remain long after she left that lonely hallway.

Shadowless. Eternal. Unnatural. Demi could not fathom what evil this thing promised, but she was certain of one thing, even before the ping on her wrist confirmed it.

She'd be needed at work today.

29
TENDRILS

FLASHES OF COBALT and white melded with a navy void as they were thrust into the world beneath the waves. With every roll in the vicious current, withered hands reached and grasped at Tarlo, though they never touched him, while oceanic shadows flickered with the accusatory glares of everyone he'd left behind. *Jontie. Carlyle. Olziyech. Velentini. Jame. Mauve. Alesio.* All the while, the eternal turmoil of the gaping maw and its warring fingers raged in the depths of his mind, tormenting him with an unknown danger.

They flew, floated, and sank within the crest of the enormous wave for what felt like hours, sustained by the constant vibrations of the unknowable masses beneath the surface. A great fear pulled at Tarlo's insides whenever he thought of the colossi beneath them, just waiting for their perilous little globe to land in the wrong place and shatter in an explosion of glassy Moonsalt and electricity. Intermittent lightning strikes flashed where Tuwia had once floated, leaving him no choice but to come to terms with the reality of its total destruction.

Somewhere, somehow, Ashelyn's hand found his, interlocking fingers as their arms trailed above them with each furious spin of their vehicle. Tarlo's glimpses of colour and horror faded into a blurry abyss.

The repeated revolutions, combined with the trauma of the day, were too much even for the stoic doctor, and by the time their R16 at last came to a halt, unconsciousness had long since taken hold of them both.

When they awoke, night had fallen.

Tarlo's first view was of the stars, and first thoughts were of Ashelyn. For once, she was the one who slept, and the gentle moonlight dappled over her weary features. Shallow breaths caused stray raven strands to dance around her lips, and Tarlo lost himself in her elven beauty.

Then he remembered.

His involuntary, despairing moan was enough to stir Ashelyn, who's eyes snapped open with realisation and concern. Tarlo rocked back in his seat, fixing his hands to his forehead. He felt so terribly small here, floating in the middle of a ceaseless ocean, at the mercy of anything that swam beneath. How many kilometres of water and darkness and death rested below him right now? How long until it claimed them? There was nowhere left to run, all they could do was wait until the great dark swallowed—

"Come back to me, Tarlo," Ashelyn breathed, and he dropped his tear-soaked fingers. Her eyes were the envy of the stars.

"It happened, again," he choked, imploring those emerald eyes for some kind of reassurance.

"It did. And here we are, again. Alive," she said serenely. "When all else fell away."

They sat in their typical silence for a long while, the terror of moving even greater than the fear of staying – but as always, just being in her orbit was a source of comfort.

"You did it, again. You saved me," Tarlo murmured, and before she could respond, he grasped at her, a wave of unbridled emotion sending his fingers streaming through her hair, drawing her towards him. It wasn't lust that he felt in that moment, but a desire, a *need* to be touched, to be close, to be *real* – a need that Ashelyn clearly shared. Their lips did not meet, nor any other piece of unbared skin, but they held each other, their shared warmth humidifying the air around them.

"What do we do?" Tarlo whispered, his head buried in her hair.

Ashelyn withdrew from him and turned to the front console. "Everything is gone. There is only one place we can go."

As if cued by her words, a heavy weight pressed against Tarlo's right shoulder.

"Back to the black."

Ashelyn nodded. "They got us out of hell once. Ever since we got here, I've been wondering if we should have left that formation to begin with. Maybe this was just a... station. One we shouldn't have disembarked at."

Tarlo's head was spinning too much for theories, but something about her words rang true.

"I think you're right, and we should go back. It's our only chance, really, but those... things are in our way."

Ashelyn shot him a little look. "You know what vehicle we're in now, right?"

Tarlo winced and nodded.

"If the *Postremus* are up here, then it stands to reason we should be able to simply travel beneath them. Right?"

Every muscle in Tarlo's body tensed, but she was right.

"Are you ready?"

Tarlo was sure the harrowed look on his face let him down, but he swallowed, breathed, and nodded.

"After last time, I swore I'd never go back down there," he whispered.

"It's different now. This time you have me." Ashelyn gave him a rare smile, and tears pooled in Tarlo's eyes. He bobbed his head again, and his breath caught as they descended beneath the waves for the last time.

Will I ever see the sky again?

Suffocating panic maintained its vice grip on his throat and chest as they fell through the gloom, but every once in a while, Tarlo felt a wave of giddy warmth. It might have been the cabin wasn't properly pressurised, and nitrogen was creeping into his bloodstream...

Or the irrepressible joy of another few moments of survival...

No. It was her.

Two hundred people had been sent to these worlds, and somehow, it was Ashelyn who still sat beside him, even after the end of all things. Something had brought them together, and kept them together, despite it all. He would do everything in his power to ensure that would never change.

"It's deep," Ashelyn murmured, and Tarlo turned his eyes towards the navs console.

A chill spread through his body as he realised what this meant.

"No Deep Scattering Layer... do you think... the creatures that were down here, they're all gone?"

Ashelyn gave a little shudder.

"Just like the tardigrades on Cahros..." Tarlo said as a dark revelation finally dawned. "Their existence began as all things do, with an attempt to stabilise their environment, to preserve and grow their species. But such was their efficacy they achieved their purpose *too* well, at the expense of all other life."

"These things are not stabilisers," Ashelyn gasped. "They're ecosystem destroyers."

"And they've been active on two life-bearing planets at effectively the same time. The chances of this cannot be conceptualised."

"Unless there is a pattern. What does this mean for any other planet down the line?"

Tarlo thought back to his visions in the formation on Cahros, of five worlds joined by a cosmic tether. "It began with Cahros, then came to Alantia. There's two more planets... and then Earth."

Ashelyn looked over at him. "But... there's no formations like this on Earth, there never has been?"

A sense of inevitability fell upon Tarlo, as the weight on his skull increased. "That we know of."

"So what can we do?" Her voice was flat. Hopeless.

"Surely, our role here is not just to observe everything falling apart?" Tarlo said.

Ashelyn shook her head. "Whatever our purpose might be, there's only one thing we can do. Stay alive, and hope these rocks will take us somewhere new."

Tarlo nodded, and all was quiet.

This new ocean, empty of any sign of life, was far more terrifying than anything he'd seen before. Even the colossal *Postremus* were something he could see, and theoretically, flee from. This empty darkness was something else, something sad and hopeless that made him feel like all life had come to an end.

Is this what death feels like?

"I'd kill for a chance to sit by the shade of a tree," Ashelyn finally said, her voice providing a small dose of relief. "To be beside something alive, and safe. Something growing."

"Maybe at the end of this, we'll plant one together," Tarlo said, and for a moment, a near-delirious hope flooded through him. He saw their hands digging at the dirt and laughing. He saw the oak rise, casting its own shadow amidst lengthening afternoons as an autumnal breeze brought with it the scent of honey.

Ashelyn's bottom lip trembled as she whispered, "Thank you."

Tarlo studied her. "Whatever for?"

"For walking with me, as first night fell on Cahros. For coming with me into the dark. For... holding me, slowly. Through chance or otherwise, you've always been at my side, and nobody before us, or after, will ever know anything like the experiences only we've shared. Nobody in the entire universe."

Her words were beautiful, but carried a chilling sense of finality.

"Ashelyn... don't talk like that. We're going to make it through this. We will," Tarlo stammered, feeling colder than ever. The darkness around them felt different to the crushing black of the last dive. Now, it felt indifferent. Empty.

As Tarlo stared at his ghostly reflection in the R16, he began to lose track of where he was. Was he even still here in the submersible, or out there? As good as dead; a spectre lost in the eternal dark.

"Do you think Mai or Terrus made it out?" he asked.

Ashelyn grimaced. "Fuck... I know they were assigned to the shuttle. I didn't see them when the base went down... but to hope..."

"Something tells me they did. Make it, I mean. Maybe it's just blind hope. But I can't accept this is the end."

Ashelyn gave him a sad smile. "Maybe you'll need to hope enough for both of us."

They continued through the abyss, seeing naught but their own apparitions in the waters around them. Eventually, the navs circuited, but Ashelyn had always seemed to hold an intuitive sense of how to navigate these anomalies, and she piloted ahead confidently.

They had been in the deeps for about an hour when the first scream ripped through Tarlo's mind. He clutched as his ears, but the sound would not lessen. Beside him, Ashelyn also buckled in pain, but she kept her hands on the nav levers, pulling them to a halt.

The screeching only grew louder. In a fit of pain, Tarlo unbuckled himself and sank to the floor, as if he could curl up and somehow block the sound, but he was powerless against the ululation.

Just as he felt his eardrums were about to burst, the cries came to a halt. A little sheepish, he clambered back to his knees but jolted in even greater alarm as he made eye contact with what was on the other side of the glass. In the exact place of his reflection, another of those ghostly whisps floated. The cabin of the R16 darkened, and he even lost a sense of Ashelyn beside him as he was drawn towards the glass, compelled to press his face against it.

Another scream rolled through his brain, and then the thing disappeared. The cabin lights restored, and Tarlo braced himself for an explanation-seeking Ashelyn, but when he looked up at her, she was gazing at a section of ocean ahead and just below them.

"Sol..." she breathed, and Tarlo realised she was looking at the sea floor. Only, instead of sand, pebbles or ocean detritus, a gigantic slab of polished stone stretched out before them. The bizarreness did not stop there, as streaks of some kind of dark, ink-like substance swirled across the surface. As Tarlo's eyes followed the swirls, he began to make out forms, shapes, and figures, some threatening and unknowable, while others seemed strangely familiar.

Ashelyn edged the R16 slowly along the sea floor. The inky tendrils mated and diverged, telling strange tales with curvaceous flourishes.

Amidst the colourless greys of the deep sea, it was difficult to accurately discern the hue of the murals, but to Tarlo's best approximation they were a combination of crimson and navy. The navy colours depicted images of a peaceful nature, rippling sea-lines adorned with boats and skiffs of a seafaring race. As they drifted further, the size and complexity of the vehicles increased, revealing ships that bore intricate designs of furnishings and shelter. Below these colony-ships streamed sleek, ovular submarine-like vessels, drawn to be spearing large, whale-like jellies.

Then came the crimson. Haphazard, jagged smears obscured and tore through the carefully drawn blues, depicting a great, bloody battle.

At the centre of the mural sat three small, navy-blue rocks. At first, they seemed similar to the ones that Tarlo and the others found in the bowels of Cahros, but these rocks were different. An arc of purple energy coursed between them, forming a dome no bigger than five feet in diameter, four feet tall at its highest point.

Sitting inside of it was a creature that he'd seen before.

It was alive.

30
THE LAST MESSAGE

THE PHYSICAL SHELLS of few things linger long after death, especially when they come to rest at the bottom of a life-infested ocean – which made the sight before them even more extraordinary.

But Tarlo had long given up on trying to make sense of the things he saw.

The thing glowed with a whiteness bright enough to scar retinae, and sat statically still, except for its eyes, which flittered rapidly from the area of the body that, on a human, would be the chest. Overall, it was a slender little creature, with finlike hands and clubby feet, closely resembling the screaming wisps Tarlo had seen all through these deepest regions of the ocean.

Resembling, but not representing – the difference was in the eyes. The screaming wisps had no such organs, and seemed perpetually frightened and aimless, whereas this one looked out at them with wide pupils that seemed almost... curious.

"What do we... do?" Tarlo said, and Ashelyn shrugged. The creature's eyes flickered.

"Not touch it. For starters." A stray current rocked the vehicle, and Ashelyn gripped the levers tightly in readjustment.

"I don't know where to start with this. What are we even looking at?"

"Could be another illusion, like all the rest."

"We're calling them illusions, now?" The thing's eyes flicked back to Tarlo when he spoke.

"Sol, I don't know!" Ashelyn exclaimed. "I'm so tired of not knowing what the hell is going on. Why can't it just be that we're losing our minds?"

The wisp's eyes widened at her outburst, and a realisation hit Tarlo. "It can hear us."

"That's ridiculous."

"I know, but look at it. It's *reacting*." As Tarlo said this, the eyes narrowed, and one of them blinked.

"Did that thing just fucking wink at us?"

Tarlo palmed his forehead. Things had gotten so strange, he didn't know whether to laugh or cry.

"Do you really think it can understand us?" Ashelyn asked.

"Not directly, I think, but perhaps contextually? I really believe it is responding to, and maybe even understanding our body language." Tarlo raised a hand and traced a large triangle in the air. Sure enough, those little eyes followed every movement.

"It is! Despite a life in the dark, it has eyes, and they work! The expressions, the reactivity... all suggests some level of intelligence. The chances of such a thing understanding our language, though, I couldn't even break it down, we're talking *infinitesimal*."

"Oh, and the chances of this white ghost thing just relaxing in the middle of a forcefield at the bottom of an ocean for Sol knows how long... that's what we call a sure bet, is it?" Ashelyn was getting frustrated, and Tarlo knew exactly why. She *hated* being confused.

"One impossible thing doesn't justify another." Tarlo stood and stretched, as if it might somehow clear his head. He dragged his fingers along the ceiling of the R16, imagining he too were trapped in a little dome at the bottom of the ocean, staring up at the endless black for eternity, counting the fishes and occasional extraterrestrial traveller as the years went by. A simple life. At least, until his sanity abandoned him after approximately five minutes. Although maybe that would be better anyway...

"Miracles aside, what in Sol *is* it doing here?" he murmured.

"At this point, what are any of us?"

They both stared at the quizzical entity, and it calmly held their gaze. Despite the similarities it held with typical biological lifeforms, Tarlo noticed that it was lacking one key organ: a mouth. Its pupils provided the only flash of colour, a speck of magenta amidst the white sheen.

"Why do you have feet?" Tarlo whispered, remembering his earlier conversation with Johann. This was followed by a stabbing pain in his stomach, and the familiar sour guilt at the reminder of another person who had died in his stead. What had Johann's last moments been like, hurtling to the unforgiving ocean while evacuation sailed away, just a few feet from him?

"Why does that matter?" Ashelyn asked.

Tarlo turned his mind back to the puzzle at hand. "Well, I can't stop thinking about the spectres back on Cahros. Those bird-like, shrouded entities? Their ultimate purpose was guiding us, long beyond their actual deaths. I can't help but feel this creature may have the same intent. I wonder if this thing is even alive, or just an... essence. A memory."

"Whatever the message is, it is more overt than Cahros. Paintings on the ground are a lot easier to comprehend than hallucinations and death," Ashelyn agreed.

Tarlo gave her a small smile. "Cultural differences, I guess. Now, back to the feet. The visions on Cahros showed that those messengers had always existed on the planet, through all its iterations from jungle, to Blackrock, to desert."

"Yes. Are you saying the story of this creature is somehow different?"

"I think so. Have you ever seen a fish with feet before?"

"Crustaceans have legs..."

"Yes, some seabed-dwelling creatures walked. But not on things like that," Tarlo jabbed a finger at the bulky, toed appendages on the end of the creature's stubby legs. "That is only a hindrance to a swimmer. Which leaves us two possibilities. Either it always lived here, but Alantia changed drastically since these creatures first evolved..."

"Or they came from elsewhere. Like us," Ashelyn concluded. "But again, why does it matter? It clearly didn't work out for them."

"It might be some clue to what the leviathans are, and how they may be linked to the *Maleficus.*"

"How so?"

"If this little creature was from this world, and the environment changed – think continental submersion, risen water levels, et cetera – then there's an element of natural selection. They simply didn't evolve well or fast enough to adapt to this new environment. That in turn may have led to the development of the *Postremus,* perfectly adapted to the pressures of the deep sea, and with endless room to grow. If all that were the case, things on this planet would neatly – though tragically – mirror the events on Cahros, where a sentient race lost its place in the rise of a super-organism."

"Patterns everywhere, I get it. Just like the two sets of formations, and the two sets of tardigrades. Sol, I hate this," Ashelyn said.

"But if they came from elsewhere, then their story is the same as ours. And there's significance to that, too…"

"United in our hubris…"

"Yes. Now as for where the *Postremus* came from, and their overall similarity with other tardigrades, size aside… Could be it's convergent evolution – where similarity is attributed to evolutionary coincidence – or some deeper link."

"Not exactly convergent. These fuckers are a little different to the *Maleficus,*" Ashelyn pointed out. "But anyway, I think we both know this can't be a coincidence."

"It all feels like we're stumbling through something so much bigger than us! Are we really just here to witness our own demise in slow motion?" Tarlo weakly smacked the R16 roof again. The little figure looked at him with alarmed curiosity.

"Falling through the starless night with nought but a broken flashlight," Ashelyn mused.

As if it had grown tired of their pontifications, the little creature began to shake. Its eyes narrowed, though somehow, Tarlo knew it was not in suspicion… but mirth? It rose from its seated position, revealing a smooth black stone beneath it, which it pressed a flaky right hand upon.

The stasis field discharged, and crackles of purple light burst forth, catching hold of the painted ink and spreading through the stones on the sea floor. The immediate impact of several kilometres of water crushed the wry little creature in an instant. Tarlo felt a pang in his heart as another connection was severed, though he could have sworn he saw a cloud of grey essence drift away with the currents.

Meanwhile, the purple charge of energy continued to spread, uniting the blue and red ink into a bright and fiery mural. Tarlo's feet warmed as the energy in the water heated the R16, and Ashelyn hurriedly ascended the vehicle to a cooler vantage. From here, they noticed something different – the artwork was no longer two disparate murals, but a series of bright purple lettering.

"The tablet, Tarlo! Capture everything!" Ashelyn exclaimed, and Tarlo scrambled for the device and followed her orders. From their new height, he was able to capture the entire message in a single frame – but he took several photographs for safekeeping.

"This is language. It is a message after all!" Ashelyn said, gazing down in awe, purple flames reflecting in her pupils.

"Was that... was it really waiting for us?" Tarlo said, hands shaking.

"Maybe just... for someone advanced enough to get down here. I wonder how long it sat in stasis like that. What kind of hell that must have been."

"How in Sol is that even possible?"

Ashelyn looked down at the mysterious message, and Tarlo followed her gaze. The seafloor was gradually dimming, and purple auroras floated up towards them. "I'm more worried by how these species with technology *clearly* more advanced than ours met such a fate," Ashelyn said.

"What chance did we ever have?" Tarlo said, standing beside her.

Ashelyn touched his arm and gave him the smallest of smiles. "As much as we ever did." She squeezed him hard as she added, "Just don't lose that fucking tablet."

Together, they watched the last of the lights peter out, paying respect to this final legacy of a forgotten race.

31
SANCTUARIAL LIMBO

THEIR JOURNEY TOWARDS the Blackrock pillars came with a peculiar sensation: it felt like they were coming home.

Tarlo grimaced. How had these foreboding, deadly rocks become his last source of comfort?

Well... his second-to-last source. He glanced over at Ashelyn, who sat in calm but pensive quiet. He couldn't imagine what he would have done if he were down here alone, or with anyone else, for that matter. But while she was beside him, the memories of blood and death only teased at the edges of his consciousness, rather than holding him in their assaulting grip.

"Do you think we'll run into the *Postremus* when we begin to rise?" he asked.

"Scanners showed the surface above us was clear before they went out. But that was nearly an hour ago. Your guess is as good as mine."

"They stayed away from here before. Everything did, for that matter. These rocks... don't seem well aligned with organics."

"Hallucinations, death, and darkness hardly make for a nice place to set up camp."

"I still can't figure out if the Blackrock is a friendly or antagonistic force."

"My growing feeling is the latter," Ashelyn said. "All these messages being left here, nearby... I think the races that came before knew that anybody in the future would be drawn here as well."

"Like moths leaving warning signs around the flame," Tarlo said.

Ashelyn laughed bitterly. "And just like those stupid insects, we've no choice but to dive into the fire anyway."

A slight grinding indicated Ashelyn had changed gears. Their final ascent had begun.

"Maybe the message the sea-wisp left for us will help make things clear. Mai would have loved a challenge like this," Tarlo said, fighting back a wave of remorse. *We didn't see the shuttle go down. They might have made it...*

"You'll figure it out, I know it." Ashelyn wasn't looking at him, but Tarlo noticed a look of sorrow sneak across her face.

"You'll?"

"I'll have my hands full keeping you alive."

Tarlo laughed, too loud, too hard. "A job at which you uniquely excel at. How many times have we now gone forth into the dark?"

She placed a hand on his leg and squeezed. "Too many, Tarlo. Too many."

She could have been moving them upwards a whole lot faster, but Tarlo understood why she wasn't. This was the safest place they could be right now... why rush back into the fray?

"We should probably suit up, right? For when we get there?" he said.

"We should," Ashelyn said, though she made no movement. "Maybe not just yet, though."

Tarlo placed his hand on hers and squeezed back.

"Would have been nice to see some of those fish you described. The red ones. Or the jellies. I always loved jellyfish. So calm," Ashelyn mused, almost absent-mindedly. "Anything other than the loneliest creature in the universe."

"I'd say it seemed rather happy to see us," Tarlo said.

"Yes. Because its suffering was over." Ashelyn's words echoed through the cabin, dire, but undeniable.

The waters lightened ever-so-slightly as their ascent continued, but this brought no solace. Every metre they travelled only drew them closer to the next challenge, the next danger. The next unknown. And where before, Ashelyn's company had given him a sense of strength and reassurance, this was slowly being corrupted by a looming fear.

He was scared of losing her.

Once, he might have been afraid only for himself – and the grief that might come from losing the source of his infatuation, protection, and connection – but as his care for her deepened, that had changed. He realised with a shock that his greatest fear was no longer his own death – it was Ashelyn's. If anybody deserved to survive all of this and go on to live some kind of life afterwards, it was her.

"You're special, you know," he blurted.

Ashelyn's eyes narrowed, but a blush tinged her cheeks. "Are you experiencing oxygen deprivation?"

"Through all of this. You've always somehow... understood these places. The way you've navigated to and through them, it's like you're one step ahead of the rest of us, in sync with whatever messages have been left behind. And I don't even know how many times you've directly saved my life."

"I'm a doctor, it's my job," she said with that absent tone again. "And outside of your case, it's a job that I've failed remarkably at doing, over and over."

Tarlo knew better than to challenge her on this. "You're so much more," he whispered.

She pretended not to hear him, but her face softened.

Their headlights, so ineffectual in the gloom, finally revealed a glimmer in the dark. They had arrived at the onyx pillars of the Blackrock formation.

"So, once we get in there, you know what we might expect. Just stay close to me," Ashelyn said.

"That's all I've ever wanted," Tarlo breathed.

There was that faint smile again.

"How far up do you think we are?" he asked, anxious dread creeping back through his chest. Soon, their time in this space between would be over.

"Far enough we should probably suit up," Ashelyn said, her words heavy. The idea of any layer of separation between them caused rivets of distress to pulse through Tarlo's stomach, but he nodded.

They had donned all but their helmets when Ashelyn paused. Even after weeks of stress and sleep deprivation, in the dark and gloom, those emerald eyes were more stunning than ever.

She closed them, depriving him of their splendour, but the taste of her lips more than made up for it. They were a little dry, as were his, but Tarlo felt only joy as they came together, feeling all her conviction in the force of her kiss, the desperation of her hands in his hair, on his cheek, pressing their caged bodies closer.

The kiss lasted an eternity and an instant. When Ashelyn eventually pulled away, the residual oxytocin reacted with the harsh feeling of a tether being snapped, and a wave of dizziness swept across Tarlo. As if sensing it, she gently assisted him back to his seat, and they floated the rest of the way in a morose, yet peaceful silence.

They passed quietly through the ruins of the Alvolito, preserved in stasis beneath these ancient rocks. Tarlo wondered if any of the debris around them was from Tuwia – could the carnage have been swept here already?

The surface of the ocean took them both by surprise. The water had stopped lightening some time before they breached, and the unchanging blue surroundings, combined with the magnetism of the formation, had led to them falling into another trancelike state. It was only the sudden bobbing of their vehicle on the waves that indicated anything had changed, and when he forced his heavy eyes skywards, Tarlo realised why.

The bright moons and gentle starscape of the Tuwian sky had been totally obscured by death-black clouds. A brutal *crack* split the world as a lightning strike erupted from nearby. This was followed in short order by many more, and it became clear they had surfaced into the midst of an apocalyptic lightning storm. Except, instead of clashing down from the clouds, these strikes raged up from the ocean, assaulting the skies with a vengeful and godlike fury.

Ashelyn's glove found his, and she held them steady. "They have us surrounded," she said.

Sure enough, the lightning strikes stretched around their island from every direction – generated by only one thing: the rage of the denizens of the deep. *Postremus Tardinata.*

"The only way is forward," Tarlo said.

Ashelyn nodded, and the two of them grimly donned their helms. While the air was still breathable, they both knew that once they descended into the caves, anything could happen.

There was no beach around the island, so Ashelyn navigated the R16 until it reached a position right next to the distress beacon, of which only the dull, red light was visible above the surging waves. Behind it, the two great black pillars stretched into the atmosphere, occasionally glowing in reflection of the violent elements.

The bio-storms raged on, sending booming *cracks* through the air that symphonised with the crashing of the vicious waves in a soundtrack of cataclysm. Tarlo and Ashelyn leapt from the vehicle together, landing in waist-deep water that threatened to consume them with each swell. As he landed, Tarlo's ankle slammed against something heavy. His momentum caused it to bob to the surface, and he caught a glimpse of a compact silver box, with a small label in red writing. *oxyGen.*

He winced. *Must be debris from Alvolito. Or Tuwia.*

Despite the climate-controlled E12, Tarlo shivered, feeling cold and wet. The filter in the helm denied him a taste and smell of the usually sweet-humid air, but he was quickly reacquainted with the scents of his own stress and angst as he reflexively gasped for air.

"Come on," Ashelyn said.

He took one last moment to feel the scene around him. Black skies, fierce lightning, turgid waters, and at the nucleus of it all, the impossible, impregnable monoliths.

What hell have we stepped blindly into?

Ashelyn grabbed his arm, and together, they descended into the maddening dark once more.

32
DEVASTATION

THIS TIME, THERE were no hallucinations. No hideous terrors or amalgamations of light. No ghostly creatures pointed the way, and no corrupted human forms assailed them. The walls did not shift, and the mud beneath their feet hid no surprises.

Still, Tarlo could not shake the feeling that they approached their doom.

The fierce noises of the world outside were just a dull echo in here, but no matter how deep they wandered, the sounds still followed, rumbling through the sensors in his boots and gloves whenever he touched any surface.

As always, Ashelyn led the way, but her gait faltered often, and Tarlo found himself helping her to her feet more than he was used to. Occasional small moans escaped her lips, suggesting a suffering he could not know.

But he knew these depths demanded silence. Whenever Tarlo tried to open his mouth to speak, a force pressed up against his jaw, clamping his teeth together so hard he thought they would shatter.

A noise, something between a gasp and a shriek, echoed through the cavern, and Tarlo realised it had come from Ashelyn. He drew in front of her and pressed their helms together. From this distance, he could see through the tint-ed glass-prene at her face, which was drawn and strained.

Then he saw her eyes. Or rather, the whites of them. Tarlo's stomach dropped as he realised what this meant – Ashelyn was bearing the brunt of the fury of this place. His entire body went cold as another pained gasp was ripped from her, and she fell against him, toppling them both to the ground. Tarlo caught her in the process, envigored by a strength he hadn't felt before, and took a deep breath. He still couldn't free his mouth to speak, but he channelled all his will into propping her back up, and with burning calves he brought them both back to their feet.

Just as once you led me through the dark, I will do the same.

He couldn't know how long they trudged through the dark together, accompanied by little other than the sounds of their boots scraping the ground and the distant *booms* from outside. Otherwise, the journey was punctuated only by Ashelyn's cries of distress, each one stripping away pieces of Tarlo's heart. He hated being unable to see what she saw, but even worse was the knowledge that he was powerless to help. Only once did she manage coherent words, a strained utterance of "Don't let go."

Tarlo swore he'd hold her until the end.

The final chamber announced itself with crushing si-lence and blinding light. The echoes of beyond no longer rang out around them, and as Tarlo's eyes slowly adjusted to the medium-blue pinpoints on the walls, he realised where he was. These same glows had glittered the walls of the corresponding cavern on Cahros – the central chamber. It was there, in the bowels of the planet, that the progenitor race had embraced its doom, sacrificing their essence to open the door between worlds.

A door that they now saw again.

Four lapis lazuli stones rose from the ground, each six feet in height, and at their centre, an even larger chunk of Blackrock sat.

The altar.

"We're here," he murmured, and to his surprise, Ashelyn responded lucidly.

"Just as we hoped."

Slowly, they approached the blue stones, but as they drew nearer, Tarlo noticed something was different about them.

"Only one appears to still be live." Ashelyn noticed it too – it was the stone furthest from the entrance they'd come through.

"It's like... somebody was here before." Tarlo's heart leapt – could Terrus and Mai have made it after all? Despite his hope, the heaviest dread began creeping up his spine.

"Yes. Let me just check..." Ashelyn extended a hand to one of the three dull rocks. "Nothing. Like they've been... spent."

"Do you think we could try the last one together?" Tarlo asked, his voice quavering. He didn't want to think about what it might mean for the Blackrock portal.

"Yes... but you should touch it first."

Tarlo didn't stop to think about the potential implications of her words, allowing his right hand to be drawn towards the soothing blue stone. Ashelyn drew up behind him, planting her hand beneath his, and a warmth rushed through his arm, pushing through his chest and all the way to the top of his head—

viii: The connection that broke

Once again, he gazed upon five worlds joined by a golden tether. The first he knew to be Cahros, the violent desert, and the last was a place he once knew as home: Earth. Last time he'd been here, the three planets in between had all been shrouded in murk, but it was different now – the centre three had all been revealed.

The second planet was a tempestuous sea, rocked by waves and lightning. Alantia. The third was a brown, fiery wasteland, whose black mesas where blanketed in red-orange lava, and the fourth was green-blue, like an algae-covered pond. He had seen glimpses of the third planet before, once home to gigantic, winged entities who sat on thrones made of skin, whose world was a screaming hell, but he knew little of the fourth. It seemed peaceful, but in the way that a battlefield was calm after the killing was done.

Through them all, the golden tether pulsed. Something linked them all together: a shared destiny. Panic gripped him as he realised the paralleled destinies of Cahros and Alantia, cleansed by different forms of the same perfect entity, might be shared by the other planets in the chain.

As he peered closer at the orbs, he noticed one last crucial detail. *The golden path is not yet fulfilled.* While the glistening line coursed through each of the first three planets, it stopped just short of the fourth world.

But it was getting closer.

Tarlo was expelled from the vision, landing in a heap on top of Ashelyn.

"Did you see what I saw?" he mustered, struggling for air as his lungs clenched and heart pounded.

"I know you saw the five planets," Ashelyn said. "The four chosen worlds of the Martellus Index. And I know you saw home."

"The first three planets in the chain have fallen," Tarlo said numbly.

"And the fourth isn't far away."

"And when it does..."

"Whatever tragedy of evolution afflicted these planets... Earth is next."

"Yes."

Silent revelation closed in on them as the blue lights in the room darkened.

"But I saw more." Ashelyn's voice glowed with an omnipotent warmth, and for a moment, Tarlo saw clouds of gold glitter in the air around her visor.

"The chain between them is gold, and the planets gain colour when they are reached. The Blackrock does not see their demise as a catastrophe. It sees it as purification. As success."

"You speak about these formations as if they are..."

SENTIENT? HAVE YOU STILL NOT LEARNED TO HEED ETERNITY'S CALL?

They both stumbled as the words were engraved into their minds, pummelling them with oppressive power. Tarlo's head was still ringing when Ashelyn spoke next.

"We have been dogs on a leash, led when and wherever these powers deemed."

"Sol... all along... we've been manipulated?"

Ashelyn nodded. "These rocks possess a will that we will never be able to contend with. They came to these worlds, *they* created these creatures, *they* orchestrated the destruction of all those races who came before."

FINALLY, ONE WHO UNDERSTANDS.

Ashelyn sank to her knees, but Tarlo felt the heat of desperate anger.

"What do you want with us?" he shouted.

All his suffering came to the surface in that moment. All those who had died, all the hatred he'd imposed on himself, all the guilt and anguish erupted into hoarse screams that echoed through the depths of the world.

"WHO DO YOU THINK YOU ARE TO DO THIS TO US?"

But the rocks were silent. Tarlo roared in pain, bellowing desperate pleas and accusations into the void.

But it never answered.

Finally, Ashelyn rose and laid a hand on his shoulder. A wave of warmth swept through him, and he quietened just in time for her to murmur:

"Why did you preserve us? Why allow this travel between worlds?"

WHAT POINT HAS SUFFERING IF THERE ARE NONE TO BEAR WITNESS? WHAT CAN BE SEEN IF THERE ARE NO EYES?

A deep vibration rumbled through the cave, and the direct communication was severed. The room suddenly felt cold, quiet, and lonely.

"What the hell are we supposed to do?" Tarlo cried. "Do these things really intend to keep us alive just so that we can watch to the end of our world? Our species?"

"Perhaps," Ashelyn said. "But they haven't finished us off yet. And, for all their power, these rocks could not stop these races from leaving their messages behind – through their sacrifice. Something tells me this entity... it does not understand such a concept."

"But these messages... How do we know they aren't just a last play to leave some kind of legacy? And maybe the Blackrock has chosen to leave them here, to taunt us?" Tarlo despaired.

"If that were the case, these things would be truly evil. But that doesn't mean we shouldn't try."

"To tell our story, even as it ends?"

"Yes. Unless... maybe there is still time." Ashelyn turned towards the final, pulsing rock. "Maybe, these things are not just eradicating us... but testing us."

"Then they've picked the wrong person to test. I have fallen short of every purpose I might claim."

Then Ashelyn laughed, a beautiful, forlorn sound that Tarlo would remember as long as he'd live.

"I know what my purpose is. What it has always been. Give me your tab."

Tarlo was confused, but complied. Ashelyn opened a blank screen, and input six numbers and two letters.

"What are you doing?"

"Just putting down some coordinates. If we ever make it back to Earth, I think they'll be useful." There was something ominous about the way she was speaking. Why would she need to write them down?

She fastened it back to his hip pouch, her hands lingering for a second afterwards.

"I think I have come to terms with my own failings. For all the people who I could not save... all that mattered was I kept you alive. Tarlo, I know what to do."

She moved too quickly for him to react, hoisting Tarlo to his feet and pushing him towards the final charged rock. He only realised what she had done when he was falling through the air, unable to halt the momentum of the shove.

Electricity surged around him as he slammed into the monument, beginning as bright tendrils that wormed around the edges of his vision. He focused for a last second on Ashelyn's outline, oriented by those beautiful green eyes shining with light and tears.

"Go, with my love," she whispered.

The energy consumed him, igniting every nerve ending on his body, flinging him through the portal to a new place, a new time.

Then he was rolling in the dark, slamming against a rocky wall. Tarlo took no notice of his pain or surroundings, flinging himself to his feet. He slammed against the Black-rock portal from which he'd tumbled, a wordless scream tearing from his mouth as his fists plastered helplessly against the rock. He sprinted through the caves, trailing his hand along the rocky walls, desperately searching for some other portal, rock, or opening. Eventually, his delirium brought him back to the same room he'd first fallen into, and once more, he laid into the central Blackrock with all his might.

It did not budge, glow, or even react.

Defeated, Tarlo sank to his knees.

Ashelyn was not coming.

He had left her in the dark.

TO BE CONCLUDED IN BOOK THREE,

DARK SKIES

COMING IN 2026.

Acknowledgements

Thank you to everybody who has been involved in this project from start to finish. To my editor, Kat, from Element Editing Services, and the absolute pros at DAMON-ZA who designed the cover, and all of the amazing bookstagrammers and authors who have shared and ARC read this novel. Thank you to Mum and Dad, who read every chapter as it was conceived, in all their initial roughness. Thank you to everybody who made the launch and release of *DARK SANDS* so special, and everyone who continues to share the love. And to you, the reader, thank you so much for reading this far, and for all of YOUR support. It wouldn't be possible without you.

After completing *DARK SANDS*, I set forth with a goal: to develop these flawed-yet-earnest characters, while paying tribute to the impacts of trauma and grief on the human soul. Thus, *DARK TIDES* came to be a story about the wonder that is life, tempered by the sadness of how evanescent it all really is. There are numerous tragedies in this novel that serve as reminders of the hardships we go through that none of us ever really deserved. Catharsis is a funny thing – sometimes, we don't need a happy ending so much as we need an acknowledgement of the pain we all feel. That's what this story means to me.

As for the future, well, there is a big finale coming your way. I can confidently say the final installment of this series will land before 2026 is out.

Until then, keep your eyes on the skies...

With love, JSH.

How To Support The Author

I am an independent author, and *DARK TIDES* was entirely funded out of my own pocket. That includes marketing, cover design, editors, you name it! I coordinate all the professionals involved in this process, manage all my social media accounts, and run my own stalls.

Just by buying this book, you've already gone above and beyond to support this Indie in ways that I'll forever be grateful for. But, in case you were looking for more ways to show support *without* breaking the bank, here's a few suggestions:

1.   Leave reviews – reviews are the lifeblood of author credibility and make a vital difference when it comes to helping us grow! If you can, please go and leave a review of *DARK SANDS* on Amazon and Goodreads, or similar platforms.

2.   Get in touch via social media – I'm incredibly active on Instagram, drop me a follow and send me a message on @j.s.harman.author! Sharing and tagging Indie authors and their books on social media is a free but powerful way to help us grow.

3.   Talk about it – recommendations are free, too. Whether it is to friends, local bookstores and libraries, or

strangers on the bus, your words are powerful and always worth sharing!

It might seem like these are small things, but the evidence is out there that they can make a huge difference when it comes to people even seeing our work in the first place – algorithms prioritise engagement. But beyond all that, just to hear from and connect with you is what this is all about, so please don't ever be a stranger.

And that's it from me! Thank you again, so much, and I'll see you in the next one!

About The Author

J.S.Harman is a new voice in the world of accessible Science Fiction. A finalist in the 2025 Aurealis Awards for Best Science Fiction Novel, Harman specialises in tales of survival, adventure and existentialism, melding classic science fiction tropes with explorations of the universal human experience. J.S.Harman's accolades also include second in the 2025 Geelong Writers Competition, a finalist place in the 2025 Verandah E40 Journal, and a finalist place in the IGWriter Awards 2025.

Heralding from Melbourne, Australia, Harman has a background in Social Work and Community Services, having spent years working in acute mental health, homelessness and disability spaces, and has maintained a passion for contributing to his community. Harman has been a passionate reader and writer since his earliest years, completing his first story at age 10, and spends his spare time playing video games, completing puzzles, assembling LEGO, and wishing he lived somewhere up in the mountains by a lake.

www.ingramcontent.com/pod-product-compliance
Lightning Source LLC
Chambersburg PA
CBHW071551030726

47593CB00001BA/112